Horizons West

Horizons West

by

Harold G. Ross

Sunflower University Press®

1531 Yuma • P.O. Box 1009 • Manhattan, Kansas 66505-1009 USA

Cover by Tom Bookwalter, Olsburg, Kansas.

Line graphics: Kansas Bluestem Grass and
Prairiecone Flower, by Rodney Hoover, Manhattan, Kansas.

Layout by Lori L. Daniel

ISBN 0-89745-242-9

Sunflower University Press is a wholly-owned subsidiary
of the non-profit 501(c)3 Journal of the West, Inc.

To Kathy

I am moved to pen the story of the Ross clan for those others of us to come, who may one day wonder why this land, America, holds such meaning for us.

In but nine more years it will have been one hundred since Grandfather John Ross left his own beloved braes and glens of Scotland in search of new horizons, with the will to survive a mighty force burning strong within him, as he longed for a national peace and personal tranquility.

I write to tell you first of where the Ross clan has been, and then to where it has now come, in these verdant hills of Virginia, after a torment anew within our adopted nation.

I pray that the Almighty would somehow finally grant, to us all, that unity and peace which we have so long sought.

James Franklin Ross, 1865

Contents

The Confederacy: Virginia — 1861   1

The British Isles: Scotland   9

America: Land of Promise   81

America: Civil War   157

America: New Horizons   223

Epilogue   239

The Ross Family

John Ross, Sr. ——————————— **Agnes Miller**
b. 1756, near Tain, Scotland — *b.* 1762, Scotland
*m.*1785, Fredrick County, Virginia
d. 1838, Loudoun County, Virginia — *d.* 1843, Ebenezer Cemetery
     Ebenezer Cemetery

John Ross, Jr. ——————————— **Susannah Thomas**
b. 1788, Loudoun County, Virginia — *b.* 1793
*m.*1815
d. 1876, Ebenezer Cemetery — *d.* 1831, Ebenezer Cemetery

James Franklin Ross ——————— **Mary Jane Gochnauer**
b. 1821, Loudoun County, Virginia — *b.* 1832, Middleburg, Virginia
*m.*1851
d. 1894, Geary County, Kansas — *d.* 1927, Upper Humboldt
     Upper Humboldt Cemetery —   Cemetery

Bruce Jacob Ross ——————— **Hughena MacArthur**
b. 1852, Loudoun County, Virginia — *b.* 1864, Kinmount, Ontario,
*m.*1882 —   Canada
d. 1940, Geary County, Kansas — *d.* 1948, Welcome Cemetery
     Welcome Cemetery

Herbert T. C. Ross ——————— **Martha Pearl Brannick**
b. 1889, Geary County, Kansas — *b.* 1891, Geary County, Kansas
*m.*1913
d. 1963, Geary County, Kansas — *d.* 1979, Welcome Cemetery
     Welcome Cemetery

The Confederacy

Virginia

1861

*O*N THE 19TH OF JULY, 1861, the silent feet of dawn came upon the edge of the woods like a ghost as a gray light swept the sky, changing the countryside into shape and distance. Far beyond my enemies, across the meadow and tree-lined creek, rose a bright sun, with its conflagration of lemon-tinged light spreading across the land.

Under normal circumstances it would have been a wonderful dawn, but the struggle ahead lay heavy on my heart, and death clouded my thinking. For many a Sunday I had heard our minister expound that all were backsliders, and unless God looked kindly upon sinners, by the next sunrise I could possibly be dead.

That day, the 19th, the men around me, most of whom were mere lads, were anxious and frightened, all troubled with the struggle to come. For most of the boys in my squad it was their first time away from family, and they were homesick. They had not yet faced the horrors of war, but they seemed eager for combat; it was the honorable thing to do, to fight for home and country. Yet, the darkness of the unknown worked against the mind, and it was a battle that one had to confront alone, for facing the terror of death was surely a solitary experience.

I was a Sergeant in Brigadier General Thomas Jackson's Brigade, a strong man deceivingly slim of body and considered tall at five feet eleven. I had grown a mustache and beard on my thin face, as most of the men around me had. And although I had never seen combat, I projected to my men along the line the confidence of one who had been battle worn.

Norse and Viking blood ran deep within my Scottish veins, and perhaps in the heat of the fray I would do well, as well as had my ancestors before me. Surely in the struggle to come the Ross tenacity would move to the fore.

From a barrel I dipped out a pan full of water, using it to wet my hair, and to wash my face and arms. I looked into a piece of broken mirror hung on the bole of a tree and combed my hair. Satisfied, I peered a moment at my reflection — James Franklin Ross, thirty-nine, and considerably older than most of the men around me.

My eight hundred acre farm was near Snicker's Gap at the foothills of the Blue Ridge Mountains. It was part of the land purchased in 1774 by my Grandfather John Ross.

My thoughts turned to my wife Mary and our four children, alone, some twenty miles west from where I stood. They would now have the care of the livestock and the land, along with their other chores. It would be a hardship on dear Mary, for my oldest child was but eight.

I grew melancholy thinking of home, and returned to my duties.

It was back in April when Tom Jackson stopped by my place. We had long known each other. To all of us, Tom's life was an admirable story of success. Born to a poor family and with his father long absent, he had been orphaned at seven by his mother's death. And though he had received little formal education in his early years, he still managed to get an appointment to the National Military Academy at West Point, after the original appointee had resigned.

Two years earlier, Tom had come by to purchase a quarter horse, and ended up buying a sorrel. It was that same sorrel he rode into the yard. He quickly dismounted when he saw me working near the barn and walked over to the corral fence. We shook hands.

"James, how are things goin'?"

"Not too bad," I expressed.

Tom Jackson was not one to fool with words, and he quickly got to the point. "It looks, James, like there's going to be a war between the states and it's getting closer every day. I want you in my brigade, the teamsters, with the rank of Sergeant. Your knowledge of horses would be worth a lot to me."

I hesitated, then replied. "Sure, I will do my duty and go . . . but only if Virginia secedes from the Union."

"It already has," Tom said. "Yesterday. I've been assigned to Harpers Ferry, and I'd like for you to join me there. I know it'll take you a few days to get your things in order, so come to camp as soon as you can."

I watched Jackson ride off against a backdrop of the springtime mountains — the quiet foothills aglow with redbud, their branches covered with racemes of pink blossoms interlaced with the misty green branches of dogwood.

Two days later I rode away from home and hoped the war would end quickly.

On the way to Harpers Ferry, I stopped by my folks' place. My Pa, John Ross, Jr., was out by the granary when I rode up on my prized black gelding, a quarter horse bred for speed and stamina.

Pa was a taciturn man, a strict Presbyterian. He took the Bible literally — no words passed his lips that were void or meaningless.

That day he took it upon himself to show some emotion. "You're doin' right," he said. "Damned Yanks anyway . . . what right do they have tellin' us Virginians what we can or can't do?"

I had never heard Pa curse before. It reminded me of the time I had caught my finger in the corral gate and blurted out, "*God damn!*" It just came out, without thinking. It was something I had picked up at school from the other boys, and I had cussed at times around them. But I had never expected to do so in Pa's presence.

Pa gave me the sternest look I had ever seen him give, and I expected a whipping; but he just stared at me without saying a word for what seemed like forever, when he finally spoke.

"From the abundance of the heart the mouth speaks." Then after a pause and a deep breath he added, "God is not the *damner*. If you must swear, say *devil be damned.*" Then he turned and walked away.

Pa was smart. Had he whipped me back then when I was twelve, as he probably wanted to, it might have made me rebellious.

This day, worry taking hold of both of us, Pa walked with me to my horse. We shook hands, and he softly said, "Take care. . ." That was the way of the Ross men — no kiss, no hug.

But Aunt Jane was a different matter. When I said good-bye to her she was crying, and hugging me with a reluctance to turn loose. Aunt Jane was really not related; she was Pa's housekeeper, and had been since Ma died. I was nine when Ma passed on in '31, two months after the twins, Joseph and Martha, were born. Pa had hired Jane to care for the house and help with us children. From that first day she had been like a mother to me.

After I mounted my gelding, Aunt Jane's tears were still flowing, and I caught an unmistakable glisten in Pa's eyes.

A month ago, in June, we evacuated Harpers Ferry. Several small, armed skirmishes with the Yankees had taken place over the last two months, but no major engagements. Most of our time was spent jockeying for position for the inevitable battle that we knew lay before us.

On the 18th of July, we had moved our brigade southeastward into an area just west of Bull Run, near the turnpike to Washington. We settled in among the other Confederate brigades already there. The day before, the Union army's vanguard had assaulted the outposts of our lines.

With our supplies and ammunition loaded, Major John Harmon, the Quartermaster in charge of the teamsters, came by my wagons. He noticed me, dismounted from his horse, and walked over.

"Sergeant Ross, Captain Forester would like for you to take command of twenty men — young boys — for the coming action. Their Sergeant has been killed by sniper fire, and we need someone older and experienced to take his place, somebody they can look up to.

"General Jackson suggested you."

I acknowledged I would do whatever I could to help, and was sent to check in with Lieutenant Garrett.

Major Harmon told me later he had made the mistake of asking General Jackson if I should return to the wagons in the event of a retreat. For a moment the precise Jackson's piercing dark eyes flashed fire from beneath the brim of his cap, and he caustically said, "Major, there will *be* no retreat."

Throughout the day, other brigades of our troops moved into the area along four miles of Bull Run, straddling the turnpike. Most were camped north of the road, as far as Manassas to the south.

On that afternoon, we had rushed into our position and set up camp along the ridge of the hill before Bull Run Creek, almost straight north of Manassas. Across the stream, Union troops were congregating for the battle — a battle to decide if, indeed, the Southern states would secede from the troubled Union.

Home was not over twenty-five miles from where I stood as I peered at the maneuvers of the enemy across the creek. They had invaded my country, and were an intruder that must be removed, just as my grandfather, John Ross, had helped evict the British from the Colonies in the Revolutionary War.

Along with the issued musket within my reach, I was armed with a Remington .44 revolver and a Henry rifle, both gifts from my father. And in my belt at my back was a sheathed twelve-inch dirk that had been carried by Great-Grandfather James at the Battle of Culloden, near Inverness, Scotland, in 1746.

Late on the 18th, as the purple twilight began moving into the underbrush and trees along the creek bed, night shadows slowly sallied across the open areas of grassland, where golden flames of campfires sprang up along our lines as did those across the brook. They were like stars on a velvet blanket draped over the countryside. Scattered and lonely, the winking flames captured my attention.

I thought of the fires comforting my enemy, and wondered if the men across the way thought of me as well. Though they were interlopers, they were men that, in truth, I hated not, and I detested the thought of having to kill a man who under other circumstances might have been a friend.

After our evening meal, and as I covered cut boughs of willow with my ground sheet, I tried to grasp the why of the conflict, and hoped that when the war was done there would be more gain than loss to civilization.

In the makeshift bed I lay with my hands behind my head and remembered what Pa had told me many years past, that if politics and the thirst for power could be taken out of the decision to fight wars, people would be better off.

I remembered, too, when I was twelve and my grandfather, John Ross, took me along to his retreat in the Blue Ridge Mountains, his secret place. There, at the high basin, he was in his element, and it became a sanctuary I would grow to love, too. A rushing brook flowed down the mountain, cascading into a waterfall of white turbulence. We camped there, in a grove of pine, where the roaring falls settled down to a deep, glassy blue pool. From the outfall, the meandering stream slowly made its way through a meadow filled with a medley of reds, yellows, and whites, pinks and lavenders — magenta and pink polygala, bright yellow wild indigo, delicate pink asters, and straight and proud lavender blazing stars, reaching for the sky — Virginia wildflowers that almost overwhelmed our eyes and our senses. And beyond the long, thick grass grew pitch pine and red oak, guarding the entrances of a dark canyon. Among the majestic oak was an ancient tree, some eight feet across and eighty feet tall.

We stayed a week camping and learning about each other — a moment in time I can never forget. Grandfather told me of his life and times in Scotland, and upon our return home I felt I had been to the sweet bonnie land myself.

As I lay by the creek at Bull Run, waiting for sleep, I thought back to Grandfather's stories, that began in 1744, twelve years before his birth and two before the Jacobite Rebellion — those passionate followers of England's James II who had fought to closure at the Battle of Culloden.

The British Isles

Scotland

*G*RANDFATHER'S ACCOUNT of recollections began with his own father, James Ross. The Ross clans had located in the northern Scottish Highlands, a swath of territory north of the Great Glen and south of Dornoch Firth, from Moray Firth along the North Sea to the Minch Sea of the Atlantic. The coastal cities of Tain, Cromarty, Melvaig, and Gairloch lay within their land.

James Ross was not related to the Ross clan Chief, but was permitted to use the Ross name, as were many others who acknowledged the Chief's authority and held loyalty to him.

Great-Grandfather James, my namesake, was a strong, supple man of weathered ruddy complexion. He appeared slimmer than his one hundred ninety pounds, and at five feet ten was considered tall. His brown hair turned blond in the summer, and he had bright blue eyes, and a full beard that nested beneath a sturdy Viking nose.

I learned from Grandfather John Ross that James had been of Irish-Gaelic descent, as were most of the Highlands' early inhabitants. When the Vikings captured the land and intermarried, their descendants became the Highlanders. By the sixteenth century, English had become their language, yet many still spoke Gaelic.

The Scottish clans were a family-formed society, with the land owned by their King, who granted property to the Chief by formal charter, holding certain restrictions and obligations to the throne. In the case of default, such as a rebellion, the ownership of the land would revert back to the Crown.

Below the Highlands Chief were cadets, from the Chief's immediate and distant family. These cadets, Grandfather had said, received grants from the Chief's divided property, forming a family network of clan territories. In turn, the cadets granted leases to tenants.

James Ross was a tenant, as his father had been before him, and had been born on the property he leased. He was thirty-one in the summer of 1744, a man who cherished life; even his routine chores were a joy to him.

He was a Sergeant in the clan army — not in the Chief's standing army of two hundred maintained at the castle, but one of the other eight hundred that were called to fight when enemies might approach and battles fought. Yearly he was required to attend rendezvous in the mountains for training. Being but a crofter — a tenant farmer — James was poor, though the small stipend he received from the army made life a bit easier.

Great-Grandfather James loved the land and it was still early that summer day of 1744 when he decided to ride to one of his favorite places higher up the mountain. He was astride his powerful shire draft stallion, some five miles northwest of his crofters cottage, in a remote part of his foothills property, on trails in familiar country, checking his pastured cattle in the mountainous hidden glens and braes. He left his horse to feed on the sparse grass and walked up the trail along an escarpment to a hanging cliff from where he could sit and see the North Sea.

James looked out upon a land that was largely treeless, a rugged and lonely land of striking beauty that leaped up from the sea into mountains as high as four thousand feet. It was a land riven by geological faults that had been enlarged by glacial action — an awesome country of escarpments, sheer cliffs, promontories, high pinnacles, narrow glens, clear flowing rivers, glacial lakes, and deep dark inlets from the sea that formed estuaries known as firths. The braes — the lovely slopes — of the glens were covered with heather and soft, downy grass. Along the brooks and rivers, in the poor soil of the glens, and sparsely scattered, were trees of pine, birch, and juniper. Although the land was considered poor and unfit for cultivation, with winters cold, turbulent, and damp, it mattered not to James. The harsh climate never entered his mind, nor the unproductive soil; it was something over which he had no control. His heart was on the tranquil beauty of the countryside, and whenever he spent time at his lonely sanctuaries, they never failed to give him a lifting spirit and a closeness to God.

As James often did from his refuge among the eagles, his eyes searched the North Sea, peering into the distance. Usually he found nothing, but this day, among the far swells, through a clearing of haze, he thought he saw three ships on the horizon of the unusually calm sea. The vessels disappeared, then moments later he saw them again through a fine gray mist. Before the mist grew dense, he knew the ships had been there — pirate ships, heading for Dornoch Firth.

James hurried to reach Tain before the pirates reached the harbor. Some two hours later, he leaped from his horse at the clan outpost to report the corsairs. The alarm was raised and a message sent to the Chief's castle, south of Tain, sited at a point above Moray Firth for the defense of his territory. The homes of the tenants paled when compared to the great castles of the Chiefs. The vast gulf that existed between the Chief and his clan was clearly discerned.

It was within the hour that the Chief, his high-ranking officers, and his standing army of two hundred men reached the town of Tain, and none too soon. The raiders came to shore from out of the mist like insidious ghosts — three galleys of twenty-four oars each.

The pirates, Grandfather Ross had told, were there to loot and rape the town, and they had to be stopped. Great-Grandfather James had rounded up the able volunteers, and it appeared that the two opposing forces would be close in number.

The pirates had rushed ashore and quickly moved forward. The clan's small army moved into line to meet them. The fighting appeared to be matched evenly, and, then, to the grief of all around, Great-Grandfather James's Lieutenant was cut down by a fierce enemy who handled the broadsword like a rapier, mutilating all who challenged him. The line began to crumble, as the Scots gave way. James rushed into the breach, where he and the corsair engaged. The slighter of the two, James nevertheless had his double-edged claymore, which he could wield as easily as his enemy did the broadsword. With a curdling battle scream, James rushed in swinging his sword and in but seconds the pirate lay at his feet, decapitated.

The enemy pirates' hesitation at their loss rallied James and the men forward with a ferocious attack, cutting down the pirates amidst the din of their frantic attempt to retreat back to their vessels. But none escaped; and to their inventory of seaworthy ships, the clan added three galleys.

From high ground above, the Chief had watched the battle, then approached Great-Grandfather Ross, and on the battlefield promoted him in rank to Lieutenant. Gathering his clansmen around him, he told them that James was now an officer in the clan's army.

A cheer went up, and James became the only officer who was not remotely related to the Chief. Yet, although he was given this special status, he remained a yeoman, farming his tenant land as before.

In 1746, a springtime sun of golden light owned the countryside as far as eyes could see throughout the Great Glen of Scotland, when Lieutenant James Ross marched his company of fellow clansmen into line to the skirl of bagpipes and rustling banners. James was dressed in his battlefield tartan, with his sheathed King flintlock pistol, claymore, and dirk in his belt. Many had abandoned the claymore for the broadsword, to carry a shield in their other hand, but James had not. He had always fought with the claymore, though it took two hands to handle the great sword.

The enemy, the Jacobite army — those who had endeavored to restore to the throne those descendants of the Roman Catholic Stuart line of James II — had encamped their men on ill-chosen grounds when they lined up in the lowlands of Drumossie Moor, yet but another showing of the Earl of Mar's poor leadership.

The struggle to ensue was only minutes away as James peered across the rolling countryside at the rebel troops coming into line. To his right was Lieutenant Sutherland's company. Farther right, on the crest of a hillock, and to the rear stood Culloden house, silent and peaceful. Further right in the distance was Moray Firth, its beautiful, deep, glacial surface waters shimmering diamonds in the sunlight.

James had thought that the alignment for battle had seemed almost unreal, more like those times when the clan members would come together at their grounds for rendezvous in preparation for war, or some peaceful gathering of the troops.

He walked the line in front of his men, who were waiting anxiously. Facing him in the distance was MacDonald's brigade of the rebel army, fierce fighters, and they alone would guarantee a hard struggle against the Jacobites.

The government army's right flank tied into the hills near the firth, its left flank to the higher hills of the lowlands. Along the plateau of the left flank rode the Duke of Cumberland, the second son of King George, overlooking the field of the impending battle; he was astride a white horse, and easily recognized by his men.

Then to the skirl of bagpipes marched a magnificent sight. The MacDonalds and the entire rebel army, dressed in their colorful tartans, with banners flying, attacked all along the Crown's line, attempting to drive a wedge through it. The attack was hard and ferocious, but the well-organized regiment with its musketry firepower slaughtered the oncoming soldiers. After the first volley, the armies moved to hand-to-hand combat and a fierce struggle. With a staggering loss of men, the Jacobite army began to slowly fall back in retreat, and then the action turned into a rout with men and officers in disarray fleeing the field.

Leading the retreat was the Bonnie Prince Charles, disappearing on horseback southwest into the erosion-slashed braes and glens.

James had been credited with killing three enemy in the heat of battle. And as he led his men forward with his claymore slashing, many surrendered while others escaped.

But it is what happened next that horrified Great-Grandfather James. To kill in battle was one thing, for it was kill or be killed; but to execute en masse unarmed fellow countrymen was a different matter.

Before his eyes, one hundred twenty of the Jacobites were executed. Later, nine hundred thirty-six were ordered sent to the West Indies, America, and Australia. Another two hundred were banished and forbidden to return to Scotland. Many of the Jacobite prisoners had pleaded that they had been forced to fight, and probably so, for there were many that felt compelled to fight for the government.

The occupation following the Battle of Culloden — a punishment no doubt — proved to be bad times for the clans. The Duke of Cumberland showed no mercy, and even the clans that had fought with the Crown were severely affected by his ordered changes, including the act that forbade the wearing of Highland tartan after August of 1747. It was a disarming of sorts, taking away the long-heralded pride of the clans, their identity through their tartans. In 1748, the act was enforced. The first offense was punishable by six months in prison, the second by seven years. This violation of their manly rights was disheartening to the clans that had been true to the Crown.

My grandfather, John Ross, James's son, had been born on April 20th, 1756, ten years after the Battle of Culloden. He had come along late in the life of his parents. James, his father, was forty-three and Elizabeth, his mother, was thirty-nine. He was the youngest of four brothers.

The first thing Grandfather John Ross remembered of life was the plain cottage that was his home, with open beams overhead and a huge stone fireplace where his mother prepared their meals. His father had carefully laid in fitted stone for their floor, whereas many of the crofters' cottages had hard-packed dirt. The exterior walls were of stone, the joints slurred with lime. The hip roof was of dried, thatched heather and resembled a haystack sitting above the ground. Grandfather John Ross recalled little of his brothers, who left home before he was three.

The Ross cottage was fifteen miles northeast of Tain. The cadet they leased from was Paul, the Chief's eldest son, and he had kept the best ground for himself in the glen of Dornoch Firth. James's land was to the south, in the rolling foothills and higher meadows, land not fit for cultivation — though heather and short grass over time had taken root in the glacial soil.

James maintained a herd of thirty head of cattle on the oasis of hidden slopes the family had located throughout the years. Other crofters marveled at how he managed to keep a herd that large on the family's available ground. The Highland cattle were large, dark, reddish-brown animals with wide and long horns, a unique breed, with heavy dewlaps and long, shaggy coats. Native to the region, they had become acclimated to the harsh terrain and weather.

James also had a magnificent pair of shire horses.

Grandfather John Ross was three years old when the King's men came to their cottage and arrested his father. James had just returned home and was still in his battlefield tartan when the officer and five men who had been lying in wait broke into the house. His father did not resist and they took him away. Why six men were needed to arrest his father, Grandfather never knew, but he guessed they had heard of his reputation as a fearless warrior and were not about to risk a loss.

James spent six months in prison, and when he was released it was well into spring and King George III had ascended the throne.

Grandfather Ross's happiest day occurred when he was six and his father told him the Connemara mare he had purchased a year earlier, and mated with his shire stallion, had dropped a foal — and better yet, the colt would be John's, along with the responsibility for its care.

"Now that he's yours, lad, what're ye gon't' name 'im?" his father had asked.

John excitedly answered, "Prince. I want t'name him Prince." After that day, John and Prince were inseparable.

John started school when he was eight. Formal education was in the hands of the Presbyterian Church, with a strict regimen of theology included in the course work. John's father went with him that first day; his mother could not bear to go. The six-month school year ran from the first of October to the last of March, and John would be staying away from home on the school premises.

His mother was crying, and Prince was anxious to go for a ride somewhere when young John had to say his good-byes. His father had their shire draft horse outside the shed, harnessing him up to the wagon for their travel into Tain. School would be fifteen miles from home, but it might as well have been halfway around the world, for John would not see his folks again until he walked home in the spring.

John and his father rode up to a rectangular, two-story stone building on a large tract of land that overlooked Dornoch Firth. To the northwest, at a lower elevation and nearer the road, was the ivy-clad stone church where the students and town people attended services. To the west of the kirk was a cemetery.

James tied the horse and walked into the spacious entryway. It was dark, cold, and foreboding. To the right, beside a closed door, hung a sign, "Headmaster."

James knocked. They entered to a strident voice, "Come in!" The headmaster stood up, a tall, skinny man with a sharp nose and receding hairline; they each shook hands.

"I am James Ross, and this is m'son, John. He'll be attending school this term."

"Aye," the man slowly replied, as he examined John with a cold look to his dark eyes. To James he introduced himself as Phillip MacDonald. "The Chief has spok'n highly of ye, and wi'out his recommendation, we would'na lik'ly o'had room here for John."

John could tell the headmaster's remark had angered his father, by the look in his eye, but James said nothing. After formulated speech-taking by the headmaster, James quickly turned to John. "Lad, I'll be leavin' now. If ye hav' any probl'ms ye can't handle, come on home, and I'll be back t' take care o' it."

"Aye, Fath'r," John replied.

The headmaster, obviously disturbed at James's icy retort, managed to squeak out of his thin, austere mouth, "Aye . . . sure, James, we'll take good care o' John. You need'na worry 'bout a thing."

It was obvious to John that the headmaster had taken an instant dislike to him and his father. After James left, the man sharply instructed John to follow him, for he would show him to his room.

They walked into the entry, then turned into a hallway that led to a wide stairway, which they climbed on their way to the far end of the building. The headmaster opened the north door of many along the hallway. It was a large room. Eight cots lined the west wall. One large table with eight chairs was placed in the middle of the room. Seven chests beside seven respective beds.

The headmaster pointed, and John put down his chest, which he had been instructed to bring with his clothes and personals, beside the remaining bed.

A fireplace along the north wall was the only distinctive feature in the dull and dismal room. The beds each had upon them one quilt, hardly sufficient for the coming Highland winter.

"John," the headmaster began, "ye will rise at four in the morning, bathe, and make yer bed. Breakfast is at five sharp, in the dining hall. Physical and military training begins at six. Theology classes at nine, until elev'n. Dinn'r in the hall is at twelve. Arts and science classes are from one 'til four. Supper's at five. Then it's t'yer room for study from six to nine, at which time all lamps ere t'be extinguish'd, and the fireplace bank'd. The schedule leaves two hours o' free time. I'd suggest it be wisely spent in the library."

Grandfather Ross had told me it was hard at first, being away from home, but as time went along the school seemed to grow on him, and he tolerated the strict way of life. He had done as the headmaster advised and spent all his spare time at the library. Books were like eyes to the world, and he could not get enough of the knowledge and the faraway places they would take him.

Grandfather studied hard and excelled in his classes. He tried to distance himself from the headmaster, solving any problems that came along on his own. Most of his classmates shunned him, because he was but a crofter's son, and thus most of his time was spent off alone and away from the others.

Nevertheless, besides the education he received, Grandfather learned self-denial and discipline, virtues, he said, that served him well in the future.

That year, he embroiled into two fights with different classmates. Nothing he had done had precipitated the disagreements; he knew the students simply disliked him, and in each case they had started the problems. Grandfather Ross had been raised to stand up for himself, and when they brought their action to him, he fought back. And even though the boys were older and more experienced, he held his own. Unfortunately, Grandfather said, a teacher had stopped the first fight, the headmaster the second. The headmaster questioned both boys, and the other combatant lied about who had started the trouble. Grandfather said nothing to defend his actions, except that they had had a misunderstanding. The other lad stood back, wary that John would blabber the truth, but he did not, and John was the one punished.

For John's first offense, he had been restricted to his room with no food for a day. The penalty for his second was a flogging — ten lashes with a whip. He took the beating with hardly a whimper, in front of the other boys. The students knew it was a wrongful whipping, and he gained a measure of their respect. From that time on, almost all of his classmates were friendlier, but he still was wary and maintained a distance.

Several times during his stay at the school, Grandfather had caught the headmaster watching him from afar, as if he was waiting for him to transgress. But he had no further trouble that school year. On the last day of March, he left school and walked home.

As he passed along the roadway raising small clouds of dust, he thought to himself how bittersweet the year had been. Sundays after church he had learned to be alone — with himself, and with God — and he became more aware of nature's beauty. On his own with nature, he could meditate in peace without interruption.

After John had been at home for a day, he noticed that his father's weapons were not in the house and he asked his father where they were now kept. Grandfather was hoping his father could work with him and teach him to use the weapons before he went back to school.

James quietly explained that he had hid his arms, lest the authorities would take them all. He had heard they were going to confiscate the weapons of anyone who had been in prison. But he left a few at the cottage, knowing the representatives of the Crown would be disappointed and disbelieving if they did not find something.

One morning, a month after John had been home, his father suggested they get some things together. "We'll be away at least a week."

John was excited and his mother helped him bundle clothes and food. James, with his staff in hand and John following, took off down the trail toward the main road. At the traveled way, instead of heading for Tain, they went southwest.

Walking along, James mused, "All yer broth'rs ere gone, scatter'd all ov'r the world in Scottish regiments. Without 'em here to help me, it's time I start'd on th' education ye'd ask'd about earlier."

"What education, Fath'r? I hope it's th' weapons."

"Aye, the education ye can only learn by experience, the education t' be a clansman and a warrior."

After walking some four miles, they came to the River Carron and took the trail southwest. They walked a narrow glen bordered by rolling braes of green. John questioned how far they had to go.

"Oh, it may be anoth'r ten miles — not too far for a Scottish lad, is't?
"No, Fath'r."

"It's my special place. Can you keep a secr't lad? Our lives may depend on't."

John was astonished, but more elated, that his father would trust him with something secret. He proudly replied, "Ye know I can, Fath'r."

James pointed to the southeast. "Ov'r there, that mountain Ben Dearg — the place we're goin' is b'fore that mountain."

Three hours later they stopped at a fair-sized brook coming from the west, where perhaps a mile away only mountains, cliffs, and escarpments could be seen. For a minute or so James scanned the road both ways. They could see close to a mile each way, and no one was in sight.

"Follow me," James told John, and quickly they entered the water, walking upstream. In moments they were out of sight of the roadway.

After about five minutes James stepped out of the fast-flowing stream onto rock, and John followed. As they ascended the north bank to a narrow game trail, James had picked up a branch and lightly brushed away their tracks while they continued west.

John wondered how they were going to climb those cliffs — and not only that, but two hundred feet ahead, a ten-foot wide fall of water gushed out of the mountain.

They continued to the escarpment, where they stood alongside and beneath the roaring waterfall. James took John's hand and stepped through the watery veil along the north side of the rift. Thirty feet later they turned north, walking in a cleft of sheer rock that widened out to about fifty feet, where they journeyed a game trail in and out of the mountain stream. Grandfather John told me it felt as if he was maneuvering along a high, narrow trench that shot straight up to a thin ribbon of sky. When he looked back at where they had entered the abyss, he could not see the entrance. Where the water hit the south wall, it splashed and filled the narrow chasm of the outfall, and the north side of the opening was nothing more than a curtain of water.

They followed the stream a half-mile north, the trail weaving in and out and around boulders like a needle stitching into a blanket. Then they headed west through the deep canyon of rock for perhaps half a mile, until it widened out to a glen.

Grandfather said they had walked into the most beautiful sanctuary he had ever seen, some hundred acres of untouched basin, with the only way out being the way they had come in.

The brook meandered across the basin guarded with intermittent pinnacles of rock, pine, birch, and juniper. The rest of the area was heather and grass interspersed with enormous angled layers of rock.

Grandfather followed his father to an escarpment near the southwest corner of the glen. The cave was invisible until John was almost on top of it, with the lay of the brae and the heather blocking sight of the entrance.

He was astonished. It was fixed like a room, with two handmade beds, an old wooden table, and two chairs. Rocks had been laid up for a small fireplace from where the smoke rose and disappeared into a cleft of the ancient granite.

Two long, wooden boxes were placed in the far corner, along with a chest. When James opened up the chest, young John could see the Ross battlefield tartan, with a twelve-inch dirk and a King flintlock pistol. The first large box contained a claymore, broadsword, two rapiers, a long bow, and arrows. The smaller but longer box held two quarterstaffs and a "Brown Bess" .75-caliber musket.

That evening as James was building a fire, Grandfather asked his father how he had found this place.

James began slowly. "I was near tw'lve, it was a year of drought, and food was scarce. I'd left home t' hunt game, and when I'd come t' th' brook that int'rsects with th' road, I spott'd a deer movin' west on th' game trail. He was headin' for th' cliffs, and I figur'd I might get close enough for a shot wi' my long bow, so I follow'd. I could see there was no place for him t' go, and I was sure he was corner'd.

"I caught a glimpse of th' deer as he reach'd th' cliffs where th' wat'r gush'd out o' th' mountain. He stood there wary and alert, then for a moment was block'd from my view as I mov'd clos'r through deep cov'r to a clearing. And when I look'd from there, he was gone. I could'na believe it; t'was like he'd disappear'd int' thin air. I walk'd on up t' where he'd stood along th' north side o' th' wat'r splashin' out o' th' mount'n. I could'na find his tracks t' th' left nor right. After studyin' on his where-abouts for a time, I figur'd he had t' go upstream through that maelstrom o' wat'r. I walk'd int' it, splashin' well o'er my head. After gettin' through and turnin' west, I could see his tracks on th' trail in th' gorge.

"That was how I found this place, and for a time I figur'd I was th' first human t' ev'r set foot here. But I was wrong, for in th' cave, I found a gold coin and th' remnants of what must have been an ancient campfire. Some-one else had been here, and from th' age o' th' coin, it may hav' been long ago, durin' th' Roman occupation. 'Tis somethin' not easy t' imagine.

"I've told no one 'bout th' glen, except yer moth'r."

James quit talking.

John was lying on his bed thinking about the glen, and later he softly said to his father, "I am grateful for yer confidence, Fath'r. I'll tell no one o' this place."

It was dark in the cave, except for the reddish glow of their campfire. John knew his training would start that next day. He thought about his father, a taciturn man of morals and principle, a God-fearing man. If given reason, he could be quick to anger, but quick as well to forgive. From what Grandfather had heard, his father was indeed ferocious in combat, and surely it must be, for whenever he was around the Chief, other cadets, or crofters, they always showed his father more than friendship. It was as though, with them, he held a high place of honor and respect.

John lay watching the flickering firelight, as the shapes transformed into legions of Roman soldiers locked in combat with his ancestors of centuries ago. He slept with the dreams of a warrior.

James worked with John all that week, starting with the use of the quarterstaff — as if it were a sword, and John was amazed at all he could do with a staff. James carried his staff as a cane. If needed, he could use it as a weapon. He was not sure of its legality, but he had not been stopped by the authorities.

Over the next two years, Grandfather John Ross attended the Tain School. He soon became a close friend of Peter Murray, the youngest son of the Murray clan's Chief. John was sociable with the other students, but not friends, and he maintained his separation.

Late during his third year at Tain, Peter told John he would be continuing his education elsewhere the following year and asked John to go along with him to the school at Beauly.

"I can'na," Grandfather John replied. "The school is for the sons and relations of the Chiefs."

As John was leaving that final day, the headmaster caught him going out the door and invited him into his office. John had developed a better understanding of the man during the past two years. He had been the son of a Chief of the MacDonald clan, and his father had been executed on site after the Battle of Culloden. Being the next in line, he had his lands confiscated by the Crown. Without a heritage, but being well educated, he had accepted the job at Tain.

He motioned Grandfather to a chair. "We haven't gott'n along well, John Ross, and as t' where you're headin' in life, I haven't a clue. In some ways we're a lot alike, for I have no future prosp'cts, and I, too, am untrusting o' others. My advice t' ye as you leave here is stay that way. Put little trust in anyone, not ev'n your clos'st friend. Then, if it turns out ye're wrong, what hav' ye lost?

"I've had my eye on ye, John, and ye seem to like yer books; they'll always be yer friend, so determine yerself t' stick with 'em."

Then, abruptly, he waved John out of the room. As John walked out the front door for the last time, he thought how sad that the headmaster had become so bitter.

For a moment, Grandfather said, he felt sorry for him. And this final effort by the headmaster — what he thought to be good and sound advice — was perhaps his way of atonement for the past three years of abuse.

In the days to come, to Grandfather John's surprise, he was accepted to the Beauly school. The recommendation from the Murray Chief and from his own, along with his high marks at Tain, had earned him the place, and he attended Beauly the following two years.

In between his schooling, Grandfather John Ross worked with his father, James, whenever they could get away to their sanctuary in the mountains. John had learned how to make his own bow and arrows and to use all the forbidden weapons cached at the glen. He had also learned from his father the arts of wrestling and boxing.

Their hunting for food was in remote areas outside the secret basin, for James did not wish to deplete the animals within, should they be needed in emergency. What hunting they did was with the bow, not wanting to bring attention to themselves with gunshots.

Grandfather learned from his father that there was always a way to win a fight, even if you had no weapons. "There's yer hands, and yer brain," his father said. "Y'must be aware o' what sets nearby — a rock, a brok'n limb, or a fence post that could be us'd as a club. In a home there'd be a pok'r, eatin' kniv's, or ev'n a brok'n chair leg. Ye must keep contrivin' and contemplatin' until ye find a way. It's what separates man from th' oth'r species."

In May of 1769, Grandfather left for the fishing village of Wick to work for his cousin, Duncan Ross, owner of a one-masted common fishing boat. They plied the North Sea, catching fish to sell — a valued experience for John. He learned the art of sailing in every weather, be it calm or rough seas.

It was in April, almost a year later, when Grandfather John Ross returned home. By this time he had turned fourteen. After a session with the claymore, his father told him he had become far stronger and more proficient with the sword.

John now stood at five feet nine, and he had grown into a strong one hundred sixty pounds. Even James had to admit that John now and then could best him with the rapier. He acknowledged that in days to come, there might be none his equal.

In the summer of 1770, Great-Grandmother Ross had wanted young John to maintain the family's traditions by learning to play the bagpipe. The bagpipe school — the "college" some had called it — was on the Isle of Skye, controlled by the MacLeods and MacDonalds. The pipers, however, were taught by the MacCrimmons and MacArthurs, though at the Isle of Mull it was the Macleans.

Pipers had a long, respected history in the clans. Their music was suited for the arid, melancholy Highlands, where it had shared a close connection to the people. And the pipers kept time for the military march, as well as for the rowers of ships that crossed the sea.

Grandfather John's mother was a friend of the MacArthurs, who trained in the bagpipe, and she had made arrangements with them, including room and board, for John's instruction. John would repay them with the chores that needed to be done, and his instruction was to last for nine months.

The sun was still behind the mountains when John left for Skye that dark gray morning. He carried the pack his mother had filled with clothes and foodstuff for the trip. He had walked five hours before he could see the Chief's castle some two miles off, on the pinnacle of headland overlooking Moray Firth. Its defensive ramparts were gleaming the golden light of morning sun. The huge stronghold was a formidable sight with its banners flying above the stone battlements. Quickly John walked by and left the castle behind him.

Grandfather knew he had to be wary of thieves as he traveled, for there were those about who preyed upon the unsuspecting. The only weapon he carried was the six-foot quarterstaff his father had made for him, but the staff, which could be taken apart into two sections and carried in his pack, had a groove at the bottom that hid a spring, releasing a tightly sheathed eight-inch blade.

"But don'na get caught showin' th' blade," his father cautioned. "Use it only when ye must. Sometimes surprise can make all th' diff'rence."

That first day, with his staff in his hand, Grandfather strode out briskly down the roadway, and by evening he came to the village of Dingwall, after having passed by Alness and Evanton. He walked on, and found a sheltered place to sleep the night, a shallow cave off from the road, where nearby spring water flowed from the mountains, cascading into a deep, clear pool. He built a small fire and roasted the grouse from his pack.

The night was dark and quiet as he listened to the water rushing across the rock in the burn, flowing on down the hillside. That was the last he remembered before falling sleep.

When he awoke, the world was still dark and after a light meal in the edging gray of dawn, as the stars were blowing out their lamps, he set again upon his way. South of Dingwall he reached the River Canon, then took the roadway west up the glen. In the distance Sgurr Mor Mountain looked down majestically upon him, unconcerned of his presence.

To the south eight miles lay Beauly, where he had gone to school, and beyond it another ten miles Loch Ness. John was thankful his traveled way would not pass close by the loch, for to travel alone was bad enough without having to contend with the kelpies, the horselike evil fairies — the goblins as locals called them — that were said to inhabit the lochs. Word told they could cause and foretell drownings, and though he had never believed in such tales, he knew he would be just as comfortable to stay far away.

Few travelers passed on the road that day, and around noon Grandfather came to the town of Garve, a busy place where he decided to take a few minutes to look inside the shops.

As he left the leather crafter, he noticed two young and tough-looking village locals loitering across the way. They watched him as he continued slowly on down the street, but when he looked back, they were gone.

John was suspicious of the unkempt youths, but he saw them no more. The way was clear to the west as he hastily made off down the road out of the village. After a mile at a good pace, he thought perhaps he was being foolish; perhaps the lads were just curious of a stranger.

Ahead the road dropped down close to the river, with dense pine and birch, a place where two thugs, if such they were, could hide in wait for a likely suspect. But it was either go on or back into town, and Grandfather was not about to go back.

He had passed the heavier part of the woods when he saw two men up ahead with what looked like clubs in their hands. But then, instead of two, there were four, as when he looked around, the two he had seen in the village were behind him. John had no chance to run, although he had been a champion sprinter in school.

The four had expected John to bolt. Instead, he turned and legged it toward the two behind him, deciding to take them on first — put them out of the fight as fast as he could — then devote his time to those at his front.

He moved in fast, and in a flurry had them on the ground. One was knocked cold and would be for some time John could see; the other was moaning, holding his broken jaw. John had heard it crack as the blow of his staff struck across the side of the hoodlum's head.

John turned and dropped his staff, so that in picking it up he might clasp a fist full of dirt into his hand. The other two ruffians were nearing, and as they moved in, they spread apart. When they had closed to within a few feet, John threw the dirt into the face of the large youth. Before he could clear his eyes, the other lay on the ground. The staff had lashed a cut across his face, laying it open to the cheekbone.

The largest offender stepped back and pulled his rapier.

"Ye've had yer way," he growled, "and now y'll get what's coming t' ye!"

"Like as *not!*" John replied.

The large bruiser was angry, John thought, and that was good. He had learned that when an opponent became angry, he became careless.

With his staff as a sword, John circled the thief's left, for he was surely right-handed. But it was a mistake, John soon found out, for he should never take anything for granted. It almost had been his downfall. Only his quick reaction — the trait of every Ross — had saved his life from the sword, as it plunged forward to his heart.

In the very final second he had warded it away with his trusty staff and suffered but a shallow gash. John could see that the leader had for certain fenced before — though he was not a master — and in moments the thug lay at Grandfather's feet, knocked cold as the winter snow.

He left the thugs to their fate, walking on, hoping they might pick a better livelihood. He made his camp that night south of Loch Fannich, sheltered within the ruins of an ancient ghostly castle. Bedded down near the fallen rubble of the keep, where prisoners of battles past were held, Grandfather's grateful prayers reached up unto a merciful God; and then he slept.

By noon the following day, Grandfather retold, he had come to the fork in the road at busy Achnasheen that would lead on to the Isle of Skye. The village folk stared as he strode down their cobblestone street. Dogs barked and snapped at his heels, but he did not turn or stop.

He came upon an inn with a courtyard and stables to the rear. He had seen few travelers on the road, and there were but four men within the common room. They glanced as he crossed to sit, his back protected by the wall. A man alone, a deep scar above his jaw, seemed to smile from across the room, as he noticed John's caution where he sat — a smile, John could tell, that the man understood, for he, too, held not a trust for strangers.

The innkeeper was a burly man — there would be no nonsense with him, John thought, although he had a pleasant enough face.

As he took in the tempting odors of the kitchen, a pretty young maiden stepped out, a lass about his age, already blossomed into a woman. Her black hair hung in ringlets about her crimson cheeks, framing her deep blue eyes and long, fringed lashes. The eyes had captivated John, a true healthy lad whose blood ran hot as he viewed any fair young maiden.

Flirtatiously she asked what he might have. As John stammered his reply, peering eagerly at her lovely oval face, he was unable to keep his eyes from her well-endowed youthful figure. She could see that he was flustered, and it pleased her.

Grandfather said he blushed at his unrestrained thoughts, then sat back to await the much anticipated meal.

As the lass came forth with his dinner, she put her hands on her shapely hips and asked, "Ere ye from 'round here, me friend?"

Grandfather explained he lived north of Tain, and was just traveling through, headed for Skye.

Her disappointment was easily perceived.

John smiled and added, "But I'll be back this way in April, and p'rhaps I'll stay a few days."

"Aye," she simply replied. "My name, I might add, is Marie."

The dinner was filling, and when the lass returned to pick up John's plate, he paid her in gold.

Amazed at the coin, and almost caressing it in her hands, she quickly expressed concern. "Ye must be careful showin' that kind o' coin, John. There're those who'd do anythin' for't . . . and hesitate not t' kill."

John thanked her for her advice. "Well, th'money came from moth'r's savin' so I might attend training in Skye. I've already had a bit o' trouble, just outside o' Garve. But I took care o' it. I don'na think they'll be botherin' anyone soon."

Marie's gaze lingered on John a moment. "Well, maybe ye're ev'n more of a lad than I thought." A moment later she returned and counted out his change in silver, then put her hand on his arm. "Be sure ye stop and see me on yer way back."

Grandfather said it was a promise he was determined to keep.

John strode out briskly from the village and took the road southwest along Carron Glen. The elevation of the country was rising noticeably, and he had hoped to reach the divide by nightfall. Throughout the day he walked uphill in the uninhabited and lonely land.

The treeless pass with the trailway winding and twisting through the barren rock was a dreary and melancholy place. The mountain peaks were precipitously rising around him in all directions, except for the trail behind and to the northeast where he had a far view of what he thought would be the Isle of Skye.

He had stopped for the night at the beginning of the southwest slope, hoping for a glimpse of the sea, but a hazy, misty fog crawled about the faraway waters below, veiling his view.

He made camp in a corner of slanting rock that nature had pushed up from its original resting place; erosion had left it like a room open to the south. He built a campfire from dead wood he found, though how it had come to be there was a mystery of nature.

From his pack he warmed over the campfire some salt-preserved beef and beans, and after eating he brewed a tea. Finishing, he lay back on his bed and watched the night capture the lowlands and slowly climb toward his pallet. Darkness came at last to him there on the pass, where he felt a million miles from home, as if civilization had disappeared.

He peered into the far distance below, where he could see three domes of faint village lights, and wondered if they might be from the town Kyle of Lochalsh, or even Kyleakin on the Isle of Skye. The distant glow gave him an undefined solitary feeling of mystery, a feeling he always had when he came upon those isolated mountain towns, as though he were a lonely vagabond and a kindred soul was waiting there just for him.

John lay back on his pallet, listening to the mountain stream of water flowing in and around the erosion-smoothed rocks, and surveyed the flat and black sky with its spattered surface of twinkling stars. They seemed to be noticing him, as they flashed off and on, perhaps wondering what he was doing in that remote and barren place, just as he was wondering what they might be doing, in their dark and mysterious unreachable habitats.

The stars were the last thing he remembered until the gray of morning, when he awoke to the music of the rushing water. He lazily stayed for a time, watching the quickly fading stars banking down their fires.

The morning air was cold, the freshness of it blown briskly down from off the nearby peaks, and he wasted no time in getting dressed in his drab brown, mottled cloak hanging to his calves, with his belt around his loins outside the fringed garment. He had the kind of clothes the Scots wore to camouflage their movements when out alone in the heather. He preferred plaids, especially of blue and purple; but, nonetheless, he would need to be wary when in unknown territory, and he dressed accordingly.

John peered over at his campfire, where one dull red ember was winking at him through the powdery ashes, and trailing a little column of disappearing smoke toward the sky. He laid his last few sticks on the ember, which after pause and little consideration raised up like flaming arms embracing the amenable sticks. They flared with force before falling together, limp and exhausted, into dust.

John walked to the rim and looked at the vast distance toward Skye. High above his head an eagle screeched and soared against a snowy backdrop of high peaks, where mighty cathedral clouds opened a window, gleaming a sunlit path through which the raptor soared and disappeared. As John stood with his bronze profile etched against the sky, he felt like anything but a crofter's boy.

He had long ago determined that as he had not been born the son of a Chief, he would have to become on his own whatever he chose. Crowns had been taken with a sword, after all, and he had a sword. And he also had wit, and words. Had not Christ become King with his Word?

John listened to the stream that appeared to be laughing at his thoughts. "That's all right!" he shouted aloud. "We will see who laughs last!"

As he packed, he wondered who could control events, for events seemed to control the person. Yet, he thought, surely God had something in mind for him, for why else would he have seen to the pathways of learning he had traveled.

He took off briskly down the path to Strome Ferry, and as he walked he thought back to his days at Beauly. He had, indeed, received a good education those past six years. But what should he do with his life? He had learned well the art of war, and was skilled in the use of his weapons. He knew the tactics, and if need be could lead a regiment into battle. With his father's teachings he was far ahead of his classmates in the use of the weapons, though he had purposely held back his skill at times in competition. For he had learned to be diplomatic, enough to know that had he won every time, he would make enemies — enemies he did not want. And, Grandfather added, his own father had always told him, "Never reveal all that you know."

Grandfather contemplated that perhaps he should join the army, like his brothers. Scottish regiments had been sent all over the world. But on the other hand, his love of learning conveyed an insatiable appetite for knowledge. He thought that perhaps when he returned home the next spring he should see about attending the university at Aberdeen. He would have to speak with the Chief about that, he knew, otherwise he would never be accepted. He had heard Aberdeen had a large library, and a seemingly endless supply of books from around the world. Grandfather really did not much care about the diploma; he just wanted access to the library, to be able to read every book he could lay hands on.

Moving quickly down grade, by sunset he reached Strome Ferry. By afternoon the next day he reached the fishing village, Kyle of Lochalsh.

The next morning, a beautiful clear sunlit day, he slowly walked along the quay admiring the hundreds of fishing boats. He stopped and talked to a fisherman working with his nets. The Scotsman took a liking to Grandfather, who hired the seaman to ferry him across the Inner Sound to Kyleakin on Skye.

The way the crow flies, it was only eighty miles to the Isle of Skye from the Ross home, but it had taken John six days to reach the island. He figured he had probably walked well over a hundred thirty miles of rough terrain. And it would take another day before he would reach the remote cottage of the MacArthurs, his teachers.

The days there flew by fast, and Grandfather John Ross took well to the bagpipe and to the tune of the Highland fling, the Scottish victory dance. It was early April of 1771 when he returned home. He had spent two days of his travel, as he had earlier promised the intriguing young Marie, at the inn west of Achnasheen.

John awoke in his own bed to sunlight gleaming through the small window of the cottage. It took him a moment to determine where he was. His room felt cold, but not a bitter air. The warm Atlantic currents along the west coast of the Highlands made harsh freezing temperatures rare.

He lay there remembering the day before, how Prince had capered with obvious joy to see him again. Then he heard his mother bustling about, the rattle of dishes, and the comforting aroma of a morning meal cooking in the fireplace.

He could hear his mother humming a favorite old ballad — a sure sign of happiness. When he walked into their common room, she beamed at him. He had piped for them the night before, and he could feel their pride in his accomplishment.

After John had a hearty repast, his father returned from the morning chores. John again conveyed the tales of his travels and his time in Skye. Later in the day they discussed the university, and his father committed to speak with the Chief.

It was but a week later when John and his father were at their special place, after a hard session with the claymore, that his father praised his improvement with the double-edged weapon. "Ye're a lot stronger than ye were."

"Aye, Fath'r, . . . I kept in fine shape doin' the chor's, and many hours splittin' firewood ."

That night, as father and son finished a modest supper, James said to young John, "Ye know, lad, nev'r t' stare int' a fire at night . . . for when ye look away ye're sure t' be blinded. It could mean th' diff'rence betw'n life 'n death." His father paused, then almost whispered, "And I know who 'twas that turn'd me in t' th' officials, John.

"Our good Alan, th' Chief's clos'st friend, his aide, last week in earnest told me th' culprit was Paul, our Chief's eld'st son."

John was not surprised, for Paul had always held his father as a bitter rival, jealous of his prowess in the battle.

"The Chief had sent Alan t' warn o' a threat on my life. Paul has aimed t' discredit and eliminate his father's loyal followers, t' gain the control o' th' clan for himself. And he plans t' hav' me arrest'd, for charges yet unknown. But we are aided by th' Chief's underground of spies, who are noting Paul's intentions.

"Amidst th' intrigue going on, th' Chief dares not come by t' visit as he's done. And if he has information for me, he sends Alan in th' cover o' night."

"If the cottage is bein' watch'd, me lad, he leaves a message in a ledge rock crevice, but a mile south o'th' hoose, and then we meet th' night next. D' ye rememb'r th' rock crevice in th' shelter'd glen — th' one where we hav' stash'd at times? "

"Aye." John remembered the place.

James wanted his son to be wary. "It would'na hurt t' be cautious, for even yer life may be in dang'r."

John was surprised. "And what would be Paul's reason, Fath'r?"

James could only surmise that the same jealousy might provoke Paul toward John that had rankled him toward James. "Ye're ev'n bett'r educat'd than he, and his fath'r speaks o' ye wi' high regard. The Chief has thought o' findin' a way t' give us each the status as a cadet. . . t' which Paul has been soundly oppos'd."

Three months after John had returned from Skye, summer was in the air as he rode to glens and braes. Wary though he had been, his father continued to warn against letting his guard down. Life was too precious to lose because of a momentary lapse.

His father had spoken with the Chief, clandestinely taken to the castle by Alan, and John knew it had been through his father's efforts, and then those of the Chief, that he had been granted the honor of acceptance to attend Marischal College at Aberdeen. Yet, with all the local infighting for power at that time, John had not wanted to go off again to school; but his father had insisted.

In late August, the morning was still dark, with a common mist in the air, when John left for Aberdeen. The Chief had even made arrangements for his shipboard passage.

When John reached the outskirts of Tain, he looked at the shrouded shores in the gray dawn. A fine cloud of haze was dimming the golden harbor lights, and farther south along Dornoch Firth a heavy fog was lifting off the sea to meet the lance of probing sunlight gleaming from the roofs of sleeping houses. From where he walked, he could see the two-masted brig waiting patiently in the harbor.

It was early in the day when they set sail. He had never been aboard a ship that size before, and spent most of his time looking it over from bow to stern. The next night they sailed into the busy Aberdeen fishing seaport from the North Sea and docked near the confluence of the Don and Dee Rivers. The university sat atop a long, grassy brae, a large, handsome stone building, with a breathtaking view of the firth.

A student showed him to a dormitory where he would sleep and study with nine others. He unpacked his trunk, then went out, walking across the Brig O'Balgoronie spanning the Don, built long ago, in 1320, and the old brig across the Dee, done in 1527, they said.

The days of 1772 passed by and Grandfather John Ross spent his spare time in the college library at Aberdeen reading the great works of Plato, Marcus Aurelius, Epictetus, as well as Lucretius and Francis Bacon. John was truly in his element.

Sundays were a day of rest, even at the universities, and many a Sabbath he would walk along the Don or the Dee. He had found a special place upstream, some seven miles on the Dee — a verdant high glen between Aberdeen and Banchory.

The entrance to the valley was secured by a cluster of rock upthrust against an escarpment, and only John's curiosity led him to find the obscured trail that lay behind what appeared in perspective to be merely a crack in the rock. As he neared the illusion, he realized it was an overlap of two different rocks, and behind that embattlement a trail some three feet wide leading to a tunnel in the rock. With some trepidation, John entered the opening after lighting a bit of heather for a torch. Five hundred feet of darkness later, he again saw daylight and a glen of brae meadows that covered some fifty acres. Heather and evergreen shrubs, their dark branches cloaked with racemes of purple blossoms, filled his vision. Out of a dark canyon, a stream rushed down from higher peaks and settled into a pool where it entered the glen. The brook wound across the meadow, with intermittent pools and riffles. John never followed the stream out of the glen, but somewhere in the wilderness of cliff and tree he knew it surely worked its way east to the river.

He often whiled away the day in this secret place among the escarpments, beside the mountain stream with falling cataracts and glacial pools. He went alone, to meditate and lay back in the grass, thinking ever so often of his parents and home.

Grandfather often had said that everyone should learn to spend time alone, so that when circumstance dictates, isolation will not be a burden. "We're born into this world alone," he said, "and we will die alone. Being alone lets you contrive and make decisions you might otherwise leave to others; you sever yourself from dependency."

Near the tunnel entrance to his glen, and higher up from a protected ledge, Grandfather said he could see the university, the town of Aberdeen, and the North Sea. Although the air was cool that particular day he had found the protected glen, the sunlight reflecting off the grass and heather issued warmth. By closing his eyes, the rich aroma rising from the earth reminded him of the place he and his father shared back home.

Time passed, and on a warm day in June of 1773, Grandfather John Ross had stopped near the entrance into his rock sanctuary, when a movement caught his attention. Below and half a mile distant was the traveled road. A wayfarer with a large pack was plodding along the trail, heading east. But down the road and out of sight from the man were four thugs, hiding in wait within a patch of tall rushes along the shallows of the river.

John determined they were thieves, waiting to rob the unsuspecting victim, and if he hurried, he might get to where the rogues were hidden about the time the wanderer did. He grabbed his staff and took off through the rock and heather.

But Grandfather did not get there in time. The lone, thin man had downed one of the thugs, but the others had him on the ground, beating him unmercifully. They never heard John run up behind them.

He let out a piercing Viking scream when he tore into the rogues, and laid out two before they knew what hit them. The other thief raced away, down the road northwest. When the others had wobbled weakly to their feet, John warned, "If ye want to stay healthy ye'd bett'r change yer line of business." He ordered them down the road, not to stop until they were out of those parts. They took off like they had been shot, no doubt thankful they were not dead.

The itinerant was unconscious, and after the riffraff were gone from sight, John hid the man's pack, then carried him to the hidden glen. When he returned for the man's belongings, he carefully brushed out his footprints and left no trail.

The vagabond was awake by the time he had returned. Though badly beaten, he had no broken bones. John fixed him food, and brewed a tea.

The man, Felix Cameron, was fifty-seven years old — not as old as Grandfather had first thought. Felix had fought at the Battle of Culloden, as had John's father, but with the Jocobites, and he had been a fugitive, fleeing from the Crown ever since — for the past twenty-six years.

Although many of the Jacobites had been reinstated to former status by this time, Felix was still wanted, dead or alive. He was certain the thugs had intended to kill him and collect the reward. And though he had many friends who would protect him, there were probably as many that would turn him in.

"Ye'd be surpris'd," Felix had told him, "how fickle those so-called friends can be at times, when money's involv'd."

Felix had been badly beaten and would not be traveling for several days, so he and John spent the afternoon together in silence as he rested. John could tell the man was someone special, and took a liking to him.

Felix was angular and skinny; he looked what appeared to be his lot in life. But his weather-beaten face belied his capabilities, and underneath the loose clothes he wore, his thin body had felt like steel.

He wore a bandanna around the crown of his head, and carried a deep three-inch scar along the left side of his jaw. The scar had not deformed his looks like some John had seen, and he could tell that Felix, when healthy, could be a tough go in a scrap.

John fixed him a bed of heather in a shallow cave, and toward evening Felix advised, "Ye'd bett'r get back t' school, or they might come looking for ye, too. I've plenty o' food in my pack. Ye go on; I'll be fine."

John agreed he had best head out, but promised to be back the next Sunday to check on Felix. When John again reached the road and wiped out his tracks leading to the glen, it was an hour from sunset. Darkness would settle in before he got back to Aberdeen. The road was empty of travelers, and his shadow went long beside the golden glow of fading sunlight.

The land was shading lovely, catching in its braes a pink brushing from the setting sun, and west above the purple rims, the last of sunlight blushed a pastel rose on gigantic clouds. Grandfather had noticed the wind coming up, as it rushed down the glen from off the braes. It moved in waves across the heather, and where it crossed the meadows, it tossed around the comely purple blossoms like an angry creature. Grandfather walked that part of the trail in the coming of night many times and it had always given him a good feeling.

Darkness had finally captured the countryside as he walked by the tombstones that sat on a plateau overlooking the river. The cemetery, a mile from the college grounds, never failed to give him pause whenever he might pass at night. That evening turned out to be no exception.

Along the road, near a large pillar-like headstone, was what sounded to be a moaning coming from the graveyard. It was always present after dark. Over time, Grandfather said, he had determined it to be the way the wind came down the glen, prowling through the many headstones, creating the cacophony. Yet it surely sounded human.

That night, there was no moon, and Grandfather could barely discern the obscure, dark shapes of the headstones. He tread softly as he passed, whistling an old Scottish ballad to appease the spirits.

When he had safely passed the cemetery, John almost shuddered with relief. He knew better than to be unnerved by unproved visions, but he wished that someone would tell his heart and his feet, for they always had that same anxious feeling whenever he slipped past graveyards at night.

The following Sunday, John was on the road west of Aberdeen when the sun began to peek above the North Sea. He was heading for his sanctuary, to check on Felix. His shadow was long, stretching on the hard-packed earth ahead of him, always ahead, always familiar, whether he moved faster or slowed; it led him all the way to the glen. He turned off the road along the river and legged a pathless trail through the heather toward the entrance to his secret place. After twisting his way among pillars of slanted rock, he entered the dark tunnel.

At the place where the stream flowed down from out of the mountain and into a glacial pool, he found Felix resting beneath a pine. Downstream several birch had rooted their feet up to the water's edge.

Felix had almost completely recovered from his beating, except for the purple bruises on his body. The day was warm and peaceful, and they talked the sunlit morning away, as the overhead pine needles whispered and danced to the slightest movement of air. At noon, sailing ships of clouds had gathered, causing the limbs and branches of the tree to move westward through the sky.

"John, you must continue bein' wary," Felix told him, "for any association wi' me would mean certain prison for ye. If we should meet again, ye must not know me. It'll be saf'r that way."

John reluctantly agreed, "But I don'na like it."

"If there's ever anything' ye ev'r need, John, a place I always return t' soon'r or lat'r is th' Wooden Buck't Tav'rn at Aberdeen. It's out-of-the-way, and tough, along th' wat'rfront — not a place o' comfort for those o' authority, nor ere they welcom'd by th' patrons.

"Walth'r Grant is th' host. Those lookin' for me hav' nev'r connect'd me wi' him, nor do they suspect it t' be a location o' mine . . . I go there in th' quiet o' night.

"Walth'r will know where I'm at, or how t' get in touch wi' me. I 've more connections than ye might think, John, and some in high places."

"Aye, Felix," John responded, "th' Crown may be lookin' for ye, but I consid'r ye a friend, and I'll not betray ye."

Felix responded fondly. "Ye sav'd my life . . . if not from a killin', then from prison and possible hangin'. I'll not be forgettin' what ye did."

When they decided it would be safer to leave separately, Felix departed first, and John waited in the glen for two hours before he started back to school.

His return was a wet and muddy one. The cumulus clouds in the sky had turned purple, and the sky had become one low, fast-moving cloud. The wind had turned to the north, from where it swept in with a veil of cold mist, whipping at the grass and leaves. It lashed his face with sharp needles of dirt carried along, and at the river the rushes were being tossed in great waves. Drops fell slowly at first, but fast behind came a downpour, whipped from all directions. Grandfather had said he would remember forever that drenching walk, and how safe he felt when he had finally entered his dormitory.

By August 17th, 1774, John had been at Aberdeen three years. More than a year had gone by since he and Felix had parted at the glen. John wondered if he was safe, trying to imagine having no home and always being on the run. It was odd that Felix had not left Scotland, as had so many others, for America, or Canada. Felix, after all, had sailed the seas; it was not as if he had never left the country before.

But Grandfather recalled his own father telling him that when you are attached to a home and for one reason or another are forced to leave, it remains like a death in the family. It stays with you. And you are forever dreaming of a return. Perhaps, John thought, Felix just could not bring himself to leave.

On that Saturday, John was in the library reading when the headmaster walked up and handed him a letter. He could see it was from his mother.

"I thought this is where ye might be," the headmaster said. "The letter just arriv'd, and I suppos'd it might be important."

Grandfather waited until he was back in his room before opening the missive, which had been dated two weeks before.

August 5, 1774.

My Dearest John, Your father, my beloved husband, has been killed, just yesterday, carried out it is thought by Paul's doing. Alan, our Chief's aide, came to give me the sorrowful news.

My laddie, ye can be proud of your father, as I know ye are, for he was a great warrior and a credit to his Viking ancestry.

He was on an errand at Paul's wicked urging, though being wary and forewarned by the Chief that mischief could be afoot, he carried with him his claymore. Yet ten armed cowards lay in wait, none with the courage to face him alone in a fight.

Though your father was but one, he took four with him to the other side. We know, with God's mercy, the difference being that they will go to a different place, for your father will be with his Heavenly Reward.

The Chief will have the funeral in but two days, and his spies are looking into the tragic events, though proof of the evil seems impossible to secure.

I am advised to tell ye, me lad, that your life is in jeopardy as well, for the Chief's spies have overheard Paul's revealing conversation. Ye must keep an eye about ye. I think ye shall be safer there. Ye must not come home at this time.

And more to our grief, the wily Paul was by the house to-day. He gave me signed papers that I am to be off the croft no later than September 30. The place will be turned to a sheep run, the fashion of the day. He has already run off the other tenants.

I have written to your brothers to let them know of their father's untimely death, though with their regiments in Canada, the American colonies, and Australia, they probably will not receive my letters for months.

Laddie, please stay in Aberdeen. Do not worry about me, for I will be safe.

Lovingly, Your Mother

Grandfather John was stunned. He could not believe that his father was dead. But as the news began to become reality, panic took hold of his mind, along with a strangling ache in his chest.

His mother had told him to stay at Aberdeen, but he would need to slow down and think through the situation more thoroughly. Rash action and foolish haste would not do.

That night he lay in bed with a crowd of thoughts rushing through his mind. He decided he must go home. His mother needed his help, with her notice of eviction, and though he doubted she might be in danger, you could never know for sure with an unscrupulous man like Paul. John knew it would be faster to travel by sea, perhaps three days, but if he could not find a passage, he would take off afoot, and that could involve some ten days through the rough Highland terrain.

He was short of money, but in the morning would go to the waterfront; surely he could sign on as a deck hand to Dornoch Firth.

A golden hue of afternoon lingered along the docks; the sun had almost dropped out of sight from where John stood on the waterfront. Earlier that day he had told the headmaster he would be leaving.

John had been everywhere along the firth, but no ships were going north, nor would they be for a month. He had even checked with the fishing crafts anchored along the quay, but they were all working the beds near Aberdeen.

Purple shadows began prowling eastward, capturing almost all of the old shanties and nondescript seaside buildings. Among the sailors' hangouts in the shade of other establishments to the west was a ramshackle wooden tavern on rotting weakened knees. John wondered what was holding up the poor structure, and he could barely make out the familiar name on its faded sign . . . *Wooden Bucket.*

John decided to return later to see if he could find Felix. Perhaps he would have a solution.

A full moon had risen into the hazy sky when John once more paused along the waterfront of taverns. Lamplights were glowing from the doorways and windows into the silence of purple darkness.

Several men were loitering along the cobblestone street. Two had walked out of the *Wooden Bucket,* staggered down the street, and disappeared into the ever-present thick gray mist.

When John was sure no one was watching, he slipped into the tavern. The common room was dark, the only light coming from three small lamps and a fireplace. He had a few silver coins in his pocket, enough for only a couple meals, but he did have one gold piece he kept sewn into his clothes. John paused inside the door for a moment, letting his eyes become adjusted to the dark. Only three men were in the common room. John assumed one, the host behind the bar, to be Walther.

Across the room two sailors, like shadows, sat at a table sharing a bottle of ale. Walther looked at him momentarily, then turned away as though unconcerned. The others paid him no mind.

It was a large room with exposed wooden beams and benches and long tables, in addition to the smaller tables. In the fireplace hung a large iron pot. John could not tell what was in it, but the aroma was wonderful.

At the back of the room was an open doorway through which he could see a long hallway with doors leading to sleeping rooms. And just inside the door was a stairway that led up to what were probably more rooms.

In the glow of lamplight, dust motes hung complacent in the stale yellow air. The smell of ale was strong, yet at that time of day almost overpowered with the aroma of food.

John walked to the bar. "Would ye be Walth'r?" John asked.

"Aye," the man replied, with a curious look on his unsmiling face. "Why would ye be askin'?"

"I'm John Ross, and a friend of Felix Cameron," John whispered.

"Of course, I've heard about ye from Felix. Ye're the laddie that beat off th' thugs. Ye needn't whisp'r, for those two over there were mates with Felix on many a voyage at sea.

"What can I do for ye?"

"I was wonderin' if by chance ye'd know where Felix might be. I'd like t' talk t' him."

"Well, ye're in luck. At times he'll be gone for months, but he's close and I can get word t' him. Chances are he'll be here within th' hour."

Walther went to the kitchen, and in minutes a wee laddie came scrambling through the common room and out the back door. John was sitting at a table near the fireplace when the lad came rushing back in through the front door and then disappeared into the kitchen.

A few minutes later, Felix came out of the darkness of the hallway. John had before him a mug of ale, and he motioned for Walther to bring another. Felix slid into the chair beside him.

After a large plate of mincemeat pie and white pudding, John explained to Felix the letter he had received from his mother and of his plans to return home.

By this time the tavern was filling up, mostly riffraff from the boats, but none in the room paid John any mind.

Felix warned, "Ye'll hav' t' be wary when ye get t' Tain. In th' populat'd areas your movements will need t' be done secr'tly and at night."

"Aye," John agreed. "But I know a few backways I can travel. And I hav' a confidant in th' Chief and Alan, his aide."

Felix then disclosed to Grandfather that he knew well the Chief, and his aide Alan as well. John was at first surprised, but then told himself he should not have been, for Felix apparently had an underground web of men across the land — a web even the Crown could not penetrate.

The two stood up and walked toward the bar.

"Lad," Felix said and paused, ". . . I'm gonna leave ye for a mite. I'll see about gettin' a boat t' take ye t' Tain."

Grandfather told Felix he had already checked. "I've ask'd all along th' wat'rfront, and there's none goin' north."

But Felix was not worried. "Leave it t' me, lad. I'll find ye a boat. Get yourself a room, and be ready to leave before dawn." He would not be seen on the streets in the light of day.

As they were concluding their conversation, Grandfather could hear a wagon outside moving slowly by on the cobblestone street. He turned to see a stranger enter the room, and when he looked back around, Felix was gone. The man moved up to John at the bar and ordered a mug of ale, peering around as he drank. Without a word, he walked out.

As the door closed behind him, Walther spit on the floor and whispered to John, ". . . A spy for th' Crown . . . the scum o' th' earth."

As Walther led the way to Grandfather's room, he reassured him that there would be no charge; it was taken care of by Felix.

Grandfather was taken back, for he wondered if Felix could afford it.

Walther chuckled. "I would'na know why not . . . he owns the place, and sev'ral more for that matter. And as for Felix gettin' a boat t' take ye home, I would'na worry 'bout that either. He owns ten fishin' craft, anchor'd there in the firth."

There was a lot more to Felix Cameron than Grandfather had realized.

John was up and into the common room by half past four with his pack when Felix appeared out of the darkness across the room. They had a quick meal of eggs and were on their way by five. In minutes they were loading onto a fair-sized fishing boat with a lone mast. Two other men were aboard — one about eighteen, the other middle-aged.

John noticed that Felix also had a pack with him. "'Ere ye goin' along t' Tain?"

"Aye," Felix answered. "I hav' business to attend, and the time seems right. My men will fish the wat'rs nearby, north of Helmsdale, where we've made good catches — cod, and herring, and haddock, ev'n a few whiting."

The single-masted boat had a cabin large enough to sleep four, and it took John but a short time to get his sea legs, for he had liked the open water — the slapping waves against the hull of the bobbing boat. It gave him a hopeful, adventurous feeling on this trip back home.

As the crew busied themselves, John helped with the lines, and in minutes they had shoved off into the darkness of early morning with an overcast sky. The water was calm, with but a gentle breeze, and the lifted sail skimmed the boat out of the firth at good speed.

They soon reached the open North Sea, and through the early morning haze, the sun lifted her glowing orb above the waves where an opening in the cloud cover splayed a golden light.

No more than thirty minutes out, storm clouds covered the window of sunlight, and the day became morose and dark. A ripping southwest wind moved them on toward their destination with shortened sail.

It was mid-afternoon when John stepped up to the bow and looked into the threatening North Sea. They were sailing straight into the heart of a storm. The wind had switched and whipped about; its raking fingers had turned cold. A confusion of boiling purple clouds lowered and swept the remaining daylight out of the sky.

John could see dimly the rocky coastline of land to the west. But the cliffs were not a welcome place to find shelter, for the rocks would tear the boat to pieces. The sea before them ran strong and rough. The waves were having their way with the boat, as it tilted steeply down the slope of one, then rose sharply to the overhang of another.

John clung firmly to the railing as great heights of sea washed up. Visibility was no more than a thousand feet, and the now ghostly coastline was inching closer as they frantically bailed water.

The fierce wind and blowing rain felt like needles piercing Grandfather's face and body. He no longer paid heed to the other men aboard, for each was trying to save his own life.

The water-burdened vessel was losing buoyancy, becoming more sluggish and slower to rise. It was steadily moving closer to the rocks at the whim of the vicious sea waves, and John recognized the fear in the seamens' eyes. They were at the mercy of the storm, helpless against the elements of sea and wind.

John saw the enormous wave come at them only seconds before it hit and swept him into the depths of a swift current. His struggles to rise were hopeless. He was held down in the turbulent depths as though by bonds, until he thought his lungs would burst. And then, when at last he thought his life was finished, he was tossed up to the surface, riding the waves like a cork, gasping for his breath.

It seems to be a narrow thread we walk at times . . . or was it a merciful God that day? Grandfather said many times that he was thankful he was an able swimmer.

He could see the boat low in the water and a man hanging onto the rail as he, himself, was swiftly carried toward the rocks. He hit a pinnacle hard, but hung on. The sea again exploded before he could get beyond the reef of rock and smashed him against the razor edges.

Quickly he began to swim to the nearby gravel beach, then lay there spent of life's energy, much of his body torn with lacerations. There were moments, Grandfather added, when he thought he might not live, but it is the nature of man to fight until the end regardless that the cause might be lost.

Grandfather laid on the shore, in and out of consciousness, then startled by an unseen action, he jumped up, realizing that Felix and the others might need help. He could see the boat, like a shadow through the haze, tossed up against the rocks. The sea was slowly, methodically cutting it to pieces. The wind and rain whipped his body as he searched along the beach where debris had already washed ashore, without any sign of life.

He swam out to check the shattered craft, then timing the waves to keep from being smashed on the rocks, he boarded. He found Felix, who had somehow managed to lash himself to the railing. His body was cut and beaten by wind-blown debris, and he was slumped unconscious. Getting him ashore without losing him would be a challenge.

But Grandfather knew that the boat would soon be completely torn to pieces, and he wasted no time. Through a merciful God he had Felix on the beach in short order, guided through the angry waters by something greater than himself, he knew. He was able to return to the boat twice again to gather up supplies and foodstuffs not yet lost, and he managed to save his pack from the battered cabin. On his last return to shore, he could see the boat taken into the sea.

John salvaged what other items he could that had washed ashore — wooden beams and pieces of lumber from the deck and hull, clothing, strips of sail, and rope. From one piece of rope a block and tackle still hung.

The narrow gravel and sand beach looked to be several miles long, and looming above it were sharply fluted cliffs some two hundred feet high. At each end of the beach the cliffs protruded into the ocean, then dropped directly into the sea.

The two men were trapped on their piece of land, with rock cliffs to the west and a barrier of reef and North Sea to the east. Grandfather knew that even if they were spotted by ship, they no doubt could not be picked up — even by long boat — because of the high waves and risk of the rocky barrier. But he dismissed the discouraging observation from his mind, and proceeded to move Felix to higher ground, and into a shallow cave-like shelter. South of their newly found cover, a trickle of spring water dropped from a hundred feet above into a small fresh pool.

John had at first thought Felix might be dead, until he checked his pulse and heard a groan, with a movement of his hand. Felix's left arm was broken and hanging loose. John straightened the arm and put on splints, then built a fire and cooked a crude broth from the remnants of their supplies. He had patiently put a trace of the soup down Felix's throat along with a bit of the spring water.

Sometime in the night, the storm blew itself out. When John awoke, a mellow light was probing into the nooks and crannies of the purple shadowy cliff. The sea was rough in the dawn, as the sun rose up like a gleaming coin in a brilliant blue sky.

John peered around the rock refuge and at its lonely beach and fluted cliffs. Now that he was calm and had his wits about him, he realized that if they had not been marooned as they were, the deserted haven would have been a strikingly beautiful sanctuary.

Felix, too, was awake and peering at John from tired, pain-filled eyes.

"How'd I get here?" he whispered to John.

"I got ye off th' boat before she went down."

Felix paused a brief moment, then stated as a fact, "I'm dyin', John; ye should've left me on th' boat, and it'd be long ov'r wi'."

"Ye aren't dying, Felix. I will'na let ye. What ye need is t' pray."

"Pray?" Felix painfully questioned. "I've pray'd most me life, and

I've yet t' hav' one answer'd. If ye ask'd me, that'd be a sure way for me t' pass on."

"Well . . . all o' my pray'rs hav' been answer'd," John replied, "one way or oth'r."

Grandfather said Felix peered over at him with a feeble and skeptical eye. He paused, then added, "Well, ev'n if I live, John Ross, how am I goin' t' get out, for 'tis certain we're trapp'd in here. Ye might make it by scaling those cliffs some way, but I nev'r could . . . and I'd starve t' death before I was well enough."

"We'll get out," John affirmed. "Did'na Christ say that faith could move mountains? Ye would'na want t' be a party t' callin' the Lord a liar would ye?

"Believe me, Felix, he'll answ'r my pray'r . . . and yours, too, ev'n if I hav' t' carry ye out o' here on my back."

". . . I hope ye can fly . . . ," Felix whispered as he lay back and closed his eyes.

Five days after the shipwreck, Felix was feeling better and was slowly and cautiously walking around. But no matter, for the men were securely imprisoned in their seaside cage. And their food would last but another week.

Grandfather said he had traversed the entire beach, and a way out looked hopeless. He had figured that first day the winds had carried them farther north than normal, and they were somewhere near the Rattray Head coastline and south of Fraserburgh, instead of near Boddam like he had originally thought.

Northwest, where the beach ran out, the tall cliff ran into the sea. But near the beach, the force of the pounding waves had tunneled through the wall of rock, leaving a window to a lovely scene through the opening.

John swam out to look farther down the coast, only to see more imposing rock. To the south was more, dropping straight into the sea.

South of where they had camped the first night lay a small glen that penetrated west some four hundred feet. At the end of the glen, wind and water had eaten away the top of the two hundred-foot ledge to where it had become at least fifty feet lower than the surrounding top.

Above, perhaps on one hundred fifty feet of abrupt rock, grew a pine tree. Gnarled and lonely, it peered at all beneath it. The fifty-foot slope from the tree to the top was steep, but almost anyone could easily climb it.

On their second day, John moved the campsite into the glen because of its high ground. He built a shelter between two large rocks, covering it over with canvas. The brae of the glen was filled with heather, which they used to make their bed, and for fuel.

John knew that if he could climb the cliff wall to the pine tree, he could hang the block and tackle from the limb and lift Felix up the rock face. Close to the tree, however, spring water trickled down, making the rock mossy and slick.

Near the north end of the beach, nature had cracked and split the rock at the face of the cliff, an opening close to three feet wide, some two hundred feet from top to bottom. Grandfather finally had decided that the vertical cleft was his only way to the top, but every time he stopped and looked at it, he was taken aback by the challenge.

Succumbing to the finality of finding no other way up, he settled within himself that this was their only way out. He walked over to the crack and put his back against one wall while pushing his feet against the other. He managed to work his way upward about ten feet, then came back down. He was covered with sweat, and in that short distance up he realized he would have to do something about his hard-soled shoes.

That night, Grandfather told, he tried to prepare himself for the climb as he lay on his pallet of heather with his hands behind his head, looking at the stars. He wondered if the twinkling luminaries believed he would be stranded along this beach — though perhaps they had no time for him, for whatever adventure he had encountered was without doubt minor compared to what the stars had seen. Still, in his small world of experience, he often wondered what were the forces that caused circumstance, the things over which you have no control.

His mind turned to the North Sea — violent at times, but now, as he lay there, calm. Only the sound of the plangent waves could be heard, slapping against the barrier rocks, reminding him of the sea's mighty, latent power. The last thing he remembered was the growling rumble of the water, and then its racing up the shore, reaching a crescendo of silence, only to rush back and meet head-on another wave.

It was the roar of the waves that woke him. He lay in comfort, peering at the dawn's disappearing stars, thinking of his father now gone, and then he returned to the business at hand — the crevice.

By the time he started his climb up the fissure, daylight was established. Not wanting the weight of the block and tackle dragging him down, he decided to carry a light line, and if he reached the crest, he would move over and drop down to the pine. From the tree he would lower the line to Felix and pull up the block and tackle with the heavier rope.

He found an old pair of thin-soled shoes in his pack and started upward. When he had reached thirty feet, sweat covered his body and soaked his shirt. To his back, he felt a small protrusion, on which he rested for a time. But he knew he would need more resting spots if he were going to reach the top, and he could see a place above him fifty feet. He would next rest when he got there.

John felt a breeze, which helped to dry his sweat. One hand was bleeding where he had cut it on the granite. He concentrated on keeping his mind off the heights, imagining he was but a few feet off the ground, never looking down.

Grandfather said he had thought of his father and mother, which also helped. Why was it we always thought of family and home when in trouble?

He had almost stopped sweating as he moved slowly upward, and within an hour he had reached the top and climbed out. He lay resting for a few moments, relieved at his success, then moved away from the cliff.

It was well into the afternoon before John got Felix and their supplies to the top. They had been isolated down on the beach for seven days. The other two fishermen had never washed ashore, and Grandfather reasoned they probably rested at the bottom of the sea.

That night John and Felix camped in a high glen from where they could see the North Sea in the distance. The only weapon they had was John's staff, which he had recovered from his pack; but they had food enough to reach across the next few days.

Despite their uncertain situation, Grandfather related, they took pleasure in the peace of the night, grateful to be alive as the firelight danced against the rocks and flickered its many tongues into the purple evening shadows.

"I'll hav' t' hand it t' ye', John," Felix spoke up, "we'd never hav' made it without yer faith. Surely ye've made me a believer!"

"Aye, Felix, like all young lads testing the wat'rs of independ'nce, I questioned for a time God's Word. Moth'r end'd me doubts wi' a question. 'Me lad,' she said, 'would ye rath'r die wi' or wi'out yer faith?' It was all th' answ'r I need'd."

They said nothing for awhile, lying back into the silence and the comfort of the night while the campfire crackled. Grandfather could see the hint of light on the horizon and wondered if it might be the northerly town of Elgin, at the bend of the River Lossie. If so, he thought, it was but thirty-odd miles east of Inverness, on the road to Aberdeen.

As he was calculating their location, Felix broke into the silence. "And what do ye plan t' do wi' your life, lad?"

Grandfather said he was both amused and briefly bothered with Felix's question, for their fate at the top of that glen was still fragile and truly uncertain. Yet he knew that his companion must have felt a surety of their return to their home.

"I've made no plans," Grandfather told him. "Some may set out their lives, but I shall let circumstance guide me."

"Wi' yer education, John, you could set your sights on most anythin'."

"Aye," Grandfather acknowledged. "And I'll know when it comes along. Wi' my training I believe I could command in an army — or build a bridge. Yet I've longed t' have a breeding farm — a special strain o' horse has enter'd my thinkin'. But I shall do what God has in mind for me.

"I hav' now t' get Moth'r settl'd, and must be wary in what I do, for it appears my life, as well, is in dang'r."

Felix acknowledged John's precarious situation, adding, "When all tha'tis done, ye could always work wi' me, lad, and I'd mak' ye a partn'r; but I hesitate ye take th' chance just now, for if ye were found out, ye, too, would become a want'd man by th' Crown. It may be ye hav' enough wi' th' Chief's son down on ye!"

Grandfather was honored that Felix would consider him as a working partner. "I would be proud," he acknowledged. "But I've had a dream . . . o' Mother and me abroad in th' Colonies. I think it's where God wants me t' go . . . a chance t' start anew with my dreams, free from th' fighting of brother wi' brother."

"Ye'll want cash, me lad, if ye be off for America. I can let ye hav' what ye'll need for the passage, but it'll take more than that t' care for yer mother.

"After Culloden, I had cach'd several pouches of silv'r and gold, secure in a cave at Beauly glen, and if I could find them again there would be plenty o' coin. I owe ye me life, laddie — twice over. Me fortune is rightly yours."

John was moved by Felix's goodness. He knew that the coins had belonged to the Bonnie Prince Charles who left the Culloden battle when the fighting had turned to favor the Crown. Told by the Prince to hide the bags, Felix finally secreted them on the upper reaches of Beauly glen, through the brae filled with heather high up the escarpment.

"When my pursu'rs came int' view," Felix added, "I dropp'd int' th' heath'r out o' sight. They were too busy watchin' th' road, for they'd found me horse and were lookin' ev'rywhere. I feared they surely would find me.

"I lay in th' bramble, the sun warm on me back. I could hear them movin' clos'r, and knew I'd have t' find someplace bett'r t' hide. Nothin' mov'd where I lay hidd'n but for the heath'r in th' wind, th' only sound th' whisp'r o' leaves and th' search o' me enemy ev'r clos'r. At times there was silence, exc'pt in me mind, which creat'd fearsome footsteps where in truth there were none — and no other sounds but th' lonely bird chirpin'. I had t' move quickly, I knew, for they'd happen on me soon. I could see 'twixt me and th' rock face, some hundr'd yards up, th' hint o' a game trail tunnel'd through th' brush and heath'r.

"I wip'd away what tracks there were and crawl'd along th' tunnel o' heath'r, draggin' wi' me th' coins, leavin' no trace o' me passin'.'"

The end of Felix's trail led to a small opening in the rock, a cave totally hidden from view. Grandfather told how Felix had crawled within the opening, and listened to the relentless searching below, determined to find him. Felix was certain his pursuers would not find the cave, but was cautiously still until finally their sounds had faded off.

Backing farther into the rock opening, Felix found a space so dark he could not begin to determine its size. All he was sure of was that he could not touch the ceiling or any interior wall when he stood.

He remained in the cave that day, often thinking he had heard voices nearby. But the following day the sounds finally had gone. Felix took sightings to the southeast, in order to find the spot again. The opening, he had determined, was straight in a line with two trees, one midway between the cave and the road, the other where he had tied his horse. But now, his horse was gone.

"That night," Felix said, "moonless and crisp, I departed, leaving the coins in the cave."

He was shortly beside the river, taking in the clear, cold water, quenching his long-held thirst.

"From the road I stood back from th' tree, sightin' across t' th' oth'r standing alone like a tall, dark shadow. Aligned with th' trees was the dark peak o' a mountain betwixt two other peaks.

"I've been back there once, and then again, but I can'na find, for th' life o' me, th' cave, for th' tree in th' brae is gone. And th' dozens o' escarpments look alike. I dare not spend time in th' area for fear o' bein' found out by th' authorities."

That was the last thing Grandfather said he remembered before he was overcome with sleep. And the first thing he thought of in the morning was the secreted sacks of coins.

Two days later, as the sun was winging into late afternoon, Grandfather and Felix came to Elgin, parting at the edge, for Felix had thought it best if the locals believed they were strangers — and especially so if he should be recognized by the authorities.

Felix would be the first to walk into the town. If he determined any uncertainty, he would return within the hour. Grandfather had hoped that it would not be necessary to bypass the town, for not only was he hungry, but he looked forward to a real bed to sleep in.

It was an hour later when John walked through the village, the streets almost empty of locals, and stopped at the inn Felix had earlier mapped for him. The isolated, gabled building sat back from the road in a patch of birch trees. West of the inn ran a robust stream, seeming to praise the world with its burbling happiness. Near the brook a giant sycamore maple towered among the pine. It was the largest tree John had ever seen and must have been eight feet across the trunk, with its dark, outstretched limbs beseeching light to a darkening sky. Before the trees, a lone rabbit in the sparse grass hopped joyfully into the woods.

When John walked into the large courtyard, sunlight was waning in the west, and purple shadows were beginning to probe into the open areas. Moving aside the inn's heavy wooden door, he walked into a landing that led down into a large common room. He paused just inside the door on the landing, to let his eyes accustom to the darkness.

A slender girl was lighting a lamp along the far wall of the room that held no more than ten others — all men, but for one young lady who sat with an older man at the end of a long table.

The patrons looked up when John entered; then, seemingly uninterested, they looked away. Felix was standing at the bar, in deep conversation with the host, and never acknowledged John's presence. As was his habit, John sat with his back to the wall, where he had good vision of the door and room.

The young blonde girl came to his table to take his order. John noticed the one unruly strand curling down along her lovely face as well as her delicately blossoming young body. When she spoke to him, her radiant blue eyes sparkled. When she had asked what he wanted, he had not answered, for at that moment he had been taken up with admiring the lass.

Unable to control the flush rising in his face, he flustered he would have the stew and the pudding. "And what about lodgin' for th' night?" he inquired.

"Ye'll have t' ask me fath'r. He's talkin' t' th' man at th' bar."

"Aye. . . an' what might be yer name?" he asked.

She was Agnes Miller, and her father, the host, was Richard. "And what might be your name?" she sweetly asked him.

Grandfather abruptly spoke his name and tried to maintain some composure.

"Well, 'tis nice t' meet ye, John Ross," Agnes replied, as she hurried off to the bar. She brought him his ale, then disappeared into the kitchen. It was not long before she had returned with his food.

Several times during the meal, Grandfather said, he had noticed Agnes curiously glancing his way. He was completely taken with her, and the certain way she had of walking across a room.

He peered over to the bar, where Felix and the host were still in conversation. But a moment later, a commotion was heard outside the door. When John looked back to the bar, Felix was gone.

In an instant, four well-armed men stomped into the room, looking around, then went over to Agnes's father. One of the men looked long and hard at John, but after a short time they left, and John could feel the tension leaving the room with the men.

Agnes returned to the table. "Father apologizes for that — they're nothin' but th' rabble o' th' earth. They're lookin' for someone want'd by th' gover'ment. Culloden was fought years ago — ye'd think th' Crown would let it be aft'r awhile."

John acquiesced. "Those I've met w'th a price still on their head ere good people; I think the Crown would be bett'r serv'd t' give 'em amnesty."

"I'll say amen t' that," young Agnes replied. "But come on, I'll take ye ov'r and introduce ye t' my fath'r. I'm sure he can set ye up wi' a room."

Richard Miller greeted John, acknowledging that Felix had already spoke about him.

Agnes walked off and through the doorway to the kitchen. Richard added, "Felix said ye'll be needin' a room for th' night."

"Aye," John responded, "and what'll be th' charges wi' my food an' breakfast?"

"It's done — Felix took care o' it. Agnes'll show ye yer room when ye're ready. Breakfast's between five 'n eight."

Agnes led John down a hallway to the back of the inn, to a small room with a fireplace along the south wall. A window also faced the south, with the covering pulled tightly down.

"And will ye be needin' anythin' else?" Agnes asked, with her pret-tiest smile.

Grandfather said he thought she must be the most beautiful girl in the whole world, and flustered at her question, he managed to mutter, "If ye're not busy lat'r, I'd like t' see ye again . . . t' talk; that is, I'd like t' get bett'r acquaint'd."

He knew he was blushing. He had turned almost speechless and felt like the village idiot, but managed to explain, "I'd like t' see ye before I leave. I won't go t' bed before ten."

Agnes smiled; she could see he was flustered, and the lass saved him from further embarrassment.

"John Ross . . . I want t' know ye bett'r, too. But it might be after ten, for I'll hav' t' wait 'til father's abed and asleep. I don'na think he'd approve o' me seeing ye."

John passed the time rinsing some of his clothes in the wash room just outside his own, and hung them on a line outside the back door.

The night air carried along a chill, and he built himself a small fire. He wondered if Felix would be back, though he doubted it. Somehow Felix had gotten wind of the authorities close by and had again disappeared.

Grandfather said he had never known anyone like Felix — he could simply disappear on a moment's notice. He hoped Felix had come to no harm, but he knew that Felix seemed to have an endless number of spies and hideouts across Scotland — perhaps even in England for all he knew.

Felix had prepared Grandfather for what he should do next. They had talked it over, and John knew he had to keep on their route to Tain. Felix would catch up with him.

When it was ten o'clock that late evening and Agnes had not yet shown, John started to believe she would not come by. He lay back on the bed and thought over the events that might lay ahead. It was an uncertain future. But he would confront each day as it came, and surely a merciful God would lead him. He was almost asleep when he heard a light knock at the door.

Agnes had changed into a pretty blue dress with white lace trim. She closed the door quietly. She was so beautiful, John thought, her dimpled smile melting away any doubts he might have had about her being the lass for him.

Near twilight, on the 31st of August, John could see Tain in the distance.

His mother would have to be out of her home within thirty more days. But it was not only his mother who was being evicted. For several years now it had been happening all across the Highlands, in the name of economic progress for those new methods of sheep farming.

Grandfather considered the result of the new sheep-walks as they called them, for they had caused the massive migrations to America and Canada. In 1773, two hundred immigrants had sailed to Lochbroom in Wester Ross; by 1776, some twenty thousand had left the Highlands.

Grandfather had many times heard of older members of the crofters' families who had nowhere to move to on their eviction date. The landlords would arrive and physically remove the poor souls from the house, stacking their possessions out in the roadway. If Grandfather's mother was not out on the ordered date, he knew, as well, that Paul, the Chief's son, was ruthless and would do much the same. Grandfather would have to make certain she was gone by the 30th.

Then John thought once again of the lovely young Agnes, and knew in his heart it was she he would like to marry, and thus she would need to be part of his future plans. They had spoken of many things before she had left his room that night at the inn.

Agnes was sixteen, and many of the lasses had been married before that birth date. She had seemed surprised that John was but eighteen, for she had thought him to be older, perhaps in his early twenties.

John skirted around Tain on obscured trails that he and his father had been familiar with. But he knew he would have to be wary, for his mother's house would be closely watched.

It was early night when he came to the heather behind the house, their branches stirring softly in a gentle wind. Lamplight was painting a golden square upon the dark ground from the lonely window along the home's north side.

It was quiet. Perhaps too quiet, Grandfather thought. Then he could hear a slight shuffling — someone outside the house and, without doubt, more than one. He could see Prince in the corral, like a ghost by the fence, his ears straight up. Someone was out there, John knew, and close. Prince would have whinnied had he caught John's smell — it had to be someone else.

Grandfather slipped on his moccasins and on silent feet went to the hiding place south of the house. What he had hoped for was there — a message and map.

The map showed a tunnel his father had built from a deep narrow gully south to the back of the house. John easily found the hatch cover hidden amidst a nest of tall bushes. The entrance was not fifty feet from the house. John knew the gully would not be watched, for there was no way to approach the house from the ravine.

The tunnel entered the house beneath the bed in his mother's room. He quietly crawled from beneath the bed and walked softly to the open doorway. His mother was in her favorite rocking chair, her back to the door.

John softly whispered. "Moth'r, don'na move, nor say a word. We may be watched. Get up slowly as if ye were t' be findin' somethin' ye need from th' bedroom."

It was the 1st of September, that year of '74, twelve days since John had left Aberdeen on the boat to return home. At least that was what Paul's spies had said — but he knew it should not have taken but three.

The eldest son of the Ross clan's Chief, Paul once had been a handsome man, but had changed through the years and the venom of jealousy and hate that had festered within, now at fifty-four, gave a ruthless, evil appearance to his eyes, with the curl of his mouth like a snarl.

His early years had been filled with all the privilege of wealth and power of the family of a Chief. His playmates soon learned that their place was beneath him.

But not until the Battle of the Pirates at Tain, in 1745, did the evil fully manifest itself. For then, at but twenty-four, Paul had been a brigade Colonel in the clan army. And it was then in Paul's life that his arrogance had invaded his soul, though he would have scoffed that anyone would consider him so.

Suitably educated and thought one of the best duelists in the army, Paul surely would be a fit leader, in the future, to be Chief. But after the Battle of the Pirates, it had been the tenant James Ross who was the hero — the one who had gained the gratitude of the men — not Paul. During the battle, the clan had been losing ground until James Ross stepped into the breech and turned the tide.

Paul had calculated it to be blind luck that had put James in the proper place at the necessary time, never admitting that he also had seen the opportunity to move into the collapsing breech.

Paul had been a brave fighter at times, though he would shirk from any challenge he thought he might not win. Only if he could see a weakness might he lead a charge; yet once the battle turned into his army's favor he could be a ferocious warrior.

And Paul would never move quickly to the fore, to fight until the best might win, for he knew that he could lose. He would not venture that gamble.

The night that his henchmen had killed James, it was only after James was down that Paul had entered the fray, to finish him off. James lay helpless, almost drained of blood, when Paul moved in to make the final thrust. A smile of recognition lit up James's dying face, as he saw Paul standing above him — a circumstance that Paul had not expected. He had hoped to find a face of fear.

Paul took James's claymore drenched in blood, and crowed, "We've got 'im, men, and when we get 'is whelp o' a son we'll be rid o' their likes for good."

That September morning, Paul was awaiting his trusted Lieutenant for a report on the progress of finding the young John Ross. Like clockwork, his man showed at seven. The aide dismounted from his roan, over to where Paul was sitting on a garden bench.

They had traced Grandfather to Elgin, he said, but from there they lost him, picking up his trail once again at Findhorn, where he had hired a boat to cross Moray Firth.

"That was two days past, and we've lost all track o' him from there," said Paul's Lieutenant.

"Where could he go?" demanded Paul.

"He's somewhere in the area," the Lieutenant assured. "He did'na go home, for I've too many men watchin' th' place. He may be hid'n out in Tain somewhere. We'll find him. I've men everywher' watchin'."

"When ye find him, ye kill him!" Paul was confident that John was not the fighter his father had been, for he had talked with those students who had dueled with him at school, not knowing, of course, that John Ross had always held back his true prowess.

"We'll get 'im," the Lieutenant boldly assured, "sure as th' cock crows an' th' hen lays. It's only a matt'r o' time."

As the man left, Paul sat back down to consider the situation. His loyal followers were to keep his actions quiet, to not arouse the rest of the clan, for James Ross and John had friends. It had been risky for Paul of late; his father had learned he was involved in James's death, and things were not well between them.

Paul was certain that his inner circle had been compromised. But he had little fear, for his father was nearing eighty, and with death surely lurking close by he would soon be teetering off the precipitous cliff of life. On the other hand, however, his father did look healthy. If matters grew worse, Paul thought, he just might have to give the spent old warrior a little shove.

"Aye," he rationalized aloud. "I should've been Chief long ago!"

Nevertheless, even if things did not turn out the way he had wanted, if John Ross could not be found, he would be rid of John's mother in only thirty days. The thought of her removed, evicted from his land, with no place to go, made him perversely gratified. No matter that his father had been furious when he learned Paul had given James's wife the notice. He had his own followers, and if his father wanted to do anything about the situation, Paul determined he would move in with his own small army, take the castle, and declare himself rightful Chief of the clan.

A half sun was streaming its golden light across the waters of Dornoch Firth, like a pathway to the horizons, when John stealthily entered the nondescript pub on Front Street. The dilapidated old building sat among others just like it along the waterfront. Riffraff and seamen were frequent patrons, and its common room was like most any along the quays. It was the kind of place in which you would need to tread softly, keep a sober head, and watch your back — the kind of place you could hire a man, for but small change, to do most anything . . . even murder.

John paused just inside the door, letting his eyes accustom to the stale barroom light. Felix was there, in a far corner, at a table. John looked over at the host, who had been closely watching him. No one else was in the room. He walked on quiet feet to Felix who stood up and smiled.

"Hello, me laddie, sit ye down and have a bite."

The host, with that, turned away, back to his chores.

Moments later a young lass came from a side room, which must have been the kitchen, and asked John for his order. "We hav' a few fresh eggs left if ye'd like those."

John would have four.

Felix introduced John to the innkeeper, Joshua Sinclair, who had walked over to their table. Like so many others, he was a friend to Felix, and John by that time had determined that Felix must know all the outcasts in Scotland.

After their meal, the men went down a hallway walled with unpainted wood panels, passing a number of doors that Felix said led to sleeping rooms. They had come near to the back door when Felix stopped. He paused, looked around, slid his hand behind a panel of rough wood, and pushed. The panel swung in, and quickly they were inside a large room. Felix closed the hidden door behind them.

John could see two beds and a fireplace along one wall. In a corner a pipe dripped water into a basin. In the other corner, was a commode, behind a hanging curtain, and a small table with chairs was centered along the west wall. Two rocking chairs sat before the warmth of the fireplace.

"This is where I stay sometimes when I'm in Tain," Felix said. "I've fix'd it up a wee bit for ye; I thought ye and yer moth'r might be needin' a secure place."

Grandfather was amazed. "Why ye've answer'd my pray'rs, Felix," he replied. "I can bring Moth'r here where she'll be safe, and then I'll have time t' set forth what I need done before we hopefully sail to America.

Grandfather admitted to Felix that he had been concerned Paul's men might use his mother as a bait to catch him. "If they did," he acknowledged, "her life would'na be worth a farthin'.

"Ye're a blessin', Felix, and I know not how t' repay ye."

"Ye already hav', laddie. Ye already hav'."

John looked away. He silently thanked God, praying for blessings upon Felix, who had fought on against all odds without bitterness or vengeance, a noble man, it seemed to Grandfather, stripped of nobility, with the courage of a warrior.

It was five the following morning when John awoke. He knew it was daylight by instinct, though there were no windows in the room. He and Felix had talked into the small hours of the morning. They had made plans for the actions John should take, moving his mother from her house, out of harm's way.

Later that night, John checked the secret place south of his mother's house. Earlier he had left a note for Alan, his father's close friend as well as the Chief's, and in the crevice he found a reply. Alan would meet him at the pine near the rock at midnight.

With three more hours to wait, Grandfather moved through the secret tunnel into the house. He would have his mother pack all she might need and be ready the next evening to leave through the tunnel.

Midnight was dark beneath the pine tree as Grandfather greeted Alan. The men talked for an hour before parting. Paul's henchmen were searching for Grandfather throughout Tain and beyond, Alan told him. They knew he had to be close at hand, but word was they were mystified as to where he could be hiding. They were watching his mother's house day and night, Alan added.

"Ye must take care, John, for they mean to kill ye."

"Aye," Grandfather acknowledged, "but we'll need anoth'r place for our messages . . . somewhere in Tain. I'll be moving Moth'r out this night."

Alan was relieved, for the Chief was also concerned for her safekeeping. "He sends his regr'ts for what has happen'd," the aide told John. "But do ye hav' a place where she might be safely hidd'n away?"

Grandfather nodded he did, and Alan gave him a surprised look, for it was something the Chief's own spies were not aware of. Nevertheless pleased, he added, "Don'na tell me where 'tis; it'll be saf'r that way."

Before parting, they decided on a place along the waterfront for their future messages.

On September 6th, John was optimistic. It had been four days since they had painstakingly moved his mother into the secret room in the guise of local farmers. Felix had sent his men to help with the move, for the large packed trunks were cumbersome as they secreted them through the tunnel and into their wagon. Her belongings had filled the small wagon, covered with grain and hay, unsuspected by Paul's thugs. Prince, who had been tied to the back of the wagon as it traveled, was hidden in a small glen some two miles from the town of Tain.

On the 10th, Felix and John returned from the glen where James had long ago cached his weapons. Felix was amazed at the beautiful sanctuary and thought it strange he had never known of its location, for he had seen nearly every piece of land in that area.

From the weapons recovered there, John kept the King flintlock pistol, the broadsword, the rapier, and the dirk. He already had with him the quarterstaff his father had given him years earlier. The other weapons, cached in the cave, he gave to Felix. John began to wear the pistol and dirk, both safely hidden behind his belt, the pistol to the front and the dirk at his back.

After they had returned from the glen, Felix seemed to have disappeared once again. John decided he would like to take those few days to hunt for the gold and silver coins Felix had left in the mountains of Beauly Glen, for if he and his mother went to America, they would need that security. Felix had assured him they both would share the treasure were they to find it.

And though the coins had belonged to Prince Charles, he was after all in exile, and John believed that the Prince had forfeited his rights to the coins. The Crown would surely have confiscated the money had they found it. He thought Felix most surely was right — the coins belonged to the finder.

John could not wait much longer for Felix to re-appear, as his situation with Paul's thugs was precarious, and sooner or later Paul would discover their whereabouts. He would wait a few days, but if Felix did not show, he would have to search for the coins without him.

Two days passed, and Felix had not returned. John was at the secluded glen south of Tain as a golden sun was beginning its flight into the eastern sky. He saddled Prince, his black stallion, then, unseen, moved down the road at a trot for several miles, finally slowing the horse to a walk.

He rode through a beautiful and lonely, indifferent land, a pristine glacial expanse of fluted escarpments and high narrow glens, plush with purple heather, and steep mountain braes clad with soft green grass. Throughout the rocky glens came down robust churning streams from out of the snow-capped mountains into the rivers and lochs. It was an abrupt land, never flat for more than a few feet in any direction.

As John rode along Cromarty Firth, the marsh rushes were changing in the wind from green to a shifting silver. Among the long-stemmed vegetation in a clearing of open water, a flock of plovers were wading, searching for food in the shallows.

Grandfather noticed, now that he was older, that as he traveled he became even more attuned to the beauty around him. The majestic landscape filled him with much contemplation.

But he would need to become more concerned, he thought, with his mother and her wishes. Grandfather knew that his mother had the same dreams, the same problems, the same failures, and the same hopes for happiness. Children seldom think of their parents as individuals, with typical human frailties; but in truth, parents were simply in a different location on the wheel of time. John promised himself that he would be more thoughtful and aware.

His mind was still racing when he reined Prince southwest at Beauly. He thought again of the wheel of time. Life surely did seem to be a circle.

Grandfather said he figured it to be nearly thirty miles to where the coins were stashed, and he could be better than halfway there by evening. It was seven o'clock when he reached the village of Cannich. The streets were empty. He stopped at an inn, stabled his horse, ate a supper, and rented a room.

He awoke the following morning before dawn and was eating his morning meal by five. Eight miles southwest of the town, on the trail of a road rarely used, he found the tree Felix had used as a marker. It was eight o'clock before he found a place with grass and water where Prince could be hidden from view. He would take care to not be seen by passers-by, for there would be too many questions that he could not answer.

From the tree John could see the road several miles each way. And though he would be away from the traveled path in his search, he was certain he could see any travelers before they noticed him, and he could drop from view into the heather.

He looked from the tree to the peak. The terrain was rough and rolling with at least two good-sized hillocks between the maze of broken escarpments to the northwest. It was no wonder Felix could not find the place again — any number of the escarpments could be the one Felix had looked at.

John picked out a slanted rock to his front for alignment and moved to it. Then he sighted from there to the peak and picked out another spot of alignment. He went over a hillock, down into a dry wash, and up the other side of a brae where he scared a flock of russet chaffinches nesting in the heather. They flew close to the ground, far away, only to settle back down into the purple blossoms and disappear. He continued on until he finally reached the escarpments.

He had seen no one on the road, but now he could not see the tree, so he moved several feet to where he could see the uppermost branches. For at least two hours Grandfather searched, but could find no sign of a cave.

He tied a purple ribbon on the rock where he had ended up and went back to the tree where he began, once again sighting at the peak. He was greatly off line, he could see, and would have to keep better alignment some way. If only he had the missing tree.

Grandfather walked out from the tree some four hundred feet and again tied purple ribbon, this time onto a top branch of heather. He had chosen the ribbon, only slightly lighter than the heather blossoms to be certain it would not stand out. Back at the tree and sighting once more, he looked carefully to find the ribbon among the blossoms. Again, his alignment was off a few feet, but even that small accounting of error if continued would be a vast distance at the escarpments.

Grandfather went back and moved the ribbon, then walked to the tree again and picked another spot some four hundred feet farther along than the first ribbon. He soon had four ribbons in line. Now he could keep aligned by looking back.

He had finished tying his tenth ribbon, and while stepping back he tripped over a fair-sized dead limb. The disturbance had scared up a lynx that raced off, leaving a wake in the waving heather. John's heart was pounding with excitement, not only from the surprise of the lynx but from the limb he had fallen over. He knew it had to be from the lost tree, and nearby could see the rotting trunk. His ribbons were slightly off alignment, but an hour later he had the ribbons once more set.

It was nearly dark when Grandfather found the cave. He made a torch from a fistful of heather, then lit it after crawling inside, hoping the lynx was not there.

The inner chamber was large, perhaps fifty feet long and thirty wide. He could see most of the ceiling, some twenty feet above him. The far upper wall had a cleft that continued out of sight — no doubt, John thought, going up and outside the cave, for the smoke from his torch lifted into the cleft and disappeared as if floating up a chimney.

West of the entrance to the cave, along the wall, John could see two bulging leather sacks. He looked inside the larger one, although he already knew what was in them both, then made a yoke from his belt to fit over his shoulders, so that he might more easily carry the bulky treasure.

By this time, much of the evening had passed, and Grandfather decided to stay put for the night. The heavy bags would be too conspicuous for the next day's travel, so he would plan for the following evening, which would return him to his room at the pub close to four in the morning, by far the safest hour to return.

He built a fire from heather and broken pine limbs to ward off the chill mountainous air, made a bed of heather, then lay back and watched the ghostly shadows dancing in the firelight along the wall.

The flowing shadows of the campfire gave him an eerie feeling — not a feeling he was frightened of, but almost a companionship, as if he was not alone . . . as if the spirits of the old ones who had passed over were still there, lingering in the primitive cave and frolicking in the firelight.

John thought back to the wee morning hours when he had slipped out of Tain. Perhaps four blocks from the inn, he had passed an alleyway of dark shadows, and though he could not see anyone there, he was certain of a presence — an instinctive feeling that he was being watched.

He knew he would have to be doubly cautious upon his return.

At three the next morning, John once again entered the concealed room at the inn, carrying the two heavy sacks of coins over to the table. His mother sleepily rose from her bed.

"So ye found th' coins, lad. I figur'd ye would."

Felix had not yet appeared, but John was unconcerned. "He'll show; he's too canny to get caught by th' Crown. Not only that . . . he has too many friends, an' th' authorities would nev'r be able t' hold 'im!"

John thought he had better not leave the coins on the table, so he stashed the sacks in a trunk. The next day before daylight, Felix finally returned to the pub. John was in the common room talking to the innkeeper, when Felix slipped in through the back.

"We were startin' to worry for ye," John told him.

Felix waved him off. "Don'na worry 'bout me, lad, for what is it they say, *A bad farthing always shows up!*"

"I know nothin' o' that," John replied softly with a smile, "I'd always heard 'twas th' smell o' mon'y." Speaking so no one could hear, John added, "I need to see ye in the room, Felix."

With the door securely closed, John walked over to the trunk. He opened the lid, pulled out the bags, then set them on the table.

"So, ye found 'em, lad!"

Felix dumped one sack on the table. Several gold pieces rolled over to the edge and onto the floor. Felix held one up to the light and whistled.

"It's a fortune in gold!" He said no more, and returned all but five to the bag. He emptied the contents of the second bag, stirred through the silver, looking closely at several, then rebagged all but five of those. He handed John's mother the ten coins.

"These ere for yer keepsake," he said, and turned to John, pointing at the sacks.

"Lad, put them back in the trunk for time bein'."

John asked if Felix had any thought what the coins might be worth, but Felix shook his head.

"No, lad, an' th' reason I don'na ere th' coins ere antiquities. Face value, I'd say th' gold was some five thousand pounds, and th' silv'r a tenth o' that. But these, me lad, ere priceless coins, and I would venture they were rarities put together by antiquity dealers as a collection for Prince Charles.

"The gold is made up of Spanish doubloons, Roman and Byzantine coins from as far back as th' first century. The silver coins ere English, French, Roman, and Byzantine."

Felix decided to take the coins to a dealer a two-day journey off, who could sell them to collectors. "He'll charge us a share, but no matter, for it would'na surprise me but what we could end up wi' six times their face — maybe more."

"And what about Prince Charles?" Grandfather asked.

"He's no need o' th' coins," Felix responded. "And wi' all th' hardship he's caus'd our fine countrym'n, he's forfeit'd all rights. Most o' me share will go t' th' poor people o' me clan. Had th' Crown not tak'n our lands I'd be Chief now. Me fath'r died twenty years past, mostly o' th' grief of the rebellion, an' worryin' for his people. The many were at th' point of starvation, and I've tried t' do what I could t' help."

Felix had been gone two days, and it was already the 16th of September. A Dutch ship was to pull into the port of Tain on the 20th and set sail for America the 22nd. Grandfather said he had heard they were going to a Dutch settlement in America, called Manhattan, a natural harbor purchased from the native Indians. He knew he needed to get passage on that ship, for each day they were still in the room it became more dangerous, and he did not want to get the innkeeper involved in their troubles.

Alan's recent notes had told John that Paul's henchman knew that his mother was gone. They had found the tunnel, and Paul was furious. His men were scouring city and countryside, trying to locate them. Alan pleaded for John to be cautious, for the Chief, he had said, was certain he could not give help if they were caught.

That night, Felix returned. The coin dealer could sell the treasure to collectors for perhaps thirty to forty thousand pounds, but it would take close to a year to dispose of that many coins without stirring the attention of the government, Felix noted.

John and his mother had no contention with Felix's plan.

Felix continued, "Then we hav' but one more problem to settle. The deal'r was able t' give me but four thousand pounds up-front. I need a thousand for pressing bills, and that leaves three thousand I can give ye now."

"No," John replied. "I'd rather we split four thousand t' keep it ev'n. Give us two now an' th' rest wh'n ye get it."

John's mother nodded in agreement.

The two thousand Felix gave to John was mostly in pound notes, along with a bit of silver, mostly crowns and shillings. John now had plenty of resources to book passage on the ship. He could even take Prince along. He and his mother could travel in comfort, and the total should not run over fifty pounds.

The problem, however, was to purchase the passage to America without being seen, for Paul's men would be watching everyone along the water-front.

John left a note for Alan laying out his predicament. He had asked in the message if someone could help him, someone whose authority would not be questioned by Paul's thugs.

"I'll give ye th' mon'y t' pay for our passage, but I'd want no one t' get int' trouble."

The next day, when John still had no answer from Alan, he decided he would have to wait until the last day before the ship sailed to attempt securing passage. Felix wanted to see to the task, but John would not allow it.

He then put together a bold plan. On the last day he would hire some seaman to move his mother's things. He would ride up to the ship and book passage. He would be seen, but hopefully they could board before Paul could organize his men to stop them. It was not the best-laid plan, but it was all he could manage. Once aboard, he would be at the mercy of the Captain, who might just turn him over to Paul. But it was a chance they would have to take.

The following day, the 17th, he had a note from Alan. He was to meet him after dark, at eight o'clock, south of Tain at the location they had decided on earlier.

After dinner there was a light knock at the door. It was Felix. John's mother was at the table sewing the antique coins into parts of her clothing. John and Felix sat down in the two rockers.

"Lad, ye sure ye don't want me t' handle yer passage?"

"I'm sure, ye're in dang'r enough; ye don'na need t' expose yourself that way. I'm t' see Alan tonight; we will hope he will hav' some ideas."

"Aye, and he will," Felix added. "The Chief had thought highly o' your fath'r, and he'll do what he can."

Two blocks south of the inn, John could see the dark shape in the shadows, the same place something had stood those times before, only now John could tell for certain it was a man.

The shadow moved when John walked toward the space between the two buildings. John felt for the handgun in his belt. It was there, as was the dirk along his back. The weapons were reassuring. But whoever it was wanted no confrontation, for he had slithered away into the deepness of the passage, and John was not about to go into someone else's familiar lair, especially in an alley where he could see nothing.

He knew the enemy was getting closer. He and his mother would have no choice now; they would have to move in the next few days.

John walked on south, watching his back trail. Whoever it was did not follow, and Alan was waiting at their location a mile south of town.

"Greetings, lad," Alan said. "The Chief wants t' talk t' ye."

"What would he be wantin' wi' me?" John asked.

"I don'na know, John, he just ask'd me t' bring ye t' th' castle."

John followed Alan; they wasted no time. They walked a short distance, then ducked into the trees and traveled a path that seemed familiar to Alan. A full moon was rising in the sky, and John could see well enough to tell it was not a well-traveled way. In thirty minutes, they emerged from the woods. The castle stood not over a mile before them.

They had somehow come in onto the north side of the fortress, and through a moonlit haze, to the south, on unfamiliar grounds, John could see the gleaming waters of Moray Firth. Before him the stone edifice loomed enormous, dark, and ominous, like a sleeping giant ready to swallow anything that came too close.

He knew that inside the lower battlement walls would be the outer bailey and the barbican, and that the high tower toward the center of the castle was the keep. Connected to the keep would be the large battlements, surrounding the inner bailey, and living quarters. From where they stood, he could also see part of the moat, the drawbridge, and the gatehouse.

After the short pause, Alan slipped down a steep incline to a cover of purple shadows. There appeared to be no path, and then they came to a stop in a dry wash, with brush on both sides of the ravine.

They turned and walked an old overgrown roadway toward the castle until they came to a stop at a high rock wall, perhaps a half mile from the parapet walls.

Alan stopped and listened. In the lull of silence the insects began to orchestrate their late summer music; then a night bird chimed in with a flute-like whistle, adding to the nocturnal symphony. Interrupting the darkness, a bat fluttered by John's head, adding a mystery to the night, as if they were close to the haunts of lingering ghosts.

Alan, satisfied no one else was close by, walked up to the wall and removed a stone. He pulled on a lever and a large door swung open. He replaced the concealing stone, and as they walked inside, into a tunnel, he closed the door. The opening was surely well camouflaged, for John had detected no door when they had stood outside.

Alan picked up and lit a torch from several in a box along the wall. It was a large passageway, John thought, at least twenty feet wide, with a ceiling that rose almost twelve feet from the rough stone floor. The door was wide enough for a horse and wagon to enter, and from the smell he could tell that horses had at times been there. After a short distance, a widened area could be seen, for stalls and mangers.

Now and again John could feel fresh air coming from some unseen outside source.

The tunnel had to pass under the moat, which perhaps accounted for the dampness he had felt in the passageway.

They had walked in the tunnel for nearly fifteen minutes when Alan stopped, removed another stone, and opened a side door, using the same type of mechanism as at the entrance. It was a narrow passageway, leading up a stairway.

They walked up the steep stairway to landings, around turns, down straightaways and more turns.

Then Alan knocked lightly, almost like a code. The passageway where they stood continued on. There had been no markings or unusual indicators along the walls they had passed, and John wondered how Alan knew where to stop.

A doorway opened, and the men walked into a large room. A fireplace and mantle took up most of the far wall. A white-haired man, dressed in battlefield tartan, stood with his back to the flames.

The door swung shut behind Alan and John. How it had closed, Grandfather never knew. It could have been another person, or maybe it had moved on its own some way.

"So ye be John Ross. Ye've grown into a strong and handsom' lad," the Chief said with a friendly smile. He walked forward with outstretched hand and pointed to a chair among two others clustered in front of the fireplace.

"Sit, John, and make yourself comfortable." He looked over at Alan. "Please come back in half an hour. John and I should be finish'd by then."

The Chief was in his eighties, and although his body was beginning to show his years, John could tell he would have been a formidable man in his prime. It was his eyes that first captured John's attention. They still had the look of youth, blue as a bright clear sky. There was no meanness in his countenance, only patience, courage, long-suffering, and strength.

John thought of the grief that must beset the gentleman, knowing his son, Paul, had not turned out the kind of man he had wanted him to be.

The Chief sat down across from John.

"Alan tells me ye want t' go t' th' American colonies."

"Aye, sir," John answered. "Moth'r and I think it would be best."

The Chief inquired of his mother, then announced, "I'm sorry for yer fath'r's death, me lad. He was th' finest man I've kn'wn. He did ev'rythin' I ask'd o' him with a joyful heart, and he sav'd th' day for th' clan many a time. We owe him more than we could ev'r repay, and I've not seen his equal as a warrior.

"It was a sad day for th' clan when he was killed, and a sad day for me. He was like a son."

John spoke quickly, for he saw a glazing of tears gathering in the Chief's eyes, and heard a breaking in his voice.

"Aye," John said, "he was a fine fath'r, a man who enjoy'd life. He had principl's, and his life stay'd within those bound'ries.

"He gave me th' best a fath'r can give a son, an honorable way t' live one's life."

"Aye, he did that, me lad, and was a man t' be proud of." The Chief continued in a melancholy tone. "I wish'd things could hav' been differ'nt . . . if only yer fath'r and Paul could hav' been friends.

The Chief acknowledged that Paul had given him many a grief, for he was consumed with the desire for power and recognition. "Had any oth'r o' th' clan memb'rs been guilty o' what Paul has done, I'd o' had 'em execut'd. But he's my eld'st son, and he'll soon be Chief."

John remained silent, then added, "For the sake o' th' clan, Mother and I should leave Scotland and go to America. We've been hunt'd day 'n night, and soon'r or lat'r we'll be caught and kill'd. It may be aft'r we've been gone a while things will resolve and ye can hav' peace again."

John did not completely believe his own words, but they seemed to give the old Chief hope, and a smile crept into his well-worn face.

"I've book'd ye and yer moth'r passage on th' Dutch ship that docks tomorrow. It's paid for, so ye'll need'na worry for that. Ye've a cabin next t' the Captain's quart'rs where ye can make the trip like royalty, and in comfort.

"Let Alan know when ye want t' board, and ye'll hav' twelve o' me guards t' escort ye both t' th' ship. Not ev'n Paul would dare interf're against me escort."

John was astounded; he could only thank the Chief.

As the tired Chief nodded, Alan entered the room. "I sugg'st early morning on th' 22nd, the day of departure, for th' guards t' arrive. I will'-na send them t' where ye're staying, for your innkeeper would have t' contend with th' trouble."

The Chief could see the surprise on John's face, and he smiled. "We've known for days where you were stayin', me lad. Our people've been watchin' out for ye day 'n night."

With the visit over, Alan and Grandfather moved toward the door.

"Aye . . . but hold fast," the Chief called as he walked to a mahogany desk. He opened a drawer and took something out enclosed in his fist. Shoving a small pouch into John's hand, he told him, "Good-bye, me lad, and may we meet again sometime."

The hour was midnight when John slipped quietly through the hidden door to his room. His mother lay asleep in her bed. He went to the table in the darkness and removed the glass chimney from the lamp. He struck his flint and steel, flashing golden sparks. From habit, he cupped the flaming tender in his hands and lit the wick, then replaced the chimney.

He removed from his pocket the small leather pouch, loosened the cord at the top, and dumped the contents onto the table. Surprised at the treasure before him, John slumped into a chair. The twelve brilliant diamonds were a breathless sight.

Grandfather stirred through the gems with his finger, isolating the largest, the size of a grape. His heart was racing as he looked at the fortune lying on the table, gleaming in the lamplight in a rainbow of colors.

He heard a movement behind him and turned to see his mother staring at the diamonds.

"It's a gift from the Chief," John managed. "I've nev'r seen such gems as these before.

"Ye bett'r hide 'em wi' th' coins, Mother. We would'na want eyes t' lay upon this kind o' wealth. Temptation might be too much for ev'n a good man."

As John's mother picked them up, she quietly advised, "Don'na forget our tithe, son."

"Aye, 'tis so, Mother. I'll have Felix deliver what we owe t' th' church."

John went to the common room of the inn for breakfast, amongst several strangers. But his eye caught upon a roguish-looking fellow in the shadows, dressed like a seaman, with a bandanna wrapped around his head. He seemed to be glancing at John with more than a casual interest.

John felt for his dirk in place behind his belt. He began to wonder if this was one of Paul's hired spies . . . or was it the chief's?

Then Felix walked through the back door, nodded at the host, and looked around the room. His eyes rested for a moment on the man in the corner who got up and walked out the door.

Felix sat down at John's table.

"Laddie, ere ye ready t' be leavin' in three days?"

"Not yet, I'm not, for I've been thinkin' of a trip t' Elgin t' see Agnes. It would'na take me more than one long day."

"No, lad, don'na do it. Paul's people are swarmin' hereabouts."

"Aye," John acknowledged. "And th' seaman who left had an interest in me — no doubt somebody's spy, but I don'na know whose."

"No worry o' him, lad; that's one o' me own."

John told Felix about the generosity of the Chief, wanting to share his bounty with Felix.

"No, John," Felix protested. "Those gems are yer gift from yer Chief. Yer fath'r earn'd their worth in service many times ov'r. I'll move 'em for ye if ye want, but if I were ye I would keep 'em. Ye've plenty o' cash, and ye could sell 'em whenev'r ye've a need.

"I know of an honest man of the law in America, a Patrick Henry o' Richmond, Virginia, and he could lead ye t' a reputable outlet."

Amidst it all, John was determined to go to Elgin, and made up his mind to leave sometime before dawn the following day. He was at the glen where Prince was pastured at the first light, and the sun was barely above the North Sea when he mounted.

In an hour he was at the coastal town of Nigg, and by eight he had hired a boat to ferry him and his horse across Moray Firth to the village of Findhorn.

It was past noon when John led the stallion down the ramp off the boat, passed through the village, and took the road south. The sun had arched around the sky to about two o'clock when he dismounted and loosely tied his horse at the inn just north of Elgin.

He walked in and down the familiar steps to the common room. After he had sat down along the far wall where he could watch the door, a pretty young lass asked what he might be needing. John ordered dinner and inquired about Agnes.

"She's not here — been gone two days," the lass stated.

"What do ye mean gone?" John could hardly believe what he heard.

"I don'na know. Ye'd have t' ask th' host."

Mr. Leslie was behind the bar washing glasses when John walked over and introduced himself.

"I'm lookin' for Richard Miller and Agnes — his daughter. I'm a friend."

"Well, I can'na help ye, for I don'na know where they ere mys'lf. Two days past, Richard came to my hoose and told me Agnes had been kid-napp'd.

"He need'd for me to run the inn while he went t' search for her. No one has heard from him since, and I'm gettin' t' wonder 'bout them meself. And what is yer int'rest in them?"

"Well, Agnes and I had a kind o' understandin'. I was in hopes t' solid-ify that before I left for America."

"Aye, a sweet lass she is, and ye couldn'na do bett'r. Ye know, a week before she was gone, a strang'r had been hangin' around th' inn, talkin' t' her, and then he disappear'd."

"The day she was taken he came back wi' four other toughs. And as soon as th' place was free o' most o' th' patrons, she was tak'n at gun-point. Richard tried t' stop 'em, but he was overpower'd and tied hand 'n foot.

"One of the locals saw the men ridin' off with Agnes, then found Richard."

"No one knows why she was taken . . . that's the mystery o' th' thing. . . . But it'd rain'd that day, and Richard found their tracks leading away from th' road. Sure it was they did'na want t' be seen on th' travel'd way.

"And Richard hasn't been back."

Grandfather asked if Mr. Leslie could show him the tracks where the horses had been tied, and the trail they took. The host took Grandfather out the back door, and upon seeing the still visible tracks, Grandfather grabbed his handgun and sword from his pack and took off riding north. By then it was late afternoon.

Grandfather said he managed to discern their trail, which followed west of the main road, heading for Findhorn. By nightfall he was near the vil-lage, and the trail suddenly ended in a tree-covered glen where the earth was torn up from the hooves of horses. It appeared, as well, that there had been a fight, and from the blood on the grasses, someone had been badly wounded.

After searching out the area, and to his grief, John found Richard and one of the henchman, both dead, in a ditch partially covered with brush.

John borrowed a shovel from the first house he came to in the village, then went back and buried both men. The grave site he had chosen for Richard lay beneath a pine overlooking the Firth. He would remember the place, should Agnes want to know.

The kidnappers' trail ended on the cobblestone streets of Findhorn, with no trace leading out of town, on any of the roads. John was convinced they had taken Agnes by boat.

He made his bed by the seashore and laid looking into the purple darkness across the ancient firth of time.

"Where ere ye, Agnes?" His words went hollow on the wind.

It was coming onto daylight when John entered his room once again at the inn. Later, when he walked into the common room where Felix was sitting at a far table, he told Felix about the kidnapping.

"There's not much ye can do, John. It's a waiting game. I'm sure 'tis Paul that has her. He's found out ye have an interest in th' lass. I'll have me men check around, maybe let it be known we can contact ye. . . . Just hold fast."

"Felix, I'll not be able t' leave for America in two days if I can'na find Agnes."

"Ye've no choice but t' leave, lad. Don'na fret; I'll find her." Felix got up from the table and left through the back door.

It was late afternoon when he returned. He softly knocked at the door of John's room. Inside, he handed John a note, which he hurriedly opened and read aloud. *"We have Agnes, and if ye ever want t' see her again, be at th' south end of Carney off Front Street at eight o'clock tonight. Ye come alone. Be there or she dies."*

"Don'na go," Felix pleaded.

John paused, looking far and away deep inside. He drew a breath, exhaled, and replied, "I hav' t' go."

"I was fearful o' that," Felix responded. "But 'tis a trap. Carney is a dead-end passage, only one way in and out. Ye'll be at th' mercy o' whoev'r holds th' neck o' th' bottle!"

"I can'na help it, Felix. I must go. I could'na live with m'self if I was to leav' Agnes in th' hands o' someone like Paul."

As always, Felix pondered a moment. "Well, if ye must, let's make some plans that might get ye out o' there alive."

Darkness had already crept into the alleyways when John moved down Front Street. A lamplighter was striking his flint ahead of him, but no one else did he see moving on the streets. Off to the southeast, the *Limfjorden* rested in the dim harbor lights with her three dark masts reaching high into the cobalt sky.

John was armed with his handgun, dirk, and broadsword. If Felix's plan did not work, he would take plenty of Paul's men with him to the grave, and hopefully Paul as well.

Though he saw no one, John knew his enemies were out there. They would wait until he found the lass, and let them both hope they might get away free. That would be Paul's twisted mind at work. He would want to kill John in front of Agnes.

He turned down Carney Street and heard the slightest noise. Back in the dark he could make out the blackened shapes of men. He walked on, uneasy, as would anyone be, yet knowing he must stay calm. Fear could alert the senses and make one more aware, but one must never throw caution to the winds; it was a prescription for dying young.

John walked some two hundred feet before he saw Agnes ahead in the distance, tied hand and foot, a gag in her mouth to silence her. The last fifty feet of the street dropped away down a noticeable decline. Only the head and shoulders of a person would be in sight of the thugs hidden at the entrance of the bottleneck. John reached Agnes unseen, and quickly untied her bonds and removed her gag. She could only speak his name as she trembled.

John warned her to be silent, and to follow him. They slipped into the shadows along the south side of the dead-end, where both dropped down and out of view of the thugs. On hands and knees they scrambled to the opposite side of the street where John counted the large stones along the base of a high retaining wall. He pushed on the tenth stone; it did not move. He pushed harder, and the stone pivoted. They crawled through an opening in the wall into total darkness, and then John quickly shoved the stone into its closed position.

Breathless, they rested, holding each other in the dark, their trembling indistinguishable from the other. A brief flash of a flint could be seen as Felix lit up a torch. He stood at the bottom of a cavernous stairway, waiting for them.

"*Come*, John . . . " Felix whispered. "We need t' get ye t' your room quickly. They'll soon be on th' other side o' th' wall lookin' for ye. Ye nev'r can tell, they may eventually find th' entrance t' th' tunnel, and we must be long gone from here . . . for they'll be searchin' ev'ry house and buildin' in this part o' town."

The ancient tunnels crisscrossed the old part of Tain, and Felix was sure Paul must have had heard of them too. The damp, narrow passage was barely more than head high. Felix led the way, as they stepped through puddles of water on the stone floor. An occasional rat raced across ahead, only to dart into a crack farther along.

In minutes they were led to an exit not far from the inn, and in no time they were back in Felix's secret room.

That night John made a pallet and slept on the floor. He awoke once during the night and could hear Agnes, in the stillness, softly crying. By daylight he was up, eating a repast his mother had fixed, along with the helping hand of Agnes.

The two women were about the same size, and John's mother had already given Agnes a needed change of clothing.

Felix came by later that morning, and the men sat much of the day talking and making plans. John's mother wanted Agnes to sail to America with them.

"Lassie, ye must go wi' us, ye've nothin' t' stay here for. John wants ye t' go, and we'll take care o' ye."

Agnes looked at John. He smiled and nodded his head. Agnes happily agreed for, indeed, with her father gone, she had no one left.

"I will go, and I do hav' an uncle in Annapolis, Maryland, father's brother."

It was eight the next morning when the Chief's guards found John at their meeting place. Six of the men were on horseback, the other six afoot — a formidable group, along with Felix's men to help carry the trunks and luggage.

John led his stallion, his handgun and his dirk beneath his jacket. That morning he had also sided a sheathed rapier.

Grandfather was dressed in his ceremonial Ross plaid, and his mother told him later that when they had walked down the street that morning, he looked every bit the gentleman and handsome warrior he had become.

They had not walked far, however, and were soon in sight of the bark *Limfjorden*. It looked to be a fine ship in the sunlight. Her crew, hastily moving about, were readying to depart. The ship's howsers tugged at the quay from the intermittent waves lapping at its hull.

The group was nearly upon the waiting vessel, a few hundred feet away, when Paul and his own twelve armed henchmen rode up and surrounded them. The Chief's guards were at the ready for attack.

Paul called out to John, "Ye go wi' me and th' oth'rs are free t' leave."

"Nay," John replied, "if it's a fight ye want, then let's duel it out now, the two of us." Before John could say more, to everyone's surprise the Chief rode up on his majestic gray stallion. With him was his second eldest son.

Paul shouted to his father, "It's 'im I want," pointing to John. "He's a traitor t' th' clan and th' Crown."

Steadily and firmly, the Chief informed him, "Ye can'na hav' 'im, Paul. I've giv'n my word he can leave. Ye go home and forg't it."

Paul was furious. "I can'na forg't it! I'll fight 'im now with rapiers."

"No. Ye will not."

John spoke up. "We can end th' deadlock and I'll fight Paul, but not t' th' death. We stop at first wound."

"No!" Paul shouted back. "To the death!"

The Chief was torn, for he knew — though Paul did not — that John, like his father James, would for certain cut down any man in his path. "What if Paul were t' pick a second t' fight in his place?"

John was willing to give the Chief this conciliation, for he knew what was in the aged leader's mind. Paul eagerly accepted, now all the more willing that they fight to the death. The Chief peered at John with questioning eyes, then faintly smiled, for he had no doubt of the outcome.

John quickly accepted — the only way out of the delicate predicament.

Paul was reputed the best swordsman around, but he had in his group the next best known duelist in that part of the land — winner of a dozen fights to the death, brutal in disposing of his enemy.

Paul was triumphant with the way things were turning out, for he knew that those who had fenced with John at school and the university had beaten him at least some of the time, and none he had talked to could come close to besting his own man. But he did not know that

John had let those lads beat him, to remain on more civil terms and to disarm any future enemies. His father's lessons in tactics had served him well. The thought of losing intentionally would have never entered Paul's mind.

Before Grandfather was ready, Paul's man thrust, and Grandfather barely threw himself out of the way of the blade. Then they joined and fought blade to blade, with Paul's man on the attack, and pressing hard. Grandfather retreated clumsily as a guise, with the hope of getting the man to make a foolish move.

The henchman lunged in, to end the match quickly. In less than a minute he had already nicked John three times, blood slowly dripping onto the cobblestone street. The man believed he was guaranteed a victory. John could see in his brutal, flashing eyes and insolent smirk his total assurance.

Each time the man extended forward, he had tried to turn his blade to the left. John's father had taught him better than that, for though it might be a brilliant move, during one slight moment it would leave the man defenseless. The combatants engaged again, and John instantly plunged his sword into the henchman's belly.

Paul shouted, "*No!* I won't hav' it!" He lunged at John with drawn sword, so fast that John was hard pressed to parry off the engaging thrusts. He knew he would have to be cautious, for Paul would not make a foolish mistake as had his substitute.

"Ye're a lucky fool, as clumsy as ye be afoot!" Paul shouted at John. "Ye'll not be so lucky wi' me!"

John glanced at the Chief, thinking he might stop the fight, a glance that almost cost his life. A blade moves fast in the hands of a crazed man, and although John had warded off the attack, Paul's blade cut a gash along his ribs. Paul was a better swordsman than the other man, but he was never as good as John's father.

John continued to retreat before the onslaught of thrusts that went to his face, his neck, his eyes. Blade to blade they fought. Before long they both had cuts to their bodies. Paul's face contorted into worry, and fear began to gnaw at him.

John smiled, infuriating Paul more. Their flashing blades engaged again, then parted; both were getting tired. Then Paul lunged forward, pressing hard and furious. But his blind anger had made him careless, and it cost him.

John's blade caught Paul's chest in not a deep or fatal wound, for it had hit the collar bone. The unwanted match could have ended there, but this had been declared to the death. John made an instant twist of his wrist, a move his father had taught him. The blade sliced upward across Paul's throat, cutting deep into his jugular. He fell and lay choking on his blood. In but moments he was dead.

The Chief sat stoic his horse. He pointed to the ship, commanding John, "Go . . . ye're free t' go."

John plodded on weary feet with the others to the ship. The crew and passengers had lined the ship's railing, from where they had watched the bitter fight. From the crowd of strangers came a shout.

"A way to go, matey! Ye must be a lad from the sea!"

As Grandfather walked up the gangway, he heard the Chief giving orders, "Take 'im t' th' castle". . . and then, "Ye men that were wi' Paul return t' your homes!" A bustling of movement could be heard as the orders were carried out.

Aboard ship John stopped, paused a moment, and looked back. Jonathan, the Chief's next eldest son and new heir apparent, was sitting on his stallion, looking like the leader he soon would be.

America

Land of Promise

A GOLDEN MORNING sun rose up from the ocean depths, and lit a gleaming path from horizon to ship. John stood at the rail looking at the calm water. For the two previous days the sea had been rough.

Light was probing the depths of reluctant purple shadows on the ship, and Grandfather was filled with hope. He did not know what might lie beyond the next wave, or be there to greet him on the new shore, but it was a challenge and his Scottish blood was racing, eager to learn that promise.

The *Limfjorden* was a magnificent ship, and John had covered every inch of it during the past five days. A slight breeze lifted the sails as the vessel skimmed through the endless water at good speed, headed west. The bow of the ship cut into the sea, slapping the backflow against the hull, then leaving a trail that eventually disappeared for no one to follow or find again.

Grandfather had said that Agnes and his mother became close friends during the voyage, and though there had been little time for the young couple to be together, they had managed a few hours on deck each evening after his mother had gone to bed.

One night during rough passage they had been soaked to the skin, as the sea washed and sprayed over the deck while the ship cut through each wave. But it did not matter to John and Agnes. They were happy to be alive, and together.

At some point they managed to talk of their future. They would marry, but not for a couple of years. He would need to get his mother settled first, and in the meantime Agnes would stay with her uncle in Annapolis.

It was October 10th, 1774, and the sun was high in the sky when a seaman from the crow's-nest of the main sail shouted, *"Land ho!"*

The crew aboard jumped to their tasks with enthusiasm.

"Port at last!" came the cry from a hand working the upper deck. An hour later, the ship docked at Manhattan Island, in the settlement of New York.

John had hired four of the seamen to help unload their belongings from the ship. On the dock they packed their things into a wagon John rented from a teamster, a large and jovial Dutchman who had come over ten years before. Several other rigs had been available for hire, but John liked the looks of the man.

Bjorn was a wealth of information. He knew where they could rent a small acreage, just a mile beyond the fast-growing city. His brother-in-law was asking six pounds a month for the house, the barn, and the grassland.

"Ye'll like the place," Bjorn assured them.

From the time they had disembarked from the ship, Grandfather said he was overwhelmed by the bustling city with its crowds of people everywhere, in the shops and walking the streets.

Agnes and his mother rode in the wagon with Bjorn on the way to their new home, and Grandfather rode Prince, who had been anxious to be out after weeks of being cooped up aboard ship.

When they had reached the new place, John bought the wagon and the team of Belgian horses from Bjorn. Though the thirty pounds was more than John had wanted to pay, Bjorn really had not wanted to sell the team, for he would then have to ferry to the mainland to replace them. In the end, however, they both were satisfied, and Bjorn went on his way.

Two weeks after their arrival in America, Agnes was in Annapolis, Maryland, with her uncle, who had come to take her to his home. Grandfather had a difficult time as she left, but she had thought the visit with family would be welcome for a while.

Just after Agnes was gone, a cold snap came in during the night, sprinkling a frost upon the countryside. It steamed the morning dawn, with the golden sunlight picking pearls off the dew-crystalled grass. John saddled Prince and reined him down the road to the town, where he had been riding every few days for their perishable supplies.

He had noticed that men in the city carried their arms in the open, but not wanting to be conspicuous he had sheathed his dirk at his back out of sight. That morning, he tied Prince to the rail outside the Atlantic Tavern, a pub owned by Patrick Stilwell, and a clearinghouse of information. People from all walks of life came there to catch up on the latest news.

For the past two weeks the talk had centered on the deteriorating relations between the British Crown and the Colonies.

As John entered the tavern he was met by the warmth radiating from the potbelly stove in the far corner. He greeted the large jovial man at the bar, then ordered a mug of coffee to start his day. It was after eight, and the place was almost full. John picked up the October 12th copy of the *Penn Gazette*, now a few weeks old, but it contained firsthand news of the ongoing crisis with England.

On the 10th, the paper reported, His Majesty James III had ordered the 47th and part of the Royal Irish Regiments to depart that day for Boston. The 10th and 52nd Regiments were to hold at the ready to sail to the same port at an hour's notice.

Four colonists, within earshot of where John was sitting, were in a heated argument over the very event he was reading about, of the opinion that a war with England was inevitable.

Parliament's continued imposition of taxes and levies on the colonists throughout the years had kindled the flames of revolution. The Sugar Act, the hated Stamp Act of '65, then the Townshend Act in '67, each had incited the Colonies to rebellion against the Crown. Skirmishes had taken place between them and British troops, Grandfather learned. And then in Rhode Island harbor, in June of '72, the revenue cutter *Gaspie* had been boarded and burned in protest of the enforcing of the disputed customs laws.

The situation had worsened since the tax of the Tea Act, for on the 16th of December, 1773, the infamous "Boston Tea Party" had taken place, during which townsmen dressed as Mohawk Indians had tossed chests of taxable tea — three hundred forty-two in all — into Boston Harbor to protest the Crown. They would not pay the tax.

John had heard that the First Continental Congress was to meet the next week, on the 1st of November, in Philadelphia, Pennsylvania, and Patrick Henry was the delegate from Hanover County, Virginia — the same Patrick Henry that Felix had told him to contact. His home, "Scotchtown," was located in the Redlands of upper Hanover County.

Grandfather learned that for the past nine years Henry had been a staunch leader in the struggle for the independence of the Colonies, making numerous impassioned and renowned speeches through the years that the Crown had damned as traitorous.

John and his mother had decided to travel south to Virginia, to

Leesburg, hoping once there they could find a more permanent home. Virginia, they had decided, was where they wanted to establish themselves. It was a state of Christian folk and of respected people like George Washington, Thomas Jefferson, and Felix's Patrick Henry, and it was farming country.

They had heard of the Blue Ridge Mountains west of Leesburg, a still sparsely settled area, with mountains reminiscent of home.

On the night of October 28th, John and his mother had almost finished packing the wagon for their move to Leesburg. The next morning, however, they awoke to a landscape neither had ever seen before. Grandfather said that a slow rain had fallen most of the night, a night that had turned bitterly cold. In the darkness, he had huddled into his warm bed, listening to the wind pelting raindrops like gravel against the windowpane. That was the last he remembered, until he awoke to a deafening silence.

By morning the wind had died to a stillness and the temperature was well below freezing. Hanging in the outdoor atmosphere was a misty shroud of frost that looked like a white world of fantasy. Everything was sheathed in crystal. The trees, clad in heavy coats of glass, were tinkling to the slightest breeze, their branches hanging and brushing a blanketed ground of thin ice. Sunlight was brushing gold throughout a rising frosty mist that slowly dissipated into a brightening sky. By noon the air had warmed enough for the ice to fall off the trees and melt.

John and his mother did not depart that day; they waited until the next, to get an early start. The remainder of the 29th was spent excitedly planning for their future and loading the last of their possessions into the wagon.

Morning had painted a bit of gray in the sky when John helped his mother into the seat of the wagon. He stepped up into the box and released the brake. With a slap of the reins they were on their way, with Prince following along behind.

The sun had climbed to nine o'clock when they reached the river crossing. They paid the crown and three shillings ferry charge. That first day they had managed just fifteen miles, but they continued on with their load, finding rest at villages as they progressed.

The night of November 4th they stayed at an inn near Frederick, Maryland. The morning darkness owned the barn where John had stabled the horses, and only the light from the lantern he held revealed the shadowy interior. He quickly harnessed the pair of Belgians and hooked them up to the wagon.

The sky was turning gray in the east when he and his mother stepped into the wagon, and in a few minutes they turned down the road to Virginia. The air was clear, except for the horizon in the east where sunlight was fighting its way through the cover of haze. It had turned the washboard clouds a beautiful pink, like magenta blossoms among dark purple branches. Slowly the colorful panorama gave way to an amber ribbon that radiated out into a blossoming crown of gold. The sunrise changed the gray sky to blue, at almost the same time that the disappearing clouds along far eastern horizons left behind a misty mauve.

John's mother acknowledged it may have been the most beautiful sunrise she had ever seen. "It must be God's way of leading us home."

"Aye, Moth'r, it certainly is a sight to behold."

It was noon when they ferried across the Potomac River. An afternoon later, as the sun was beginning to sink behind the hazy Blue Ridge Mountains, they reached Leesburg.

The Colony Inn sat on the west side of town, an impressive old structure of timbered frame construction with a large courtyard and stables. John parked the wagon and loosely tied the horses to a rail. He moved lightly up the two steps and opened the door leading into the spacious common room of the inn.

There had been few travelers, and the inn was nearly empty. Three men and a middle-aged couple occupied the room. Two of the men shared a bench, drinking tankards of ale. The other sat alone at a table.

John and his mother walked past a door leading to the kitchen then sat at the empty table next to a well-dressed gentleman, who appeared to be in his late thirties.

The room had a high, open-beamed ceiling with a large stone fireplace blazing warmth along the far wall. The innkeeper stepped out from behind the bar and walked over to their table.

John stood and held out his hand, "I am John Ross, sir, and this is my mother, Elizabeth."

They soon had made arrangements with their host for the stabling of their horses, a room for the night, and supper. They did not know how long they might stay, but it could be a while, they thought, until they could permanently locate.

After a bit of polite conversation, their host returned to his duties, and a pretty young girl came out to take their order.

As she left, the gentleman nearby stood up, addressing John and his mother. "I could not help overhear your names, and that you've been in the Colonies but a short time. Allow me, please, to introduce myself. I am Patrick Henry. I believe we have a friend in common, a Mr. Felix Cameron."

"Aye, sir . . . we do," John responded with amazement at the coincidence of their meeting. "It is a pleasure t' meet ye."

Grandfather said he could only believe that it had been Divine intervention that had brought him into the presence of Patrick Henry that evening. And he could not deny the Divine hand in his life as a whole, for how else could he explain the fortuitous connection with Felix, established so long ago.

The renowned Henry continued, "I'm just now returning to my home in Hanover County. A week ago I was attending our First Continental Congress in Philadelphia.

"You will find, my young friend, that as you become part of our new land, you will learn of our passion for independence from tyranny. It is said that we posture war, but we only seek justice and liberty for our Colonies."

After the meal, John's mother retired to their room. John stayed to talk with Henry, for he knew this might be the opportunity of a lifetime. After John had related some of his life in Scotland, Henry studied him for a moment.

"You know my own uncle, the Reverend Patrick Henry, my namesake, completed his work at Marischal College at Aberdeen University, and my father, John, attended Aberdeen as well. How unusual that we have these many ties of commonality."

"Aye," Grandfather responded, "I have been blessed with a fine education, but nevertheless I've much yet to learn."

Henry nodded his understanding, then grew more sober with his voice.

"I must warn you, John Ross, I have heard your name before — just recently, in fact. The Crown has put a price of five hundred pounds on your head, dead or alive, for the murder of your Chief's son, Paul Ross."

Grandfather was dispirited, though not surprised. "I had fear'd that might happ'n, but I'd figur'd the Chief would not press charges. The fight was fair, and a fight I'd not ask'd for."

Henry admonished Grandfather, "It's not your Chief that filed charges, John; it's the Crown."

"Well, like Felix, now I am also a fugitive on th' run."

"Well, have no fear, John, it's not well known around here, and the colonial authorities will suppress it as they can. Most colonials would have no concern for anyone wanted by the Crown."

Henry looked intently at John. "You have the values I like in a man, and you've had an excellent military education. How would you like to join the seekers of freedom, the colonists, and fight for what you believe?"

"Aye, I would be honored to fight wi' the Colonies, sir, for I like what I've heard, and liberty is surely a worthy cause."

Henry was pleased with his able new recruit. "I'll notify the Loudoun County Militia. Look up a Colonel Gifford; he lives here in Leesburg."

The two new acquaintances talked of many things, and the hour became late before they called it a night. John told Henry about the diamonds he needed to sell, and as Felix had predicted, Henry had an honest man they could deal with in Richmond. John gave him one of the gems to take to the dealer on his forthcoming travel there.

Henry recommended a banker for John and his mother, located close by in Leesburg.

"You'll never need worry about the integrity of Boles," Henry told him. "You will know your money is safe."

Henry then told John he would send the money from the sale of the diamond to the banker Boles, to be deposited in John's name.

Late that night, John lay in bed thinking of all he and Patrick Henry had discussed. Henry was truly a great and honest man, and a patriot probably none might equal. The many happenings of that day ran through his mind, and shortly he went off to sleep.

On the 10th of December a deep snow had covered the ground as they slept. In the morning John was heading for Snicker's Gap, in the western part of Loudoun County. From what he could learn from banker Boles, the property advertised in the local paper was in the foothills of the Blue Ridge Mountains — fifteen hundred acres of grassland, a small house, and abundant spring water — two thousand pounds sterling.

It was seven when he shouldered into his sheepskin coat and stepped outside, the temperature a good twenty degrees below freezing. Grandfather had not seen winters that cold in Scotland. He saddled Prince and tightened the girth, waving to his mother who had come out to see him off.

"Be car'ful, lad, and keep warm. I've pray'd for your saf'ty."

A mile down the road, Grandfather turned to look back, but the inn was far out of sight. Much had happened the past month. He now had an account with the banker and four thousand six hundred pounds sterling to his name, with three thousand two hundred from the sale of the diamond, even after the dealer had his share.

He had gone to see Colonel Gifford after his talk with Patrick Henry, and found that Henry had already stopped by to see him.

"I understand you have a military education, and some line experience as well."

"Aye," Grandfather replied, "though not in a military settin' — just a few small conflicts. But I'm certain I could handle most anythin' on the battl'field. I've been trained at all lev'ls of command up to that of an army. Whatev'r field position I held I would surely know what t' do."

Colonel Gifford was pleased. They wanted John in the militia. "Your knowledge of tactics and command would be invaluable to us.

"What rank do you think you should have?" he asked.

"Wherever ye want, sir. Private, if ye think that's where I should be."

"No, no, not Private. That would be a waste of your knowledge. I'll start you as Sergeant, where you can be in the thick of things and also a leader."

In the days following their conversation, he and the Colonel had attended two militia meetings. The militia met twice each month, on weekends. Each man furnished his arms, and though they were a ragtag and undisciplined sort — mostly farm folk from those parts — they knew how to handle guns.

Grandfather's squad ranged from old men to young boys, yet none seemed to resent the young new face coming in with the position of Sergeant. They knew little about drill, or tactics of warfare, and they seemed eager to absorb his military instruction.

That cold day in December, three miles outside Leesburg, Grandfather rode across an empty, frozen land, a soundless world except for his horse's squeaking footfalls. The strumming music of the winds came to his ears through the leafless trees and frozen tufts of grass, sounds that rose and fell along the surface of blowing snow, dusting across the country slopes, and humming lonely songs into the distance.

Past mid-morning the wind had died down and the far southern sun was busy at breaking through the gray haze of overcast. Slowly the mist of crystals filtered away and disappeared into a welcoming sky.

The sun was now claiming a silent winter ownership upon the land as Grandfather rode by a farmhouse. Two large black dogs leaped from their shelters and barked angrily at his passing. He wondered if they were at the business of protecting their passing-by roadway, or if they resented his right in entering the heartland of intimate grass and lonely hills.

Miles later he turned into the property that was to be sold. It was a fair land of long grass peeking through the snowy foothills against a sudden backdrop of snow-covered peaks, escarpments, and canyons. He was excited as his eyes quickly surveyed the snow-clad countryside. It was reminiscent of Scotland. It was beautiful.

Grandfather knocked at the farmhouse door and a gray-haired woman answered, with her husband close behind. He was a lanky patriarchal gentleman with a graying beard.

John introduced himself, and they invited him into the parlor, a room rarely used, flaunting its pristine condition. It was all John could do to control the joy he felt. He wanted to blurt out his acceptance of their advertised price, but he managed to contain himself and politely accepted their hospitality and talk.

After riding over the land, John was even more in awe of the property — four hundred acres of cropland, eight hundred acres of grass, and the remaining three hundred acres of mountainside. An energetic mountain stream wound its way through the acreage, along with several springs.

An hour later, John was again on horseback, returning to Leesburg, a landowner in the colony of Virginia.

Two weeks later, on New Year's Day, 1775, John and his mother had finished moving into their new home, nestled in the foothills of Virginia's Blue Ridge Mountains.

The first week of January came in with a relentless blizzard. Throughout that winter, whenever the weather would let him, John made improvements to the place. He repaired the barns, fixed fence, and built a large corral using poles of pine he had selectively cut along the mountain slopes.

The militia was now meeting once a week, but John was on call at all times. The men in his squad were becoming good soldiers, and he felt they would do well in combat.

His mother had worked inside the house, buying the things she needed in Alexandria. She loved the mountains at her back door, wishing her husband had lived to share the beauty.

On the 10th of March that year, the temperature hovered near a mild fifty degrees as Grandfather traveled the road to Richmond. It was two and a half days on horseback from home, and he could finally see the town in the distance. He was planning to visit the gem dealer, for he carried two diamonds in his chest pocket.

That mid-afternoon, John had fifty-four hundred pounds in notes from the sale of the two stones, and he was on his way to visit Patrick Henry, who was staying at Richmond's Tidewater Inn. It was coming onto dark when John entered the inn. He could see Henry sitting at a far table.

"Sit," Henry said, after their greeting, surprised to see John in that area.

"I came t' sell a couple stones, and t' buy a mare t' breed with my shire-Connemara stallion."

Henry complimented John on his English horse, describing what they had there in the Colonies — the quarter horse — developed from an English-Spanish cross, the Spanish from an Arabian, the English horses similar to John's own stallion. Henry knew a plantation owner near Williamsburg, some fifty miles to the east, who owned Arabian horses, but he warned John that they were expensive.

Daylight found John on the road to Williamsburg, passing through the rich Virginia farmland. Sunlight was in its afternoon hue when he traveled the roadway to the large plantation house. Its impressive, tall, white columns welcomed those who approached through the lane of large oaks, with their arching limbs spread wide, festooned with wisps of Spanish moss.

Arthur Fields came to the door, a handsome man in his forties, and looked John over then smiled. He obligingly held out his hand.

He was a man John immediately liked, a man with appealing character.

Grandfather explained he was looking to purchase a mare, detailing his breeding plans and why he wanted an Arabian.

Fields had not planned on selling any mares right then, he told John, but perhaps the next year he might sell a few.

John explained it was Patrick Henry who had told him of Fields' stock. "And I plan to raise a type of quarter horse, to breed a line with th' speed of th' Arabian and Connemara and with th' stamina of a Shire."

Fields seemed to appreciate John's explanation, saying, "Come with me; I'll show you what I have."

The plantation's large barn and two single-storied gabled-end sheds were north of the house, all busied with the activity of hired help and slaves — at least Grandfather assumed they were slaves — tending the many stalls of horses. Fields courteously greeted the handlers as he and John walked down the aisles of the shed, and he was greeted with kindness in turn.

The barn had a hearty smell of leather, manure, and native grass, its loft bulging with stacked hay. The men went on through the barn and out the large wooden doors that were swung wide and latched open.

John noticed that the earth of the pole corral was worn from the hooves of many horses. On the far side of the pole fence, in a holding area of some sixty acres of grass, John could see at least fifteen young Arabians romping and racing at play. Fields pointed to the horses.

"Look 'em over; tell me what you like."

They took hold of the top rail and climbed over the fence, walking out in the grass toward the horses. Admiring the animals, Grandfather said, "I'd be interest'd in that black mare next to th' gray." He had obviously picked out the best of the lot, for Mr. Fields acknowledged, "You know your horseflesh all right."

John would have wagered that whichever he would first point out, it would most surely be the one Fields would not want to part with. The one Grandfather really wished to have was another black, a few inches shorter, with a conformation that seemed a better match for Prince.

Fields responded to Grandfather's first selection, as he had thought the man would. He would not be selling that mare, he stated. "She's my pride and joy."

"Well," John murmured, as he slowly swung his arm around and pointed again, "How about the black ov'r yon."

Fields smiled. "She's an excellent five-year-old that I hadn't wanted to sell, but your bein' a friend of Patrick, and him recommendin' me, I'll let you have her for two hundred pounds."

Grandfather politely protested it seemed a little steep. "Ye sure ye could'na come down a bit?"

But Fields would not come down, and after the shock had worn off, Grandfather felt guilty for haggling over the cost of an animal that could be priceless to him. He was about to tell Fields he would take the mare, when Fields declared with a frown, "Well, if it'll help you, I'll take one hundred fifty pounds."

"No!" John replied. "I'll pay th' two hundred."

"No!" Fields said emphatically. "I'll take one hundred fifty."

"No! I'll pay th' two hundred." After John had repeated the "two hundred" again, he began to laugh. "It looks like I'm arguin' with ye to pay th' original price!"

Fields joined in the laughter, the start of a long and close friendship.

John stayed the night at Fields' invitation, and the next morning he stepped into the saddle and started on his way back home. Behind Prince, on a line, trailed three beautiful Arabian mares, a harem for the stallion.

Fields had decided John would need more than one mare to get a herd started, and let him have two more, a white and a chestnut, almost four-year-olds. "I'll take four hundred pounds for the three."

John was pleased. He had the seed for producing a new breed of horse, and the fertile ground to produce that offspring.

On the morning of March 18th, and after three days riding horseback, John could see his farmstead in the distance. Delicate yet majestic was the sunlight as it danced among the purple shadows beneath the trees. It was a day unusually warm for that time of year. John thought that spring was but a few days away; with all her beauty and charm, she would be welcome.

Thirty minutes later, he rode into the yard. He had no sooner dismounted when his mother came out of the house, and he displayed the beautiful trio of mares.

"Lad, ye did well," she told him. "And while I think of it, Colonel Gifford came by to see ye two days past. He wants ye t' come by t' see him."

John decided to ride into Leesburg in the morning. He led the horses into the barn, fed them a bit of corn and hay, then rubbed them down, spending careful and patient time with each. Before he went in to dinner, he turned them loose into the eight hundred acres of pasture.

"Ye're on your own," he shouted as they flew out the barn door and through the opened gate of the corral into the rich, long grass. They raced off into the distance with tails streaming in the wind, Prince racing joyfully along with the three young mares. John noted that for a twelve-year-old stallion, he ran like a youngster.

It was two o'clock when John stopped by Colonel Gifford's house. He had already been to the bank, deposited forty-eight hundred pounds into his account, and had his supper in town, at the inn.

He moved onto Gifford's front step just as Gifford walked out the door.

"Well, John . . . I've been wantin' to see ya. We must increase the pace of our training, for word is it won't be long until war is declared."

Grandfather had heard the same, though had wished that it need not be so. He asked the Colonel where they might want to rendezvous.

"Rendezvous?"

"Aye," John answered. "That's what they call'd our clan meeting and training in Scotland."

The Colonel decided they would meet on Saturdays, at seven in the morning, north of Leesburg on the Graham place. It had the many different terrain and water crossings they might come upon in battle.

John stepped up into the stirrup, then settled down into his squeaking leather saddle.

"Saturday 'tis," he said, and then he rode west and out of sight into the light of afternoon.

Four days later, on March 23rd, the second revolutionary convention assembled at the St. John's Church in Richmond on a dreary, snowy day. Patrick Henry moved to arm the colony of Virginia and delivered a haunting and motivating speech.

"There is no longer any room for hope," Henry declared. *"If we wish to be free — if we mean to preserve inviolate those inestimable privileges for which we have been so long contending — if we mean not basely to abandon the noble struggle in which we have been so long engaged, and which we have pledged ourselves never to abandon until the glorious object of our contest shall be obtained — we must fight!"*

Henry declared the war to be inevitable, and concluded his impassioned call to arms with the words that were being repeated north to south, east to west, across the thirteen colonies — *"I know not what course others may take; but as for me, give me liberty or give me death!"*

Grandfather said that things must have seemed hopeless to Patrick Henry at this time, especially after a resolution had been put forth that was far too weak. Henry then had proposed his own resolution, which left no doubt as to the outcome. *"An appeal to arms,"* he said, *"and to the God of hosts is all that is left us!"*

On April 15th, John awoke at sunrise. The radiant dawn of the Blue Ridge Mountains filled his vision as the night retreated in reluctant shades of purple. He was carrying his handgun, with his dirk sheathed behind his back and out of sight. He was armed at all times those days, as were many of the militia.

By seven o'clock he had finished his morning meal and was outside where the horses waited near the barn. He had made a practice of feeding them a bait of corn in the mornings, and they were always there at daylight.

John had turned the two Belgian draft horses loose in the pasture along with the others. The male was a gelding, but John had wanted Prince to sire a foal for the mare.

After his chores, he walked over to a place west of the house where he often sat to meditate and pray, a glen of grass, among the large, imposing oak trees.

The white, two-storied house was off to his left, as he sat looking south toward the mountains. To his right was a tree-covered dry wash that went as far as the main traveled road a half mile away. He needed to clear out some of the trees, for they offered far too much cover if an enemy were to approach the house.

The night before had been just above freezing, and while the cold bench was stealing warmth from his body, the sun's rays on his back felt warm.

Redbud and dogwood were in full bloom, their branches covered in pink and white. The quiet scene gave him a feeling of well-being, yet though he owned this beautiful place, it still did not stop the melancholy that swept over him when he thought of Scotland. It was a feeling that would hold him for as long as he lived.

John was also feeling the need to see Agnes. He had written twice, but had not heard from her. The thought that something might be wrong would not leave him.

He leaned back on the bench to catch more sun, as he listened to a slight breeze whispering in the budding branches. The sky had turned a brilliant blue, and the sunlight lay warm and golden upon the greening grass and the mist of newborn chartreuse leaves.

He listened to the softness of silence, nature's lonely song, soaking in the day until in an open space of sunlight he spotted a mass of ugly black against a backdrop of misting green and purple shadows. The snake was repulsive to his soul, as he watched the serpent lay, catching the warm sunshine.

He shouted and threw a broken limb at the snake, which was coiling to strike if John should come closer. Then slowly the creature slithered away and disappeared into the underbrush. With the snake out of sight, John settled back on the bench to relax.

He wondered if the snake had been an evil omen, and instinct caused him to instantly roll off the bench as a shot from the ravine echoed loudly across the countryside. The ball had just grazed his right arm as he fell to the ground. He lay still for a moment, hidden behind the bench.

He heard running in the brush of the ravine away from where he lay, then jumped up and grabbed his handgun from his holster. Bent over, he raced north along the top of the long ravine where it made a horseshoe bend. He cut across and dropped down into the dry wash. A middle-aged man hurried into sight.

John shouted at the man, "Hold up!"

The startled assassin slid to a stop to fire his gun, and a blast of flame spurted from its muzzle. His hurried shot missed; but John's did not. It penetrated the heart, and the man lay on the ground dying.

The man tried to speak, sighed a deep breath, then died.

Leaving him lay, John found his horse north in the ravine tied to a dogwood tree.

John's mother called to him, inquiring what the shots were about.

"A man took a shot at me," he replied, as he approached her. "He is in the ravine . . . dead. I don't know who he is, but I'll tie him on his horse, and the horse will likely go home or to where he was last fed. I would like to know who wants me dead."

It was nine that morning when John gave the strange horse a hard slap on the rump and a flap of his arms. The horse ran down the road toward Leesburg for a half mile before it slowed to a walk.

John followed the horse, which stopped at intervals to try the grass along the roadway. By noon, John could see Leesburg in the distance. At the next crossroad, the horse turned and continued on south.

Five miles farther along, the gelding turned into a private roadway leading to a large plantation house. John could see the horse walk up to the barn southeast of the house and stand in front of the barn door.

It was not long before a man walked out of the house, passing around the horse several times as he examined the man hung over the saddle. He then glanced down the roadway, surveying the countryside, when he spotted John some thousand feet away on the main road. John waved a sweeping arm, and the man appeared startled at John's presence. He dropped the reins of the horse from his hands and rushed inside the house.

After ten minutes of waiting, John decided that the man was probably barricaded within his house, his weapons at the ready. He moved about the road in sight of the house, the dead man still on the horse by the barn. Now that the plantation owner knew he had been found out, John was certain that the man would be frightened of his own shadow for a long time to come. Either that or it would make him more angry, depending on how bad the man wanted John dead.

Later, when out of view, John rode away from the plantation. He wondered how long it would be before the man was brave enough to come out of his house.

John rode into Leesburg to talk to Colonel Gifford about the happening, and was told that the plantation belonged to Blaine Fitzgerald, a well-known Tory.

Gifford surmised that Fitzgerald had learned that John was wanted by the Crown, and probably thought that by having John killed, he would do the Crown a service and, in turn, collect the generous reward.

John was not to worry about killing the unknown bushwhacker, the Colonel advised. It most certainly would not be reported, for who could Fitzgerald report it to without implicating himself?

John planned to do nothing more about the attempt on his life unless Fitzgerald took further action to have him murdered. He would once more have to be wary.

On April 20th, 1775, Grandfather John Ross was nineteen. He was glad to be alive, and knew he had surely been blessed by God.

A day earlier, war broke out — it would be heralded as the American Revolution. Some one hundred thirty colonial minutemen had clashed with one hundred eighty British at Lexington. The minutemen were armed and ready, thanks to Paul Revere's determined ride in the dark of night, spreading the word of the approach of the British.

When the third revolutionary convention assembled in Richmond, Patrick Henry was appointed commander-in-chief of all the Virginia forces. The Second Congress had met in May 1775, with Colonel George Washington as a delegate from Virginia.

Boston came under siege by the militiamen, after they had routed the British in April from Lexington and Concord.

On May 6th, 1775, Patrick Henry returned as a delegate to the fifth revolutionary convention, where he had called upon the congress to make a declaration of independence. It was a "cast off the yoke" speech. There he was elected the governor of Virginia, the first governor of an independent state.

On May 10th, 1775, militiamen captured Fort Ticonderoga, and on the 25th the British frigate *Cerberus* dropped anchor in Boston Harbor. Aboard were three Generals appointed by the Crown to conquer the rebellious colonists: General William Howe, General Henry Clinton, and General John Burgoyne.

By June, Grandfather still had not heard from Agnes — nearly eight months without a word — and thus he decided to go to Annapolis. He left on an overcast, dreary day, with clouds rolling low overhead. He had saddled up Prince, waved good-bye to his mother, and rode off at a brisk walk. The horse was spirited, so John let him run, first a canter, then a full, ground-eating gallop into a mist of fine rain.

By noon the next day the sky had cleared to welcoming sunlight as he reached the home of Agnes's uncle in Annapolis. It was a large two-story white house with two tall, round columns guarding the front entrance.

John knocked on the door, and the uncle, a tall, slim man with thinning hair and silver-rimmed glasses answered. John was reluctantly invited into the house, and as he followed Agnes's uncle into the parlor, the man muttered, "Agnes is busy with her daily chores, but I'll see if she has the time to see ye."

John was bewildered at Mr. Miller's attitude, for he had not seemed unfriendly in New York when he had met Agnes at the dock. Shortly, Agnes entered the room. Her eyes lit up when she saw John, but almost as quickly they were full of sadness and almost fear, John thought.

The two talked for a time and then John suggested, "I'm nineteen, and ye've turned seventeen. I thought maybe now would be a good time to get married, Agnes."

"I had thought so, too," she replied, "but when I mentioned it to Uncle Bruce, he told me I could'na marry for at least a year."

"Well," Grandfather replied, "I can wait a year longer if I must." Then he asked, "Did ye get my letters?"

Agnes seemed shocked. "No!. . . Did ye receive mine?"

"No, I did not, Agnes."

It was then that John realized Mr. Miller had no doubt intercepted the letters, wanting to break up their plans for marriage. But after a pause of silence and thought, John changed the subject.

"Colonel Gifford tells me the militia could be called up anytime t' the front lines, Agnes. Hopefully this war will not last long. . . .Will we ever be at peace?"

"I hope so, John; and I hate the thought of ye havin' t' go."

Grandfather asked Agnes if she would like to have a walk in the pleasant, warm day, but she refused.

"I can'na, John. Uncle Bruce would not let me, not without a chaperone."

An astonished look appeared on John's face. "Ye mean ye can't even walk with me alone? That seems out of line for as long as we've known each other."

"Aye . . .," she replied whispering. "He is quite strict, and he'll be listenin' t' what we're sayin' from the next room, so keep your voice down on anythin' ye don't want him t' hear."

John nodded his understanding.

With a forlorn look Agnes continued. "Uncle believ's I can make a bett'r marriage and wants me t' see oth'r men. He's introduc'd me t' some, against my wishes, though I've told him I am not interest'd, and the only one I want t' see is ye. I have not been visitin' wi' anyone of yet, but he keeps insistin' . . . and he's a forceful, stubborn man."

"Aye, Agnes . . . let's both of us walk away from here now and get married."

"I would, John . . . but I can't without Uncle's permission. He would put a stop to it."

Unable to hear what John and Agnes were whispering, Miller suddenly walked back into the room. He sternly blurted, "That'll be enough visiting for today. Agnes, ye hav' housework to do. And a good day to ye, young man."

John quickly interrupted, speaking sternly as well. "I thought Agnes and I might go for a walk."

"No!" the uncle declared. "She has her work to do."

John looked toward Agnes as she was leaving the room. "I'll be back, Agnes."

"Ye needn't both'r," her uncle protested.

Agnes paused, turned for a moment, then disappeared through the doorway. John was sure he had seen tears in the eyes of the woman he loved.

Miller walked John out of the room. But at the front door, John spoke firmly. "I'll be back, Mr. Miller."

As the uncle closed the door, he angrily replied, "I told ye not to both'r; and ye'll not again be welcome here!"

John stood outside, looking at the closed door, and for a moment he thought about breaking it down and removing Agnes from the despot's control. But he quickly reconsidered, for he surely did not want the local authorities after him. He walked away with a desperate ache in his heart.

John mounted up and reined his horse north, pondering what Miller was up to. Why was he so hostile . . . and Agnes so frightened? Perhaps his mother would have some thoughts.

John awoke to sunlight streaming through his open bedroom window. A soft breeze blew aside the white lace curtains and passed across his face and arms where he lay covered with a sheet. A feeling of contentment rose within him, and he anxiously dressed for the day. But then he thought of Agnes, and anger took hold.

John and his mother had talked into the late hours, the night before, and though they could not determine why Agnes's uncle was so fiercely protective, John's mother had suggested patience. "The lassie loves ye, lad, and things will have a way o' workin' out."

John knew that patience could only last so long, but he determined to give it a couple months and then return once again to the Miller house. He would not be turned away the next time, and he would take her out of there, by force if necessary.

On the 14th of June, 1775, the young colonial lawyer John Adams proposed that the congress appoint George Washington commander-in-chief of the Continental Army. Adams was a strong believer in both the law and in what he called the obligations of morality and religion. The vote was unanimous for the unassuming but capable Virginia gentleman.

Though Washington had commanded his own regiment for five years, and though he did not seek the appointment, he wrote to Mrs. Washington that *"the American cause shall be put under my care . . . a kind of destiny, that has thrown me upon this service."*

On the 17th, the American colonists fiercely fought at Boston's Bunker Hill, dismaying the British regulars with their nearly unending stream of musket fire.

The rebel cry, *"Don't fire until you see the whites of their eyes,"* from General Israel Putnam, would echo across the Colonies. And though Bunker Hill ended a stalemate, it gave the colonists a false confidence for a quick and easy war.

General Washington arrived in Cambridge, Massachusetts, just outside of Boston, on the 2nd of July, and on that warm and rainy day he took command of an undisciplined army — an army of officers wanting to curry favor with the men. Washington quickly tightened up the ranks, insisting that his officers enforce tighter discipline, and he soon had his Generals placed according to their talents.

Nathanael Greene, a Rhode Island Private, was pulled from the ranks and promoted to General. Greene had a bad knee, and his limp had cost him command of the Rhode Island Kentish Guards. But not willing to be left behind, he enlisted as a Private. Washington could see that this man's talents could be better used.

The brassy sun of summer had moved into August, filling the day-time sky, when Grandfather again rode his gelding with determination into the streets of Annapolis. Two months had passed since he had seen Agnes.

He dismounted and tied his horse to the hitching rail, then taking his time, he observed the house as he walked the flagstones to the front porch. He was certain he had seen the curtain move in the downstairs window north of the front door.

He knocked and waited for a time, then he knocked again. He waited several minutes and knocked again, louder. Nobody answered. He knocked once more, much louder than before. Finally after several more minutes, Mr. Miller appeared at the door.

"Oh, it's ye!" Miller said, trying to act surprised.

"Aye, it's me. I've come t' see Agnes."

"You cannot!" he exclaimed. "I told ye last time not to both'r comin' back."

"Aye, ye did, but I don't listen t' threats. If ye don't invite me in and let me see Agnes, I'll find her myself!" John had hoped that a stern bluff would get him into the house, for in reality, he was hesitant to do something he would later regret.

Miller glanced at the holstered gun on John's side. "Agnes isn't here. She's visitin' her cousin in Ge — . " He hesitated a moment. ". . . In South Carolina. Ye can look through the hoose yourself if ye don't believe me."

Miller looked madder than a nest of bees, but John thought perhaps the handgun had prevented a fray. He searched the house, but, in truth, Agnes was gone. He thought Miller was about to say Georgia when he had earlier hesitated, though he doubted she was in South Carolina. But where in Georgia might she be?

Shortly he was back on the road to Leesburg. The day had grown hot and sultry as he moved across dusty backroads with brush and thickets encroaching his passing. He loved the sweet aroma of the leafy vegetation that filled the air. Toward evening, clouds began to gather in the west. A strong wind rolled in, pushing along a swirling cloud of dust down the road. A timber of oak and cottonwood waited patiently maybe a mile ahead, and he raced to beat the oncoming rain. He had no sooner found a downed tree next to a clay bank to use for a shelter when large drops came down, turning into a downpour and tattooing the earth and veiling the countryside. Through the maelstrom, he could see but a few hundred yards ahead, the trees appearing as dim ghosts, stranded along the countryside. In an hour, the rain stopped, and after sleeping through the cool night, John greeted the morning's clean and fresh arrival, with the sky a brilliant blue.

Grandfather mounted his gelding, and in a few hours he was crossing the Potomac River.

John stopped to see Colonel Gifford, at Leesburg, on his travels home. Gifford rushed out the front door as he dismounted.

"John! . . . I've just received orders. The militia is to report to the front lines near Boston!"

"I've been expectin' it," John nodded.

His commitment to serve meant that Agnes would have to wait. He would find her when he was able, even if he had to turn the state of Georgia upside down.

But once again for John Ross, duty had called.

By August 10th, Grandfather John Ross and the Virginia militia were two days out of Leesburg. At eight that morning the air was already turning sultry. They were moving north between a sun-baked sky and a lingering dust that passed for a road — a dust that choked the lungs and covered the body gray.

John had been promoted to Captain two days earlier, and he was riding a five-year-old quarter horse strain he had purchased in Leesburg — a beautiful chestnut gelding built for stamina. He had his handgun at his side, and sheathed along the saddle was his father's broadsword.

It was coming on to six o'clock when the line of men stopped for the night in a clearing of oak near York, in Pennsylvania.

On the 28th, the men of Virginia reached the lines near Boston and were assigned to General Nathanael Greene's command.

The colonists controlled Dorchester Heights, just outside of Boston, and the siege of the city became an example for the war. The British had meanwhile moved unchallenged along the Atlantic seacoast with their warships, and the colonists moved at will by land, except for the isolated impediment of British strongholds.

Grandfather spent the next few months versing his troops in his Scottish battle knowledge, training the men in hand-to-hand combat and in the use of the sword and bayonet. At other times, he was out on patrol, keeping tabs on British General Howe's redcoats.

The British army was pinned down by the colonists' Continental guns from the heights that overlooked Boston, and the British seemed content to stay put in the city for the time being. Then, on a golden day in September, Colonel Gifford stopped by John's tent with orders that he report to General Greene at headquarters. It was a day when all was peaceful, except for an occasional rattle of musket fire from the Continental Army's advanced pickets.

John made his way to headquarters, behind the lines perhaps half a mile, in an abandoned house, where he knocked on the door. Instructed to enter, he walked into the room and saluted. General Greene was sitting at a desk covered with maps.

"Sit!" he said, pointing to a chair a few feet away.

"Captain Ross . . . I've been watching you with interest ever since you arrived here. Colonel Gifford conveyed to me your education and experience in Scotland, and I believe you are the man I have been looking for. I have an assignment — a special charge — for someone. I would like for the job to be yours, but before you answer, you must hear me out, and then you may decide.

"I want you to be my eyes away from the army. It will be dangerous.

You will have to travel light and forage off the countryside. You will operate autonomously, unless you have direct orders from Colonel Gifford. At least once a week I will expect a courier, with reports of your operations the week previous — more often if necessary.

"The information would be sent to me immediately and with great dispatch regarding any enemy movements. You would be free to harass and disrupt the enemy when possible and at your discretion. You might want your men to dress as do the local backwoodsmen, to blend into the countryside.

"If you should accept my charge, you would be given one hundred to one hundred fifty soldiers in your company, though I would also ask your opinion on the number of men you might need."

Grandfather did not hesitate a moment. "Aye, I'll accept your offer of command. 'Twould be an honor, sir. And I have looked at th' terrain hereabouts; it's mostly forested. To operate secretly, and efficiently as possible, I suggest, sir, the smaller number of men, perhaps a hundred hand-picked, good men acquainted with th' country. Too many would be cumbersome t' keep together if time is of importance, especially in th' wilderness."

Greene nodded as he took in John's words, mulling them over. "Yes, I will agree! You will have your orders in the morning. Move out when you have picked the men you'll want in your command, and when you are ready. I will see to it that the quartermaster outfits you with your requests."

"Aye, sir," John replied as he saluted and then walked out, closing the door behind him.

John found twenty men from Scotland, three from Tain. The remainder of the new command — the Blue Ridge Boys — would be made up of local valley boys and men from his militia.

In late September, with banners snapping in the wind, John's company of one hundred two enthusiastic men rode out of camp in double column and disappeared into the green wilderness north of Boston.

That same day, Benedict Arnold's army of one thousand men shipped away from Fort Western to fight the British in Canada. And while Arnold was moving against Quebec, Captain John Ross was harassing any garrison of redcoats he could find.

By the end of October 1775, the Blue Ridge Boys had made seven raids on enemy outposts. Grandfather's company had five killed, eight wounded, and nine captured. The enemy had twenty killed, thirty wounded, and fifty captured, along with staples of food, four cannons, one hundred rifles, one thousand rounds of ammunition, and two hundred head of cattle.

In late November, Grandfather heard a rumor that the British were holding a herd of three hundred cattle near Burlington, Massachusetts. General Greene's last message had indicated that the army's food supply was low. Grandfather thought he could help, and determined to round up the cattle, moving them on the hoof, rather than afterward.

On the 3rd of December, at dusk, John's company had moved to within ten miles of Burlington. The pre-winter weather had been fair, but the sky had an ominous look to it along the distant horizon. John had sent two scouts into Burlington to see what they could learn.

The Blue Ridge Boys camped in a glen where birch trees lined a cheerful, crisp, bubbly stream with high banks. The trees had shed their leaves by this time, except for the very stubborn few clinging to the branches. Dark skeleton limbs fringed the gold fading sky, like knitted lace. The midnight moon was full and streaming silver light through the delicate cobwebs of branches, lining a path to John's tent.

A scout rode in to report that the cattle were just south of Burlington about four miles, in a meadow. A large timber following a creek lay east of the herd, and a company of armed British soldiers guarded the cattle.

"It's a lot of firepower," he told John.

The second scout reported the same observations, adding that a colonial sympathizer had confided that twelve prisoners of war had been marched into town by the garrisoned troops two days before, and they were now being held in the local jail.

"Aye," John acknowledged. "Ye've done a good job; but ye better get some sleep, for we'll be movin' out early in th' mornin'."

John woke his second-in-command, Lieutenant James Fulton, a Shenandoah Valley boy and a good officer, with orders to have the men eat and be in the saddle by five.

Grandfather had decided to split his small army, and at four-thirty he held council with his two Lieutenants and six Sergeants. He would take Sergeants Kirkpatrick and Ryan with thirty men. Fulton would take the remaining officers and sixty troops. Lieutenant Fulton would stealthily move his men into the timber east of the cattle before daylight.

Grandfather would confront the jail at the break of day and release the prisoners. Their musket fire, he hoped, would pull most of the British away from the cattle.

"At daylight," he told Fulton, "ye should hear our rifle fire comin' from Burlington. Wait until the redcoats pull out for th' city and are out o' sight before takin' th' cattle. Drive them west by southwest to the Concord River, then turn south t' our lines at Boston. Leave Lieutenant Cary and fifty troops just inside th' timber, which is some five miles west o' Burlington, and have 'em wait for me there. I may need 'em if the Federals are in hot pursuit. If not, we'll catch up wi' ye in short order.

"And, Lieutenant, do not run th' cattle to death; we need 'em surely inside our lines. Ye're a farm boy, and ye know what t' do."

Lieutenant Fulton nodded, but asked, "Captain, could I not put Cary or a Sergeant in charge, for I'd hate to miss the action?"

John knew how Fulton felt. "I know ye do, Lieutenant, and I want ye with me; but th' cattle are too important t' General Greene for me t' trust anyone else."

Fulton acknowledged his task, and agreed to prepare for moving out. The Blue Ridge Boys left together, then split five miles west of Burlington. They would regroup there later, to hold back any pursuing enemy force.

It was six that morning when John reached the outskirts of Burlington. He and his men paused for a time, until John could see a hint of gray on the eastern horizon. He quietly moved his troops into the village. Surprise would be their best weapon.

The scout pointed out the jail in the still dim light, and John placed his troops, with orders to hold or stop anyone approaching the building. He took ten men with him, drawing his handgun and carrying it in his right hand. A broadsword swung along his left hip.

Two guards stood outside the jail, slumped over, groggy with sleep. Dressed in their butternut buckskin, the colonials were almost invisible in the dim gray light. John quickly walked up to the two guards and announced. "Ye're under arrest by th' orders o' General Greene."

The startled guards blinked and peered at each other. One reached for his rifle, then thought better of it, as ten guns were aimed for his heart.

The commotion must have been heard inside, for when John kicked open the door, a shot blasted through the doorway.

"Take 'em now!" John shouted, as he led the men through the opening in a rush. He turned a fast left and at once fell to the floor as a bullet whistled past his head.

John fired his pistol, and a redcoat dropped, blood dripping from his temple. The Blue Ridge Boys were firing, and men were dropping in the large room that must have garrisoned twenty. John had his broadsword in his hand and charged into two men brandishing swords. They were no match for Grandfather's speed and skill and were down and out of the fight with serious wounds.

A British officer quickly shouted, "We surrender!"

John recognized the man as the Captain who commanded the small out-post. He had spotted him earlier, when the Captain had quickly scribbled what appeared to be a note and handed it to a courier who had slipped out the back window.

John knew what that meant — reinforcements would soon be on the way. He would have to hurry and move out, for the British would be quick-ly upon them.

With no way to care for the surrendered troops, he released the colo-nials and locked the redcoats in their own cells. Of the ten men with John rushing the prison, two had been killed and three wounded, in addition to John, who had a slight injury to his left arm.

The released colonial prisoners asked to join up and ride with John's men, and he agreed, telling them, however, "Aye, ye shall go . . . but ye'll have to find your own mounts."

The colonials scurried outside and secured the redcoats' horses that had been stabled out back. With mounts at hand, they soon armed themselves, as well, with the captured British weapons.

Checking through the jail one last time, John peered through a small opening into one of the smaller cells. In a dark corner lay a full sack of something that looked like it might have been ammunition. He unlocked the door to check, and found instead a man, unconscious, his clothes dirty and tattered. He had been severely beaten, but his heartbeat was fairly strong.

John picked up the man and carried him out, ordering the Sergeant to take care of him, "And bring him along! For some reason th' Federals want this man dead." John looked at the poor soul again. "*Wait* a minute!" He was astounded. . . . It was Felix.

"My God! I know that man. Sergeant, check his wounds. He's goin' with us, and I do not want him hurt more than he is, however ye may manage it — stretcher, or in th' saddle, held or cradled by someone."

"We'll take care of him, sir." And then the Sergeant looked up at a sky of falling snow.

"Aye . . .," John acknowledged the Sergeant's concern for the weather. "Let's move out. We'll have us a hot time with th' British before long, so let's get t' our line o' defense. If everthin' goes as planned, th' other troops will be waitin' for us at th' woods, and the cattle hopefully farther west."

The Burlington woods were a tangle of heavy thickets, along with birch, maple, walnut, oak, and pine. When Grandfather arrived at the pre-arranged location, Lieutenant Cary quickly showed him several ways to withdraw from the entanglement of forest if the battle turned against them and if retreat became necessary. Then they returned to the front of the timber facing east. The line of trees along the meadow was in the shape of a crescent moon. The middle, where they stood, was some five hundred yards from a north-south road.

John determined that the enemy would be unaware of his true strength. He and thirty-two soldiers would defend and hold the middle, and to his left and right he placed thirty men on each side, out of sight, in the dense grove of trees. They were not to open fire until the redcoats were completely within the bowl of the crescent and when his men had slowly fallen back into the timber.

The men were building embattlements when the British came into view — perhaps two hundred, that charged into the meadow. They crossed the road into the long grass with banners flapping in the wind, colorful flags speckled white in the falling snow.

John and his men, armed and ready, stood waiting. The air was not a bitter, biting cold, but one of those winter days that felt halfway pleasant, energizing the troops. The scene John looked upon was like the setting of a beautiful painting, except he had the feeling that the landscape he peered at had the blackened brush marks of death.

John rode his chestnut gelding before his troops, encouraging them to stand and wait for the right moment.

"Wait until we can see th' buttons on their coat. Fire low men . . . fire low, and wait for my order t' fire!"

The redcoats were led by a Major on a beautiful gray-white stallion. The Federals were getting closer, and as the first group kneeled to discharge a volley, John shouted "*Fire!*"

The blast was deafening. Men fell to the ground in both lines. The British realigned closer, led gallantly by the Major who was everywhere shouting orders. Both sides fired their second volleys, and more men fell from the ranks.

The colonials slowly retreated, as their lines were about to be overrun. John rode back and forth, shouting at his men to hold. The third volley scratched John in the fleshy part of his left arm. His horse went down, and the chestnut lay dead.

The fighting was close now, hand to hand, bayonet to bayonet. John had pulled his broadsword from the chestnut's saddle. Like a madman he waded into the enemy. So furious was his attack that for a moment the British stalled. John then realized he needed to retreat into the woods for his plan to work, and he began falling back toward the trees.

The Major, seeing the colonial commander fighting on the ground, dismounted, leaving an aid to hold the reins of his stallion. He, too, drew his sword and approached John with the weapon pointed up. They slipped blades and fought in earnest, as John retreated closer and closer to the timber. John did not know who that Major was, but he soon learned he was an excellent swordsman.

When John was within a few feet of the timber, the Major looked around at his position; a startled look came over his face. He shouted at his men to fall back, for he had realized, too late, that they now were vulnerable. Volleys of gunfire hit both his flanks, his men falling like cord wood onto the field.

What followed was pandemonium as the remaining British retreated, in panic, as fast as their legs could carry them. They left behind sixty-nine dead, wounded, and captured, including the dying Major, who John ordered taken to a shelter, where he comforted the man as best he could. The Major's servant never left his master's side.

As John and the Major talked, the Major complimented him on his handling of the broadsword. "I've known but few men who can fight with a broadsword, and they could never have stood up to you. . . .Who are you? You must be of the gentry."

John told the Major his name, where he had grown up in Scotland, and a quick detail of his education and training.

"I knew it was something like that. So your training was not only that of the gentry, but from your father, who it seems was a master." The Major's pain was evident as he continued. "You can go a long way in this world, John Ross."

Though John had duties he needed to attend to, the Major appeared to want to talk, and Grandfather decided he should not disappoint such a brave soldier. He had no fear of the British, for he was sure they would not return — at least not until they could reorganize.

By noon the snow had stopped, and by mid-afternoon the sun had burned away the remaining haze. The air felt warm near the ground, in the bright sunlight. The Major asked to be carried to an area of deep grass nearby, and his servant brushed away the snow, then fixed a pallet. They carried the officer to the bed and gently laid him down. His servant made a pillow from the grass, wrapped with his own coat.

The major spoke weakly. "The smell of the grass reminds me of my childhood, playing in the meadow." He and Grandfather talked of many things the remainder of the day, until the sun moved from out of the sky.

Grandfather had sent most of his men on ahead to catch up with movement of the cattle. He held twenty men with him to accomplish the cleanup. His troops had come out of the brief battle with only ten dead and twenty wounded.

John learned that the Major was Count Richard Sheffield, young and wealthy, with a bright future before him, if not for the fatal wound in his belly.

"No, . . . I'll not recover from this wound," the Major disclosed. "The knighted would say there's nothing better than to give one's life for his country, but I've always noticed that those saying it were not exposed to the dangers of dying." He smiled weakly from his pallet.

He spoke of London and the beautiful women there, and of all the places he had been, and those he had not yet seen.

"I wish," he said, "we could have met under other circumstances."

"And I as well," John replied, turning away, the circumstance beginning to mist over his eyes.

Under his breath, Grandfather swore. "The damned politicians. I could only wish they would face enemy bullets; perhaps they would not be so quick t' fight their wars."

The Major wanted John to have his horse, his sword, and whatever else was in his pack. His Turk-Arabian stallion's name was Prince.

"Aye!" John replied. "I'll treat the horse with all kindness. And now I will have two horses named Prince."

The Major weakly smiled. "I knew you were nobility, John. A King, no less! For only Kings can have two Princes!"

It was dusk when the Major died in a purple hue of fading light, his head in the lap of his servant. John had tried to return the Major's pack and sword to his servant to take home to the Major's family, as he accompanied the body, but the man had refused.

"No, sir, the Major wanted you to have them, and I would not dare to go against his wishes. I have been with him from the day he was born. I knew him as well as any person could. I can tell you, from what I have watched here today, he respected you more than many of his friends.

"You're a good man," Grandfather told him. "If things do not work out for ye, return t' America. I live in Loudoun County, Virginia. Most in th' area know will know my place."

The three inches of snow blanketed the ground with fresh promise. With his escort of twenty men, Grandfather rode snow-lit trails until four that morning, then bivouacked his troops.

On the 14th of December, Grandfather's Blue Ridge Boys drove their cattle into General Greene's garrisoned camp. John turned in his report to the General, who smiled after reading it. "I knew I could count on you, Captain — a job well done."

After Grandfather had reported to Colonel Gifford, he went to check on Felix. The camp doctor had him laid out on a cot, and he was asleep.

The doctor was wiping his glasses, and he carefully put them on before addressing Grandfather. "Well, Captain, he will make it all right. He's suffering from exhaustion, starvation, several broken ribs, and cuts and bruises. He needs rest and food, along with a little gentle care for a change."

The following morning John ducked inside Felix's tent to see if he was awake. Felix was sitting up on his cot, smiling.

"Looks like I owe ye my life again, John."

"Ye owe me nothin', Felix. Nobody could kill ye anyway, ye old codger."

The two friends talked most of the morning away, and John learned that Felix had reached America after a hasty escape from Scotland, for the antiquities dealer he had known and trusted there turned out to be an enemy. The man had schemed to avoid paying the money owed for Felix's coins, then had turned Felix into the authorities, to collect the Crown's ten thousand-pound reward on Felix's head.

Felix had been imprisoned for less than a week before he escaped, with the help of his men on the outside and a well-placed bribe to the jailor. Then he left for America with the reassurance of his colonial connections.

On November 1st, a Dutch ship had sailed into the harbor at Tain, and while supplies were being loaded that night for the Colonies, Felix had slipped aboard, making passage by paying the Captain in cash.

In America, the ship had docked at Marblehead, Massachusetts, to unload supplies, before moving down the coast to Boston. Felix thought it prudent to take his leave of the ship at Marblehead, for Boston would be too dangerous, with the town being occupied by redcoats.

He had spent the first day at Marblehead, and had purchased a reprobate of a horse, the only creature he could find. All the good horseflesh had been rounded up by both armies.

He was in Burlington by noon the next day, where his cousin, a Crown-loving Scotsman, lived. The man had never married, and it had been years since Felix had seen him, forgetting that even back then he had been a snake in the grass.

Felix knew when he walked in the man's house that he should have started running as fast as his legs could carry him away from there. But he decided to stay on a few days, for they were blood. Yet blood did not matter to the cousin, for the next morning a squad of British redcoats appeared at the house and arrested Felix. They searched his room and went through all his belongings, finding nothing.

It was not an hour later that Felix was in the jail, locked in a cell — the very cell at Burlington where John had later found him.

Around noon that first day, however, Felix was interviewed by the commanding Captain. The questioning began cordially, and then the Captain bluntly asked, "Where do you have the treasure hidden?"

"The treasure?" Felix incredulously asked.

"Do not play games with me! The Bonnie Prince Charles's treasure. The Crown has posted rewards for you, and for information leading to the treasure."

Felix acted bewildered. "I don't know what you're talkin' about."

After an hour, the Captain got up to leave the room. "Think about it, Felix. It will do you no good to stall. I'll get the information from you one way or another. After a night without food or water, perhaps you'll have a change of heart."

Alone in his cell, Felix's mind was racing. The man said "treasure." Could there have been more than the antique coins that he knew about? Certainly they were worth a goodly amount, but he had not considered them the kind of "treasure" the Crown seemed to be after. And apparently the antiquities dealer had not told the Crown about the coins he had bought from Felix and had in his possession. He would want them for himself — as well as the reward for turning Felix in.

The questioning started again the next day, but the Captain was getting nowhere, and once more got up and angrily marched out of the cell. Some minutes later, Felix heard a click of the cell door lock. Two burly men entered, and in short order they walked out, leaving Felix in an agonizing heap on the damp, cold floor.

The third day Felix asked the Captain what kind of treasure he was talking about. "If ye tell me, then maybe I can be of help."

The Captain's eyes gleamed with hope, but his face showed his distrust, for it was the first time Felix had cooperated.

"All I know is what I've received from the Crown, that the Prince had chests of old gold coins and precious gems. Rumor has it the gems are diamonds, rubies, emeralds, and pearls — thought to be the finest in existence . . . and truly worth a King's ransom!"

Felix looked at the Captain. "What you've told me hasn't helped; I am only more confused."

The Captain angrily left the cell. Minutes later, the thugs once again entered and gave Felix another furious beating, leaving him unconscious. It was the following morning, by some amazing quirk of fate, that Felix would be found by Grandfather, almost dead in his cell.

That next day at Grandfather's camp, Felix was feeling better and he began to sort over the things the British Captain had told him. He recalled the days after the battle of Culloden, in that long-ago race for his life. He knew that the coins were a part of the Prince's treasure, but obviously only a small portion. At the time, Felix had thought the coins were all that the Prince had with him. He should have known that Charles would not have trusted him with everything.

He went back in his mind to that day at Culloden and remembered something else. Before the Prince had shoved the sacks of coins into his hands, his back had been to Felix. Recalling the scene, Felix now thought that perhaps the Prince had also transferred something into the hands of his trusted servant. The three men, at that time, were being fiercely pursued by the loyalists, as they pushed west up Beauly Glen. But at the crossroad, the Prince's servant had veered off, and took the road north toward Dingwall. . . . *Why?*

At the crest of the hill, Felix had looked back. All the pursuers were behind the Prince and himself, except for a beautiful white stallion and a black horse that raced after the servant, ridden by the clan Chief Ross and his devoted companion, Alan.

The picture was becoming clearer to Felix. He wagered that the diamonds the Chief had given to John were some of the Prince's precious gems referred to by the Captain. Felix was sure that with the swift horses they rode, the Chief and Alan would have captured the servant. And the Chief would have confiscated the gems, as would any Viking warrior. He would never turn them over to the Crown, for they were the booty of war, and rightfully his.

The whole scene took on a new twist for Felix. The precious treasure sought by the greedy fingers of the Crown was actually in the hands of the Clan Chief Ross! Instead, the Crown, like a thirsty bloodhound, was chasing the wrong man — an innocent man. The only connection Felix had was the hiding and the selling of the coins of antiquity, and even then he had been fleeced of the proceeds of that sale by the charlatan dealer.

Colonel Gifford's Virginia Regiment was one of several whose enlistments expired December 31st. On the 24th, General Greene spoke to the regiment with an impassioned plea for them to stay. Almost all the young men in camp were farmers, particularly the Shenandoah Valley boys. The regiment voted to return for another enlistment after their fields had been plowed and planted in the spring. Greene could not be too unhappy with their decision, for after all, the army would need the food grown in the valley.

On Christmas Day, John lay on his cot in his tent. It had been two weeks since his Blue Ridge Boys had returned with the cattle, and he had spent his morning talking with Felix, who was up and around and finally as spry as ever.

In the corner of Grandfather's tent lay the Major's — Count Sheffield's — bag. Grandfather had not opened it before, as he felt like he would be invading the Major's privacy. The bag was made of leather, and hand tooled. Grandfather had never seen another one like it — a long bag with a leather strap for carrying. He laid the bag out on the cot.

Inside was a rifle, inlaid with gold on a mahogany stock. Engraved on an ornate gold plate were the words, "*To my son, Richard Sheffield, for honor.*" Grandfather saw as well a handsome sword, sheathed in gold, and a pair of valuable dueling pistols. In an interior section of the bag were suits of elegant clothes, fit for a count. A small mahogany box contained letters from home, personal and intimate, along with some money, close to a thousand pounds. Another box contained about forty small, red uniformed toy soldiers. Apparently these carried sentimental value, perhaps a childhood gift.

Grandfather thought he simply could not keep the Major's possessions, for they were too personal. But he would, he decided, keep one of the toy soldiers as a memento and ship everything else to the Major's father. He wrote to the Duke, offering some solace at the loss of his son.

Your Grace,

Your son, Count Richard Sheffield, Major in King George's army, was a man I had the privilege to know but a short time. We were on opposing sides in the present conflict in America, and it was my company that had brought about your son's death, and the tragedy you must feel.

Before he passed away, Richard and I talked some six hours, and I have met none more brave, more honest, or more honorable than he. For those few hours, we became warm friends.

Your son had asked me to keep his belongings, but after inspection, I feel I must return them to you. I have kept for myself but one of the toy soldiers in his bag, as a memory of Richard.

Richard wished that I take his own stallion, Prince, to my place here in Virginia's Blue Ridge Mountains. I will honor that request and hopefully use the stallion to sire a line of quality.

If you wish to contact me, Your Grace, your correspondence may be sent to John Ross, Leesburg, Virginia.

Your Obt. Servant
Captain John Ross
Continental Army

On New Year's Day, 1776, and as Benedict Arnold convalesced in Boston's Lower Town from his leg wound at the Battle of Quebec, Grandfather's Blue Ridge Boys were leaving the lines at Dorchester Heights. He had purchased a roan gelding for Felix, and by daylight they were in the saddle and heading for the lonely hills of Virginia.

The new year had welcomed the troops with a banner that flew above the American lines on Prospect Hill, overlooking Boston. With its thirteen stripes and crossbars of the Union Jack, General Washington had told his men that the new flag had given a sense of unity to the Continental Army.

And meanwhile, the battle would continue, for King George III had hired thirty thousand German mercenaries — Hessians — from Duke Karl of Brunswick, to help defeat the colonists.

That January, General Henry Knox's army began moving to Boston the captured cannon from the British at Fort Ticonderoga. He followed old native Indian trails, pushing through snow and ice with a train of forty-two sleds, pulled by hearty oxen. A January thaw thwarted the move for a time, when ice and snow gave way from the heavy weight of the artillery.

But in early March the cannons were placed at the top of Dorchester Heights, bringing an end to the British occupation below. On March 17th, British General Howe abandoned Boston, withdrawing seven thousand troops to New York, where the Hudson River cut off New England from the southern colonies. Howe had realized that Boston was now undefendable with the added firepower of the colonials.

General Washington had won his first battle, with the enemy's retreat from the field.

March 15th, 1776, found Agnes in Georgia. Her uncle had sold his home in Annapolis and had moved to Savannah. She had been crying most of the morning after another furious argument with her uncle, for she loved John, but her uncle would under no conditions accept him as her husband. He had made arrangements for her to marry a wealthy plantation owner, Jerome Stanton, in April.

Agnes was a prisoner in her uncle's home. Twice she had tried to escape, only to be caught and returned to the custody of the tyrant. But she was helpless, as she would not be eighteen until May.

Agnes was not certain, but she thought the arrangement made with Stanton would make her uncle a wealthy man. She had met and talked with Stanton on several occasions, though he was not the first man to whom she had been introduced. Earlier she had met a Simon Armstrong, also a wealthy plantation owner. But Armstrong was a disgusting, vulgar person of forty-five, whose lustful eyes surveyed her shapely body each time he came to visit. She had a deep dislike for him. Stanton, by contrast, was a kindly old man of seventy-five, whose wife of fifty years had recently died. He had seven children, four boys and three girls.

Agnes was glad Armstrong was no longer a suitor; he apparently did not have deep enough pockets.

Stanton owned several large plantations that he had managed himself until recently, when he had turned over the operation to his eldest son. Agnes had met most of Stanton's children, all older than she, though she had taken an instant dislike to Henry, the eldest. He was a dark-eyed, arrogant, pompous, and swarthy man, fifty-four years of age, with a wife and eight children. She could tell by the way he looked at her, he had unwholesome thoughts.

At two that afternoon, Jerome Stanton had come by to visit, and relaxed in a chair across from Agnes on a red velvet sofa. As always, Stanton was the gentleman.

"Are you coming along with preparations for the wedding?" Stanton asked.

"Yes . . . everything is fine," she replied. Not one to live a lie, Agnes continued, "Mr. Stanton . . . I like ye . . . but I don'na love ye."

"I know, Agnes," he replied, pausing with a smile. "I've known from the first time we talked that your heart already had been taken. It was your uncle that came to me with the proposition of marriage. I had not planned to ever marry again, but out of curiosity I agreed to meet you.

"You have impressed me from the beginning, and I would have refused your uncle's proposal, but I was horrified to think that he might even consider having you marry someone as base as that Armstrong. You would be no more than a slave. I could not stand the thought.

"Only then did I decide to make an offer to your uncle for your hand in marriage. You would be much better off with me than with Armstrong, or your uncle, who holds you here against your will.

"When we are married I would appreciate you becoming the lady of the house, managing the household help. You will have your own bedroom, Agnes, for in my heart I am still married to Helen."

Agnes was stunned. Tears filled her eyes.

"Ye've been someone pleasant among my days of sadness, sir . . ."

"It will be all right," Agnes. "Things usually turn for the best. And since it seems we are to be wed, I think you should call me Jerome."

Later, after Stanton had left the house, Agnes mulled over her predicament. She knew she had to make one more attempt to escape back to Virginia, to John.

But as the joyless wedding day came nearer, she was watched closer than ever. Only a week remained for an escape. And if nothing presented itself by then, Agnes knew she would have no choice but to go ahead with the marriage. Things could be worse — much worse — but Agnes was in no mood to think so.

By April of 1776 it had been a little over three months since John and Felix had left the lines near Boston. Back in Virginia, Grandfather had finished his spring plowing and planting.

He had given Felix a diamond, and from the proceeds Felix was able to purchase five hundred acres two miles south of John's property. In no time he had settled into his new home.

Time and circumstance had brought other changes as well. Prince had died; the beloved stallion John had brought from Scotland had been struck by lightning. Grandfather had buried his long-time companion in a high canyon, covering him with dirt and rock, in a place that overlooked the house, the barns, and the grasslands.

But it appeared that Prince had accomplished his mating, as the new Arabian mares were plump with impending motherhood, and they would be dropping their foals sometime in May. John would have liked to have been present when they had birthed, but he was committed to return to the war. The mares would have to manage their birthing alone.

Grandfather decided to leave Major Sheffield's horse to mate with the mares after they had foaled, though as before, the horses would be on their own in the freedom of the grasslands.

John had been melancholy for the past few days. He had gone again to Annapolis, hoping that Miller would tell him of Agnes's whereabouts, but the man was nowhere to be found. The neighbors knew nothing, except that he had sold his house in the fall of '75 and moved.

One neighbor suggested John check with the post master for a forwarding address, but to no avail. John was almost out the door, when the man shouted to him, "Wait! I don't know if this means anything, but he mailed a package about a month before he left town. I remember because he grumbled about the cost. It was mailed to somewhere in Georgia."

John was appreciative. "It might mean somethin'." He had the hunch all along that Agnes might be in Georgia.

Early on the morning of the 20th of April, Grandfather's twentieth birthday, he saddled the bay gelding he had purchased from a neighbor. He was to meet his Blue Ridge Boys and command at Leesburg. The brigade was headed back to the front lines.

The golden sunlight infused the countryside, except for the early morning dark purple shadows that danced with golden dapples beneath the forest of newborn leaves. John rode along the high banks of a long pool of creek water that was reflecting an endless blue sky and catching its moving white clouds in her deep net. Patches of blooming redbud and wild plum dotted the far bank, their branches covered with bountiful white and pink flowers.

Birds were singing and darting in and out of branches, casting falling blossoms into a placid breeze. Like snowflakes, the petals drifted down to float upon the surface of the clear blue water slowly moving downstream. In the distance the trees were misted with the chartreuse of spring's new life.

Except for the war, Grandfather thought, and for not knowing the whereabouts of Agnes, life could not be better.

At the end of May, General Greene again ordered out the Blue Ridge Boys to harass the enemy and confiscate anything of value that could be used by the colonials.

Then in mid-August, John's patriots were called in by Greene, and on the 27th they began what was called the Battle of Long Island. General Washington had mustered ten thousand troops to face General Howe's thirty thousand.

General Clinton of the Tories outflanked the Continental Army's Generals Sullivan and Stirling, and both, along with eight hundred men, were captured. Washington then moved to reinforce his foothold on Brooklyn Heights. Defeat looked imminent as they anxiously awaited Howe's attack; but it never came. Then the rain began to fall, and the British naval forces could not enter the Hudson River against the bitter force of the northeast wind.

Before General Howe could gather his men for attack, darkness had settled over both armies. Under the cover of night, with the help of fishermen, sailors, and tradesmen, Washington's army escaped across the East River. John Ross's Blue Ridge Boys were among the last group to withdraw. Behind a cover of thick fog, all of the colonial army's nine thousand men and equipment were safely across the river.

On September 22nd, Nathan Hale was hanged by the British as a colonial spy. Hale, a true American hero, had remained calm and bore himself with dignity, as he told the hated British, *"I only regret that I have but one life to lose for my country."*

In October, General Howe moved his army once again against the Americans, as Washington moved his forces north to White Plains. The colonials were in a desperate struggle with the redcoats as they retreated across the Croton River, and a few days later the redcoats crossed the Hudson River in a surprise raid on the colonials garrisoned at New York's Fort Lee. John's men barely escaped capture, and again the army left behind a warehouse of armament and supplies.

The cause for the colonials looked to be lost, and desertions had become rampant. In November, when they retreated across New Jersey, General Washington could muster only four thousand troops. In three short months the army had lost five thousand men. Things had never looked more bleak for the Continental Army.

On the last day of November, two thousand enlistments were up and John's band of Blue Ridge Boys was down to twenty men. Fifty of those had returned home with the promise to be back after spring planting. The remaining thirty had given their lives for the principle of freedom.

Years later Grandfather had said it broke his heart to see so many good men die, on both sides of the conflict, men that were selfless enough to make a better world for others. They had asked for nothing they were not prepared to work for, or die for. After the sacrifices he had seen by these men, it made him angry at those who thought that the country owed them something without their own portion of sacrifice.

The colonials' fight for freedom was facing its darkest hour, and by appearance the war was over.

The depleted American Continental Army retreated across the Delaware River into Pennsylvania, where they would be safe and could recover from the disaster of the fall campaign.

December was well upon them, and as was the British custom, General Howe's army went into winter quarters. He was confident of victory in the spring. General Gage had stationed his crack Hessian guards at the army's outpost in Trenton to oppose any threat from the war-battered colonials.

General Washington had become desperate, and desperate men sometimes take chances. But it would take an attitude of boldness to turn the tide of the war. As the British rested in their quarters, Washington was busy making plans. His surprise attack on Trenton the day after Christmas of 1776 would become his first field victory.

On Christmas Day, John and his renewed company of fifty men readied their mounts to forage the countryside for larder. That evening, General Washington's infantry marched toward the ferry at the Delaware River. It had been a bitter cold day, with a snowstorm setting in. Many of the two thousand, four hundred soldiers were without shoes and had tied rags around their feet. From where Grandfather mounted his horse, he could see Washington standing on the snow-covered bank looking across the ice-clogged river with unbending determination on his face.

In retrospect, Grandfather later declared, he realized what a miracle it was that the Continental Army's eighteen field pieces and a number of horses had managed to cross the ice-clogged Delaware. Surely God had intervened that cold and snowy morning, for by three o'clock, long before dawn would break, they were on the far bank.

Washington was fearful he would be too late to surprise the Hessians, but the overconfident Germans had celebrated all night, drinking and playing cards.

In the light of dawn, General Washington attacked. By nine-thirty, the Hessian commander, Colonel Rall, was mortally wounded and had surrendered his sword to the Continental Army.

The surprise at Trenton was evidence of General Washington's abilities at work, and it seemed to turn the war around, giving the troops and colonials a needed lift of morale. Washington had hoped to push on north, but the snowstorm raged. With one thousand prisoners and armament to attend to, they retreated back across the Delaware.

On the 30th of December, Grandfather's company had returned to camp with fifty head of cattle, forty hogs, and a wagon load of canned goods. They had found the colonists more than willing to give what they could spare.

On the last day of '76, Washington again crossed the Delaware, with five thousand two hundred men. From there they regrouped at Trenton to move against Princeton.

British General Cornwallis, with eight thousand regulars, was on the move south to meet Washington.

On January 1st, 1777, the Continental Army marched muddy roads, and by the next day Cornwallis had the colonials pinned down and desperate, with their retreat cut off by the Delaware River. The situation once again looked hopeless for Washington's army.

The night turned bitter and cold. The British were ready to destroy Washington's men . . . but in the morning light, they faced no army. Cornwallis had been the victim of a hoax. Washington's army had slipped away on hard frozen ground, boldly moving around the British flank during the night.

The Continental Army moved on from Trenton and surprised the British garrison at Princeton. The thin British lines broke, and the spirited Americans moved on through Hackensack and Elizabeth.

On January 6th, the Continental Army rested at Morristown. General Howe was forced to fall back before the colonials, and in eleven days Washington had liberated New Jersey.

In late March 1777, Grandfather went home for a month, as did the rest of his men. He was to report back no later than May 1st.

John awoke his first day at home to the aroma of his mother's cooking. There was always a feeling of contentment when he was at home. He wished he might have the luxury to stay, though even a month away from the grinding war would seem like heaven.

After breakfast, he went out to check on the horses that he had been forced to so long abandon, and he looked upon an endearing sight — Prince, the gift of Major Sheffield, was prancing among his harem, then necked around the black colt and two white fillies. The three mares were full of belly, and in a month or so would foal with the stallion's offspring.

At the end of the second day at home, Grandfather rode over to see Felix, now recovered and well rested. It appeared that a farmer's life was just what he had needed. The spring evening had a chill to it, and as they were sitting in front of the fireplace, Felix declared he would like to go back to the front with Grandfather when he was ready to leave.

"Why . . .?" John asked.

"Well, for one, I'm bor'd; but the main reason is that I believe in the revolution. What Patrick Henry has said is proper and correct, and all men should have liberty. It is worth fighting for this America. . . . And if I'm going t' benefit from this country, then the least I could do is t' help fight for her liberty."

John nodded, understanding well how Felix felt, and then asked, "How old ere ye Felix?"

"I'm sixty, John. But of what matter is that?"

"Well, . . .come t' think of it, none at all. And if ye want t' ride with me, I'll make ye a Sergeant."

It was settled. The two would ride out in four weeks, Grandfather determined, then added, "Felix, I've been givin' thought of Prince Charles' treasure, and I still cannot figure why th' Crown would connect ye with more than th' coins?"

"As near as I can see, it must be the diamonds, John."

"The diamonds?"

"Aye . . . they must've found out from th' minist'r of th' kirk back home."

"Ye mean th' tithe?"

"Aye . . ."

"Ye think the crown found out through the kirk?"

"Well . . . they must hav'. I gave th' tithe t' th' reverend, and he was quite pleas'd t' receive it. I'd heard lat'r when he tried to sell the gems for cash, the Crown got wind o' it. I learned from me sources that the authorities confiscat'd the two diamonds, claiming they were part of a treasure that belong'd t' th' Crown. I believe th' minist'r finally reveal'd our names, yours and mine.

"Aye, Felix, it makes sense now. And that's why word had been circulated in this country for my arrest. But we mustn't ever let it be known our suspicions, and who had given me the gems."

"It would've been bett'r not t' hav' giv'n th' church the diamonds," Felix added. But Grandfather did not concur.

"No, Felix, my tithe was due. I did my part, and God knows I did th' right thing. If it went awry after leavin' my hands, then others are responsible. In this case, the Crown will have t' answer t' God. The Royalty would have been better served by leaving th' tithe where it belonged. It's th' very thing that has brought th' Crown t' part of its troubles in America — its levies on th' church — for believe me, there will be no interference in th' church in this country once we've severed the cord."

Grandfather left for the war's front on his twenty-first birthday and reported to General Greene on May 1st. The following day he received his orders to once again harass the enemy, as far west as Ohio, to capture what goods and arms he could, and to forage for food to return to the needy troops at the front.

It was a Monday, beneath a brilliant sky, when John's command of one hundred twenty men left camp for the wilderness. In moments, they had passed into dark woods, riding on the virgin cover of last year's leaves crunching softly beneath the hooves of the columned horses. It was a pleasant day in a lonely land that knew nothing of wars familiar to men. The conflicts of the woods were none but nature's own, yet, in truth, the same struggle man had confronted since time began.

The spring was at its fullness, changing into its summer green, along with the glowing wildflowers blooming on the beginning curve of life. Only the closeness of his men brought John back into the present and the nasty business at hand.

Grandfather John Ross's Blue Ridge Boys had been off and away from General Greene's army for forty-five days, and they had captured armament, cattle, and other foodstuffs — supplies badly needed by the Continentals — all accomplished with fast and hard assaults on the outlying British posts scattered throughout the northeast.

It was the second time John had sent back captured goods. It was dangerous duty, and he had given Felix, along with twenty men under his command, the responsibility of getting the plunder to General Greene's army.

When Felix and the men returned to John and the troops, they brought the news that the Continental Congress, now back in Philadelphia, had now adopted a thirteen-star flag as a standard for the thirteen Colonies of America.

After Felix had returned, Grandfather and his men rode through Pennsylvania, crossed the Ohio River, and swung south as far as Cincinnati, Ohio, before turning north by northeast to Lake Erie near Sandusky. From there they continued northeast, bypassing Cleveland, then through a portion of Pennsylvania into New York and on to Lake Ontario.

On July 10th, John's command of Blue Ridge Boys captured a British outpost at Sackett's Harbor near a settlement that would become Watertown and the Black River, swiftly hitting the surprised enemy. The British had ten dead and twenty wounded. The two hundred redcoats thought they had been assaulted by a regiment and had retreated quickly into the forest, abandoning their supplies.

John's command had five dead and eight wounded. They captured five cannons, four hundred muskets, and enough food to fill five wagons. They found and rounded up two hundred head of cattle, and released fifteen prisoners held by the redcoats, most who were frontiersmen. Some wanted to join up with Grandfather's command, and he eagerly accepted their enlistment, for they would replace most of the men he had lost. His command now mustered one hundred eighteen.

The beautiful mountain country of New York state abounded with forests of maple, birch, oak, pine, and cedar, as well as graceful bending willows along the streams. Deer, black bear, and turkey roamed the forested mountain slopes, along with rabbit, squirrel, raccoon, pheasant, and quail.

John had heard that the Colonies' General Horatio Gates was now garrisoned at Albany, some one hundred sixty miles southeast. He would head there and turn the cattle over to Gates, if he could get through. Then from Albany he planned to turn south, with the remainder of his supplies to rejoin General Greene in Pennsylvania.

The Blue Ridge Boys traveled the beautiful forested land on an ancient trail, with a view of the Adirondack Mountain peaks along the sky. The cattle slowed their pace, but still they made twelve miles that first day. From then on, those well-traveled days would be few and far between.

That first night out, the men camped in a clearing of maple along the Black River. Each day, John and Felix would ride on ahead into the countryside to locate the best campsites for water, grazing, and routes to travel.

On the fifth day out of Watertown, at dawn, when the purple shadows were racing for the trees and canyons, John rode out alone to the east. He had sent Felix south. The trail they were to follow had suddenly become narrow, choked with brush, and almost impossible to traverse. Men, horses, cattle, and equipment were forced to move single file beneath the canopy of forest.

John rode his gelding up a winding path, searching for a better trail. But as he pitched the horse over the trunk of a downed tree and breasted a steep slope, he had an unmistakable sense of foreboding. Something was amiss.

From out of the deep forest he felt eyes upon him. He stopped to rest a moment — or rather that was what he wanted whoever was watching to think. He surveyed the dense wall of trees, but could see nothing, for nothing was visible over fifty feet ahead.

Yet, Grandfather's instinct, passed down through generations, had told him an enemy was afoot. He dismounted from the bay, then busied himself nonchalantly with his pack, slipping on his moccasins. In moments, he was out of sight. Clandestinely he moved through the thick trees, keeping a watchful eye on his horse. He was not worried about the gelding being taken, for the horse would never let a stranger come close, let alone ride him.

Grandfather had found tracks where a lone native — an Iroquois — had obviously lain in wait, a fierce enemy helping the British. But something had scared the warrior away — probably John's disappearance from sight.

John mounted his gelding, traveling southeast about a mile until he lost the Indian's trail. He decided to move up the mountain to better view the country, and at a far higher elevation he followed a mountain stream that ran into a meadow of wildflowers.

Ahead some two hundred yards was a clear view to the southeast. John dismounted, and the bay eagerly waded into the meadow, trailing his reins.

The stream merrily wandered across the colorful meadow to the rim, where it pitched off into space, creating a roar from far depths below. John walked to the rim to take in the striking view, and melancholy raced through him as he thought back to Scotland. He remained for some time admiring the scene and watching for surreptitious movement below.

In an instant, from the corner of his eye, to the south, some fifty Iroquois were slowly moving to position themselves on both sides of the narrow Black River trail. They were readying for an ambush, and it was his men they were laying for. With his Blue Ridge Boys strung out along that trail, they would have no chance.

And then John gratefully realized that it was but a few minutes from dusk, and his men would be in camp. The fierce Iroquois would also go into camp once they determined that the soldiers would not reach the point of ambush until the following day.

They would be waiting in the morning.

John's horse clung to the steep trail down from the heights. Along the way he could see a clearing, from there he looked back at the majestic waterfall. What a sight it was in the fading light. The churning water must have fallen two hundred feet before hitting a plateau pool; from there he had counted six cascades of falls before it reached the bottom plunge of splashing white that settled out into a dark, quiet pool of water.

With a thankful heart, Grandfather moved along in the darkness, aware of the disaster that had come so close to befalling his men. The full moon was high when he rode into camp and met with his officers.

By midnight, John and his troops were nearing the bedded Iroquois. After scouting the camp, John placed his men for a frontal attack, to prevent his troops from getting separated in the dark. Stealthily they moved within three hundred feet of the camp. The ambushers themselves were about to be surprised.

John shouted, *"Fire at will!"* and pandemonium broke loose. Charging and shouting, the colonials overran the Iroquois camp and what few were left alive had frantically scattered into the night. Some twenty had escaped; thirty lay dead. The Blue Ridge Boys had no casualties that night, except for three men slightly wounded.

Five days after the battle, John's troops bivouacked along the Spruce where it ran into the Mohawk River. The river was low and some of the men seined a deep hole of water, coming up with a mixed net full of trout, catfish, perch, and carp. That night the men ate heartily all they could want. Those fish left over were smoked, to eat later.

The next morning at the break of dawn, John left camp alone. He had instructed Lieutenant Fulton and Felix to move the men out an hour later, after the men had eaten.

It was a beautiful day in the woods, riding in the deep shade, like twilight. The only visible light was the brilliant dappling of golden sunlight that had somehow penetrated the green canopy overhead, dancing on the carpet of last year's leaves, and on the green of scattered new foliage. In the serenity of the forest, it was difficult to imagine a brutal war not far apace.

The day was scorching hot when riding through the open meadow, but the deep, thick woods was soothing and cool. By mid-afternoon, John was ten miles ahead of his men, scouting any problems. He knew he would need to be returning to his column.

In the silence of the forest, he once more felt he was being watched. He was certain it was not the Iroquois; but his instincts called for caution. Eyes followed him, he knew, but for some reason he did not feel a danger. Nevertheless, he made no sudden movement, and reined the bay to a stop. As he dismounted, he feigned a look at his horse's hooves. He slowly peered around, eyes searching in all directions. No one was in sight, nor was there movement to catch his eye. The curtains of leaves throughout the forest made it impossible to see very far. But John knew . . . someone was watching.

The gelding's ears were up, and he was expanding his belly. John grabbed the horse's nose to keep him from whinnying. Whoever was out there was not afoot.

John fussed with his horse for a time to keep him quiet, then remounted and boldly spoke aloud. "Ye can come out now. I'm friendly. And ye must be friendly, too, or ye'd have taken a shot at me."

Not over a hundred yards away, a redcoat moved out from behind a clump of birch trees. The soldier rode his black Arabian stallion, neck proudly arched, where John sat loose in his saddle.

"Good afternoon, Major," John greeted the officer.

"And good afternoon to you, too, Captain." the stranger responded. "Might you be Captain John Ross?"

"Aye, that I am; and how would ye know my name?"

"I am afraid your reputation precedes you, Captain, in the wilderness. Perhaps I should have shot such a noble figure. Who knows how the Crown might have rewarded me for your death?"

John stoically watched as a smile spread across the Major's face.

"I'm much obliged ye did not, Major. And whom do I have th' honor t' be talkin' to?"

"Major Patrick Ferguson, at your service. . . . I had intended to shoot ye, but for some reason I could not do it."

John had heard of the Major, as well — the determined redcoat called the "Bulldog" by the colonial woodsmen. John was also aware of the breech-loading rifle, with its renowned firepower, that Major Ferguson was said to have invented. "And I also know why ye could not shoot me, Major," John responded.

"God stopped ye!"

"I see," said the crusty Tory. "Perhaps I'm fighting on the wrong side."

The men visited for about an hour, each knowing the other was the enemy, but intrigued with each other's skill, as friends would be. Had they met on the battlefield, they would have been at the ugly business of trying to kill each other. While they visited, Ferguson let John examine the breech-loading rifle, and John was predictably impressed with the weapon.

"It has been a pleasure," the Englishman said. "And . . . you might want to take your men south of the river if you're heading east."

Grandfather thanked him. The Major's suggestion sounded like the sensible thing to do. And as his command crossed the river, nevertheless they rode wary, though his instinct told him the suggestion was not a trap.

Later Grandfather learned that a large British force had been concentrating in the area that Ferguson had told him to avoid.

It was late July when John's Blue Ridge Boys rode into Albany and reported to General Gates' army. The General wanted John's company to stay with his own command because of their experience. Within four days, General Gates had received permission from General Greene, by courier, to keep them.

Now under Gates' command, John's company swelled to one hundred forty men, and John was assigned to the regiment of General Daniel Morgan — another Virginian — made up of mostly frontiersmen.

From June until September 1777, the Blue Ridge Boys were harassing the enemy and capturing supplies. It was a hot day in July when they had attacked a garrison of redcoats at Saratoga, New York. It turned out to be a disaster. John's company attacked at dawn in the gray of morning before the sun had risen above the forest. The attack should have been a surprise, but the British were ready and waiting.

Grandfather had ridden by several farm homes the day before, and he had surmised that one of the inhabitants must have been a Tory who had gotten word to the enemy. When the Blue Ridge Boys made their assault, the awaiting British volley killed fifteen of the men and wounded nineteen others. After the volley, the redcoats came rushing out of their breastworks with mounted men at the ready, and in the running battle that ensued, Grandfather lost another five men. But some eight miles from Saratoga, he regrouped his men at a strong position and made the British pay for their head-on assault.

The loss of so many men was a saddening experience. Grandfather limped back to camp with only seventy-five of the one hundred four men who had started the attack.

On September 11th, British General Howe's army of sixteen thousand troops crossed Brandywine Creek and defeated General Washington's eleven thousand troops of the retreating Continental Army.

Washington and Greene had galloped their horses to the front, where three thousand colonials held the high ground against six thousand British and German troops. The colonials clung fiercely to their position, but at sunset they faced the inevitable and retreated, with General Greene handling the intense rear-guard action.

Meanwhile, at Bennington, Vermont, to the north, the colonials led by General John Stark killed two hundred of General John Burgoyne's men and captured seven hundred prisoners.

And at about this time, young Jane McCrea, the minister's daughter who was to wed a redcoat in General Burgoyne's army, was murdered by two of Burgoyne's own brutal Indians. Outrage sped through the Colonies at the killing of an innocent and fueled an enlistment of volunteers seeking vengeance on Burgoyne's army. Colonial militia by the hundreds now made haste to join General Horatio Gates' command at Albany.

On September 19th, Burgoyne made his attempt to clear Albany and the area of the northern Hudson River of all colonials. He knew that if he could get past the colonials at Bemis Heights, he would control that area to the north. But a surprise awaited the redcoats.

Colonial frontiersmen, including Grandfather John Ross's company under General Morgan's command, were waiting in the trees, camouflaged in their hunting shirts, just north of Freeman's farm.

At midday John's men opened fire, and the British suffered great losses. The colonials pursued the fleeing British only to be met with a countercharge.

The men fought desperately, and the control of the twenty-acre Freeman farm position changed several times. The arrival of the German von Riedesel, however, saved the British from total defeat, forcing the colonials to withdraw.

But Burgoyne had lost six hundred men killed, wounded, or captured. From the 20th of September to the 7th of October, Burgoyne wrote, the two armies were so close together that not a day went by without a skirmish.

Meanwhile, General Gates' Continental Army was increasing in numbers, and by October he had mustered nine thousand five hundred men. By the 17th, General Burgoyne had surrendered to General Gates; it was his only option.

During the winter of 1777-1778, General Washington camped at Valley Forge, in southeast Pennsylvania, some twenty-two miles from Philadelphia. Compared to the previous winters of the war, this one was somewhat milder. Had it been an exceptionally severe winter, the Continental Army would not have survived. Their food supply was scant and hunger was the army's greatest danger.

Of the nine thousand troops, a fourth of them were reported unfit for duty, being barefoot and without clothing. Smallpox and typhus also were a threat, with five hundred dead bodies found in the camp. At about this time, Nathanael Greene was named the new Quartermaster General, and Grandfather's company was occupied as before with foraging the countryside, seizing cattle and foodstuffs.

It was the first winter that Grandfather had not gone home. Because their larder was so scarce, General Greene had asked him to stay on and once again search for food for the troops.

Grandfather's Blue Ridge Boys unit was down to sixty men. The other seventy had promised to return after spring planting.

As the new year progressed, on February 6th, 1778, France recognized the independence of the Thirteen Colonial States, and the French were now at war with Great Britain. Grandfather and his men spent most of '78 harassing the enemy and capturing supplies.

The fast-moving, lightly packed Continental Army pushed to overtake British Major General Henry Clinton's rear guard, and on June 28th near Monmouth courthouse, the Americans attacked.

When General Washington rode up, however, the Continental front was collapsing and falling back. Washington halted the retreat, riding his beautiful white horse until it was exhausted. He was everywhere along the lines cheering the soldiers on amid their shouts. With General Washington's determined example, the tide of battle changed.

As the conflict raged hand to hand, bayonet to bayonet, the heat of day was intense. Out of the smoke and parching heat also of the battle, Grandfather described the brave women water-bearers, who aided the thirsty, spent men — the women they called "Molly Pitcher."

With sundown, the fighting halted. The exhaustion of both sides necessitated a truce. Men unable to move slept at their position.

But as midnight approached, the British troops withdrew into the cool darkness to continue their march. Neither side had won a clear victory in what became known as the war's longest and most fierce battle, the last large engagement between Crown and Colony in the north.

A year later, in June of 1779, the armies were still fighting. South of Albany and ten miles north of where General Morgan's command had bivouacked along the Hudson River, one of Grandfather's scouts returned to camp in a rush with the news of a group of redcoats in the wilderness. The scout had been seen by a British outpost, however. The Tory had fired at him, though he escaped and was not followed.

At around ten that morning, and within the hour, all of Grandfather's horsemen were on the move. It was a pleasant warm day with the sunlight painting golden dapples on the dark ground of the emerald forest. The only sounds were the steady drum of horses hooves, the jingle of bridles, and an occasional squeak of leather.

The Blue Ridge Boys rode into a clearing, and in the open grass ahead appeared a column of redcoats. The surprised Tories spurred their mounts north. Johns's troops followed in pursuit, and then he halted them in a shallow gully. He had seen a reflection of sunlight from something within the woods. Suspecting it was a rifle barrel, John realized they were rushing into an ambush.

In the depression and unseen from the trees, John sent half his men to outflank the enemy. The rest moved down the road to where they could open fire. At the same time, the British flanks were hit by the Blue Ridge Boys, and the brief fight was over — a potential defeat turned into a blessing of victory.

Throughout the remainder of '79, Grandfather's command was busy harassing the enemy.

At about this time, the colonists' war was taking another turn. Benjamin Franklin, a patriot and statesman, had handled many different posts for the colonists, including Minister to France and Secretary of the Navy. Franklin had outfitted John Paul Jones with three small ships and a brigantine Jones had named the *Bonhomme Richard* — "Good Man Richard" — in honor of Franklin and his *Poor Richard's Almanak*. Jones had served in the exceedingly small colonial navy since 1772. He was from Scotland and considered by some to be nothing more than a wanton corsair — a pirate. By September of 1779, his infamous raids along the coastal cities of Great Britain had instigated a panic along the shores.

On September 23rd, Jones had spotted the Baltic Merchant Fleet of England being convoyed by the frigate *Serapis* and a sloop of war. The British frigate could easily outsail the brigantine, so Jones attacked the enemy with a blast of firepower from his cannon.

It was after sundown when Jones ordered the firing of a broadside at *Serapis*. Men fell by the scores. When the British Captain, thinking Jones might surrender, called out asking if his ship had struck, Jones' gamely replied, *"I have not yet begun to fight!"*

Jones realized that his only chance was to grapple the British ship and board her, and thus he ran his brigantine into the stern of the frigate and fixed his ship to the *Serapis* with the fearsome grappling irons.

By the light of the moon, the British frigate's main mast could be seen to sway. The Captain struck his colors, conceding to Jones his sword and ship.

The new year of 1780 in the American Colonies was ushered in with snow and winds leaving four-foot drifts in its wake. By March, eight inches still lay on the ground.

General Horatio Gates now commanded all the patriot forces to the south, and Grandfather's company of Blue Ridge Boys had moved to South Carolina. His command worked independently most of the year, continuing to harass the enemy and capturing supplies.

On May 12th, the British had finally taken Charleston, South Carolina.

Later, on September 23rd, three Continental militiamen stopped a civilian near Tarrytown, New York. They found on the man papers of the military inventory of all of West Point, and a pass signed by West Point's commander, Benedict Arnold. The courier was actually Major John André, in charge of espionage for British General Henry Clinton.

The colonials knew that the loss of West Point would be disastrous. British cannons placed there would cut America in two and control commerce on the Hudson River.

When General Arnold learned of André's capture, he escaped the colonial authorities and joined the British. Grandfather had said all the men questioned why a hero like Arnold, who had fought so gallantly for America, would suddenly turn traitor. Even those who thought they knew him asked that question, for they were baffled. The most logical answer would be money, as many of the officers and men had not been paid for their services, and the only spendable money was the hard currency of other nations. American currency was worthless. Perhaps, Grandfather speculated, that was Arnold's motivation.

Meanwhile, British Major Patrick Ferguson, the officer that three years earlier had befriended Grandfather and his command near the Blue Ridge Mountains, began meeting stiff resistance from the colonials. Ferguson and his redcoats had stopped at Kings Mountain in South Carolina. His position was the dominant high point of the area. He knew well that one never wanted to position himself below an enemy's firepower, but he mistakenly thought there was no way he could be forced out of his defenses.

The local backwoodsmen were joined by other volunteers from Tennessee who had ridden their horses all night to get to the battle. At three in the morning, Ferguson noticed the added firepower, and that below him they were surrounding his position. His brigade made several charges with rifle and bayonet to escape his mountaintop fortress, but to no avail.

Major Ferguson's men were being picked off by the rebel sharpshooters. They were so well camouflaged in the trees that his situation became untenable.

Ferguson mounted his horse and led a charge to break through the surrounding colonists. But he was fatally hit by the colonial sharpshooters, and the battle of Kings Mountain was over.

In December of 1780, General Nathanael Greene relieved General Gates of the southern command, with its over fourteen hundred troops. But their appearance, Greene reported, was "wretched beyond description."

Greene went to work in his steady way. He picked Virginian Henry Lee to be one of his commanders. And he had heard so much praise from his own men about the Virginia frontiersman General Daniel Morgan, that he picked him as another commander, along with Colonel William Washington as his third officer.

Confronted by Cornwallis's thirty-two hundred regulars, Greene separated his three armies. He had learned well the advantages of traveling light and moving swiftly. The men would eat off the land and harass the British.

The first week of 1781 still found Grandfather's company of Highlanders and mountain boys in South Carolina with General Morgan's command. It was now the fourth winter that he had been away from home. Grandfather told me it had particularly pleased him that he had been moved permanently to Morgan's regiment, for he had grown to like the tough, hard-as-nails soldier and man of the country. He was the kind of man you would want on your side in a desperate fight. Even General Greene had said that Morgan was an officer he could count on.

That first week of January, General Morgan was on the move. He had been ordered west by General Greene to fight the enemy, to give protection, and brighten the spirits of the people.

Grandfather thus had his men up at daylight, and after a light repast they were in their saddles by eight o'clock. The regiment struck the British post Ninety-Six in western South Carolina, killing one hundred fifty loyalists and taking forty prisoners.

After the battle they lay back to rest, waiting for Lord Cornwallis to retaliate. They did not wait long.

Cornwallis divided his forces into three groups. One was to hold Camden, the second was to be his command, and the third was to find, push, and punish General Morgan's command.

Banastre "Bloody" Tarleton's command closed fast upon the colonists and General Morgan retreated, holding the Tories at bay in a moving rearguard fight. Tarleton's green-clad British dragoons were experienced fighters, and they were pushing Morgan hard to the west.

January 17th was a cold and bitter morning. Morgan had retreated the night before to a rolling plain famous for cattle roundups, called the Cowpens. Morgan decided he had been shoved far enough, and that was where he would make his fight. With no way to retreat, the Broad River at his back and open woods to his front, it appeared to be a poorly chosen battleground favoring the British.

Grandfather had said he was sure that Tarleton's mouth must have watered when he saw where Morgan had decided to fight. The wily Morgan deployed his men perfectly, for he understood them and what they could do.

As the British closed in, Morgan ordered two skirmish lines of militia to fire and fall back, then to withdraw to the rear, slipping past the main line of regulars. Tarleton charged full force ahead, confident of victory. The third line of tough regulars held and in the confusion of hand-to-hand combat, Morgan sent Grandfather and his Blue Ridge Boys to the right to outflank the dragoons.

As the colonials were pushed farther back, the British thought they had won the battle. Then at General Morgan's command, the colonials counterattacked. At the same time, William Washington's cavalry smashed the British right, as John's mounted militia hit the left. The flanks of Tarleton's army disintegrated, and the British Army was in panic, fleeing in confusion.

Tarleton tried in vain to rally his troops, then was forced to flee himself with the colonials in hot pursuit.

The Battle of the Cowpens was over and General Morgan had scored a brilliant victory. Nine hundred British were killed, wounded, or captured — ninety percent of Tarleton's forces were destroyed. Twelve colonials had been killed.

After the battle, a verse emerged, sung by the Continental troops, to the tune of "Yankee Doodle":

> *Cornwallis led a country dance,*
> *The like was never seen, sir*
> *Much retrograde and much advance,*
> *And all with General Greene, sir.*

After the defeat of Cornwallis at the Cowpens, General Greene united his forces and with dispatch moved north to the Dan River.

Yet Cornwallis was in hot pursuit, confident he would trap Greene at the river, knowing there were few boats in the area. But General Greene was too smart for that, Grandfather recalled; the General had prepared for the movement in advance.

On February 14th, Greene's army slipped across the river leaving Cornwallis stranded behind.

In April of 1781, Grandfather's company was now kept busy raiding enemy positions throughout South Carolina. On the 20th, Grandfather celebrated his twenty-fifth birthday camped along the Ogeechee River, fifty miles northwest of Savannah. He and Captain Dooley of the Georgia patriots had become good friends. It was a fair moonlit night when they sat by a campfire talking about the things men do when they have been away from home a long time.

Grandfather had heard that Dooley was from Savannah, and he peered over at him. "Are ye acquainted with th' people around Savannah?"

The Captain acknowledged that he was.

"Would ye know of an Agnes Miller, niece of a Bruce Miller?" Grandfather asked.

"Well . . . I know of her, not personally, but I had seen her a time or two. She was a beautiful woman, though there was something strange about her situation when she first moved to town. Her uncle seemed to never let her out of his sight."

John then told Dooley about his relationship with Agnes. Dooley looked shocked.

"John, I don't wish to have to tell you this . . . but Agnes is married. If I remember well, it was an arranged wedding that took place around the first of April in '76."

John sat silent and crestfallen.

"I'm sorry to be the bearer of that kind of news," Dooley sympathized, and after a pause continued. "She married Jerome Stanton, a very wealthy plantation owner. If I remember right he was a widower in his seventies, and from what I've heard he's a decent man."

"Do you think she's happy?" John asked.

"Well, I couldn't tell you about that, for it's been several years since I have seen her."

John lay back on his pallet, thinking of Agnes. Five years, he thought . . . married for five years. It was hard to believe, but there had been no time for him to try and find her. The war had kept him captive as well.

Grandfather usually listened to the night sounds as he was falling off to sleep, but that night he listened to his pounding heart.

In late October, the French relieved the Continental Army with three thousand troops put ashore at Jamestown, to keep Cornwallis bottled up. Later, on a cold and blustery day in November, John and Felix took winter leave, and mounted up for Virginia. Little did they know that when they left the war this time, it would finally be for good.

In December of 1781, General Washington prepared his offensive for 1782, but it never developed. Instead, a British mercenary began negotiating peace in April.

On the 10th of April, 1782, Grandfather was at home. His militia had been notified it would not return to active duty unless hostilities were to flare up again. The war appeared to be winding down — at least he hoped so.

It was a Sunday, and daylight was tugging at his eyes to wake him. He could hear his mother in the kitchen, and it would be the last time she would be fixing him breakfast at home. She was getting married to Felix at the nearby Presbyterian church that day at two o'clock. John felt melancholy, but at the same time shared a happiness for her. She would be moving into Felix's comfortable one-story home he had built and furnished over the past six years.

It had been a shock when Felix had asked John's permission to marry his mother. But after he had thought about it awhile, he realized that it should not have been a surprise, for Felix was his father's age, resourceful, and intelligent.

After breakfast John went out to look at the countryside. In the foothills, redbuds were cloaked with beautiful pink blooms patched among bold emerald pine. Scanning to the east, he could see the trees along the waterways clad in a new growth, like a chartreuse mist, along their dark and shapely branches.

He thought back over the years. He would soon be twenty-six, and he felt like he had lived a hundred years. Scotland, the land he had loved so dearly, was in another life and in another world far away. Hopefully his second life, fighting the war in America, was finished, for he felt he was at the threshold of his third, a life that he prayed would offer peacefulness for the rest of his days.

But could he be happy without Agnes?

Grandfather's rambling thoughts were interrupted by the sight of his herd of horses on a nearby slope, heads down eating grass, a vision of contentment.

Prince, the gift from the British Major, was tossing his head in anticipation along the corral fence, waiting for John to take his morning ride. John had not planned a ride that morning, but then decided he would have plenty of time before they would be due at the church.

Prince was frisky, and John decided to just let him run. The stallion took off for the mountains, heading southeast, for the steepest escarpment of the property, along the range. John was bewildered — it seemed as if Prince had a destination in mind — and he gave the stallion his head.

It appeared as if Prince was going to walk right up to the escarpment, when he turned in behind an upthrust rock. They were on a trail about four feet wide, so narrow John could reach out and touch the rock face on each side. He must have ridden a half mile through the cleft of rock, always upgrade, when suddenly the narrow opened up into a valley of deep, plush native grass, some three hundred acres of high hidden meadow. Far and away below, to the northeast, he could see his house and barns in the distance.

From beneath his hat brim he peered at the sun and determined it was near ten o'clock. He would have to hustle back to get ready for his mother's wedding. From the looks of the horse tracks going back toward the house, he could tell that Prince must have been bringing his offspring to the meadow for some time.

The mountainside meadow was southwest of what Grandfather considered his own property line. He determined to find out who owned it.

The following week Grandfather explored the new meadow. He had found only one other place to ride out of the canyon, and it was a narrow way covered with pine. That Thursday he went to the land office at Leesburg and discovered no one owned the mountainside, and it was considered unsuitable wasteland. He could buy all he wanted for fifty cents to the acre.

When he left Leesburg, he owned four thousand additional acres. He wondered how many more hidden meadows he would find.

Grandfather called Prince's hidden meadow the upper pasture. It took but a small amount of selected pine to pole fence the two narrow ways where livestock might find a path out. When he had finished his fencing, a gate hung open across the narrow trail, to separate the two pastures.

By December of that year, on the 30th, the British and the Americans signed a separate preliminary peace treaty in Paris. Great Britain recognized the independence of the United States of America — but the revolution was not officially over.

The final treaty was formally signed in Paris some nine months later, on September 3rd, 1783. Grandfather said that on December 4th, General Washington, at Frances Tavern in New York, embraced each of his officers with tearful eyes. His words could not be forgotten: *"With a heart full of love and gratitude, I now take leave of you. . . ."* The General then rode to a waiting barge to cross the Hudson River to the New Jersey shore onward to his home, Mount Vernon, on the banks of the Potomac, just outside of what would become the new nation's capital.

General Washington was fifty-one, and he had not been home for eight long years. The prime years of his life had been spent in the service of his country.

George Washington was truly America's greatest selfless patriot, Grandfather had declared — he would take no pay, and had accepted only his out-of-pocket expenses.

In September of 1784, Grandfather John Ross was returning from Richmond, where he had been visiting friends in Tidewater country. He had spent a pleasant day with Patrick Henry, now the Governor of Virginia, who lived at "Leatherwood," in Henry County. He had spent another two days with Arthur Fields, the breeder from whom Grandfather had purchased his mares long ago. And he had taken Fields a beautiful, white, five-year-old stallion, whose dam was one of the Arabian mares purchased from Fields. The sire had been Prince, the Arabian-Turk stallion. Grandfather did not know if Fields would accept the stallion, as he was not purebred Arabian; but one only had to look at the animal to know he was something special.

To Grandfather's satisfaction, Fields was pleased with the gift, and gave John another Arabian mare when he left.

While in Richmond, Grandfather also sold two more diamonds. He had been in the saddle for two tiring days. He almost rode by the Courtyard Inn, just outside of Alexandria, which sat back from the road in a grove of oaks, but twilight was moving on to purple, and the soothing golden light from the lamp posts was too inviting to pass by. The inn, at the north, was a large structure of stone and heavy, darkly stained beams, with a spacious, landscaped courtyard. To the east were the stables.

John rubbed down his white gelding and new mare, gave them water, and pitched them some hay. He grabbed his saddlebags and walked wearily up the flagstone path to the door of the inn.

He paused at the entry and peered around. The patrons looked up for a scant moment, then went back to their business. Yet, something did not feel right to Grandfather, and he was wary. He dropped his arm to his waist and felt his money belt beneath his loose shirt. At least his forty-eight hundred British crowns were safe. He did not have his handgun, but he was comforted by the feel of his dirk resting against his back.

Amidst some ten people in the room was an empty table in the back corner, not far from a doorway. Grandfather took it and kept his back to the wall. He wondered what the problem was with him, why he was so nervous. He thought of Blaine Fitzgerald, the loyalist who had long ago sent the assassin to kill him. But Fitzgerald had sold out and, after the British had surrendered, had gone back to England.

The proprietor of the inn was building a fire to counter the cool autumn air, and a maid was striking lamps on the tables and along the darkening walls. The red glow reflected on the high-beamed ceiling, and the golden light of the whale-oil lamps penetrated into the large shadowy dining room, accentuating its mystery and charm.

When the maid came over, John ordered a mug of ale and dinner, then made arrangements to stay the night. Her smile and questioning seemed familiar, John thought.

As he took a sip and sat back to relax, he thought that perhaps he had been too particular about what he wanted in a woman. Now, at twenty-eight, he should already have been married. He had called on several pleasant women, but just could not develop an interest. Perhaps the lovely fair Agnes had spoiled him.

As John peered across the room, the maid again was looking his way. From out of the dim lamplight, he could see she was quite attractive, her black velvet hair hanging in ringlets that curved along her pretty sun-darkened face and red lips.

From between long lashes her smoldering eyes peered inquiringly at him. He was stunned for a moment. As she faintly smiled, he quickly turned his eyes away, then looked back for but an instant, to make certain he was the one she was looking at. The maid smiled again, with a slight nod of her head.

John looked around the room. Other men were there, and she wasn't paying them the slightest bit of attention. What did she want?

He felt for his money belt again and wondered if she somehow knew about it, then concluded that he doubted it.

When she brought his food, he was startled as she put it on his table.

"It's been a long time, John."

He looked at her questioningly, and began turning the memory pages in his mind. They were blank.

The lady continued, "It's hard to believe twelve years have passed."

The twelve years took him back instantly to the inn at the edge of Achnasheen, in Scotland. Marie Mackenzie . . . he could see the resemblance now! Her features had matured, but the years had been good, and she had grown even more beautiful.

"Ye don't know me, do ye, John?" she purred teasingly, placing her hand on his. John quickly recovered himself.

"Aye, I know ye, Marie, though to be honest I did not until ye mentioned that it'd been twelve years. In some ways ye've changed, but ye're even much more beautiful than ye were back then."

Marie laughed, "Ye've such a way with words, John; I'd hoped ye hadn't forgotten our night together in the moonlit brae of heather." She looked into his eyes. How is it ye've slipped the bonds of marriage all this time?"

John blushed in the dimly lit room. Then his brain struck a wary chord. How did she know he was not married?

Suddenly he became skittish, and felt like he was falling into a trap that had no bottom. What was the matter with him anyway? This beautiful, sensual young woman was apparently interested in him, yet his practical senses were telling him to run. But his feet would not move; they were hooked up to the renewed desire racing through his mind.

Marie had arrived in America the year before, in the fall of 1783. She was staying with her aunt, her father's sister in Alexandria.

For a year she had been trying to locate John, and only the last week had she learned, through discreet inquiry, that he lived near Leesburg.

Marie had been married for a time, all of five years. She had hated it, she told John. The man was a good person, but he had demanded loyalty, and loyalty, Marie smiled at John, was not one of her strong suits. When she had salted away enough money, she walked away from the marriage and left for America.

Marie had learned that John left Scotland after killing Paul Ross, the Chief's son, in the duel; and she heard the rumors, from her source, of a treasure that John had acquired. She had no doubts she would find John somehow. She had remembered him as handsome for such a young lad, and well educated; and now, even better, he was wealthy.

After polite conversation, mostly about their days in Scotland, John suddenly stood up. "Marie, it's been nice visiting wi' ye, but I'll go to my room now; it's been a long day."

Marie grabbed his hand. "Not yet, John . . . I've so much I want to tell ye!"

John pulled away. "No, . . . not tonight. Good night, Marie."

John could tell she was upset at his leaving, but he moved over to the host and got the key to his room. As he walked to the stairs, he glanced back at Marie. She still stood by the table, but by then she had regained her composure. She lifted her hand into a wave.

Grandfather's room was small, but comfortable. The lamp sat dark on a small table, and he removed the chimney, struck a flint that flared the tender with a golden flame, then lit the wick and replaced the chimney. The bed was immaculately made and covered with a fine handsewn quilt. A window with lace curtains was along the east wall. Alongside a fireplace was a rocking chair, and against another wall stood a dresser with a mirror, reflecting a large white porcelain bowl and water pitcher.

John looked into the shadowy dim and dark mirror. He thought he looked pretty good for all that he had been through, but then the darkness of his reflection may have concealed his true appearance.

"I'm a fool," he told the reflection. "She all but offered herself t' me and I refused!"

"*. . . No . . . ye did right, John Ross, for it is strange she knew ye were not married,*" the mirror seemed to reply.

Nevertheless, Grandfather said, he decided to think about it. Perhaps he would call on Marie. After all, he had no one else in his life, and truth be told, he was lonely.

He looked at the time. It was early. He would wait for a while, then check the horses, and have some tea before he turned in. He started to hide his money belt under the bed, then thought, *No, that'd be the first place anyone would search.* He went over to the dresser and pulled out the three drawers. There was no way to hide anything in the dresser, but there was something strange about the drawers that he could not instantly discern.

Then he realized that the depth of one was different from the other two. One had a false bottom.

John finally found the hidden spring that released the pins at the back of the drawer, then he slipped in the money, closed it, and replaced the drawer. Leaving it partly open, he neatly placed inside some shirts, underclothes, and socks. He doubted even the host knew of the secret spot, or he might have kept the piece of furniture for himself!

It was nine when John went downstairs. Marie was not in the dining room. He went out to the stable, watered his horses, gave them each a bit of corn, and went back to the inn. Only two other people were in the room when he returned.

He ordered a mug of tea from the host. Marie was nowhere to be seen — probably in the kitchen, from where he heard the rattle of dishes and pans.

It felt good to sit in the late evening quiet, as he sipped on his tea. He had thought of having another ale, but he was a light drinker.

After perhaps a half hour of mellow relaxation, John retired to his room. As he opened the door and walked inside, he could smell perfume. He peered around and saw Marie sitting in the rocking chair.

Startled, John asked, "How did ye get in here?" as he turned up the lamp on the table.

"'Twas easy. I just asked the host yer room."

"I locked th' door," John flatly stated.

Marie got up and slowly walked over to him. "No, John, ye're mistaken. The door was unlocked. Do not be mad; I had to see ye again before ye left in the mornin'."

John was positive he had locked the door, but her presence had him completely confused. And then she was in his arms, and he surrendered to her eager passions.

The sun was rising in the east when he rode away from the inn. He was not sure what time Marie had left his room, but it must have been close to midnight.

Someone had searched his room. The things in his saddlebag and dresser were not replaced as he had laid them. It was probably Marie . . . but the money had not been disturbed.

John told Marie he would see her again, but made no commitment. He still was wary of her, and it was impossible for him to think clearly when they were together. He had been helpless and stricken with overwhelming desire the night before, and he rode the morning away with his conscience weighing heavily on him.

In the future he would need to be more cautious, he determined. What if Marie were to become with child? They would have to marry. He would have no choice. And he was not certain that was what he wanted.

John waited two weeks before he went to Alexandria. Marie's aunt answered the door and greeted him warmly.

"So ye're John Ross. Marie can not seem to get ye off her mind. I'm surprised ye're such a young man to be so wealthy."

"I'd hardly call myself wealthy, Ma'm, but I do hav' my own place in the foothills of the Blue Ridge Mountains."

"Marie said ye'd say that, I suppose to play it safe," the aunt whispered softly, and winked.

John took them both to a supper at the inn, and on the way home Marie whispered in his ear that the next time they would have to go somewhere to be alone, then squeezed his hand.

On a warm day that November, Grandfather rode Prince to the upper pasture where the water came down from out of the mountain through a slope of rhododendron that filled with beautiful purple blossoms in the summertime.

A waterfall dropped off into an emerald pool, surrounded by a meadow of grass where he would go and lie back, dreaming of the past. On such an afternoon, when the low sunlight was casting familiar shadows, he had decided it was time to head for home.

He whistled, and Prince trotted over to the basin. The stallion was thirsty, dropping his muzzle into the cold water, and champing at the bit when John mounted up and started for the lower pasture.

On the ride home he thought of Marie. It had been a month since he had seen her, and in that time he had decided she was not what he wanted for a wife. It looked to him like she could be more misery than a patch of poison oak.

He could not get Agnes off his mind. She still was the woman he wanted to marry. He would never have to worry about her with another man.

And he knew that Marie had heard about Prince Charles's treasure and was convinced it was in his possession. He was also sure she would drop him the minute she knew he did not have it.

Grandfather rode Prince into the barn, rubbed him down, and pitched some hay into the manger along with a handful of corn. He left the barn door open to the pasture and walked out of the large swinging door. As he approached the house, he could see a black mare tied to the hitching rail — it was Marie's. Grandfather surmised she had decided she had waited long enough. When he walked through the door, she rushed to him.

"John," she said, "why haven't ye been to see me? I stood it as long as I could. When ye hadn't come I thought I'd come to ye — silly lad. I'm a warm and passionate woman; I could not stand bein' away from ye another minute!" She looked into John's eyes, with her arms wrapped around his waist.

John started to speak, but before he could begin, she interrupted.

"When we're married, John, ye're doubts will all vanish." She looked around the room. "Of course, ye'll hav' to build onto the house, and we'll need new furniture. French would be nice; I love French furniture."

John thought it would be a good time to bring up the subject of the treasure.

"Marie, I know ye think I have the Prince's treasure . . . but I do not."

She peered up at him, and her face showed some doubts, but John could see in her eyes that she was considering that perhaps he really did not have it. Then suddenly her look turned to a smile and she put her long-fingered hands on her shapely hips.

"John Ross, ye almost had me there; I know ye dare say nothin' about it for fear o' th' Crown, but ye'll not be havin' me believe it for a minute."

The dark of evening came quickly upon them as they visited, and the more John listened, the more he was convinced he would not marry Marie. But he felt an obligation to her, and hesitated to break away abruptly. It was not in his nature to hurt a woman's feelings. He would have to decide what he should do.

"Marie," he said firmly, "I'm not interested in marriage now. I will come see ye, but I'll make no promises."

He had extended his hospitality to Marie for the night, and the following morning, she rode back to town. She could not believe it when he put her in the spare room; the idea of it galled her.

At first she had been upset, and what bothered her the most was that she had not accomplished what she had set out to do. Late in the night she had gone to his room, but found him asleep. She stood by the moonlit window for a time, then thought it wiser to leave quietly, for she was sure he would know nothing of her entering his room.

But John, indeed, had heard her. He lay awake, feigning sleep, his loins in agony, desiring the woman that stood in the moonlight, yet fighting the very idea. His blood raced, and he would have been helpless if she had moved into his bed. But she left the room, and he gave a sigh of relief.

As she neared town, Marie decided she would have to try a different tactic with John Ross. He was too skittish, and she would have to give him more room. But sooner or later, she was determined she would get him to the altar, and then she would have all the money she would ever need. He could stay on his old farm and she would move to Europe, live in a mansion — anything was possible once she had her hands on the treasure.

For the kind of money she knew he must have stashed away, she could be patient.

In early March of 1785, Grandfather was in Leesburg. News was being circulated around town that King James III had restored the Jacobite lands in Scotland. Grandfather, a man of great faith, told Felix, "I knew it would be." Both men were filled with hope for the future of their homeland, for the clans could now restore their customs and dignity.

In April, Felix heard from his brother, Augustus, who had been made Chief in Felix's absence. Felix could return and claim his birthright; and if he did, Augustus would step down as Chief.

The Crown had removed the wanted status that had hung over both of their heads, for it seemed that most of the Bonnie Prince Charles's treasure had shown up in jewelry shops in the major cities of Scotland and England. It had been scattered, as the locals were wont to say, to the four winds, and the Crown had thrown up its hands.

But Felix replied by letter to Augustus that he would not be returning to Scotland, for he was happily settled in America, where his hopes and promises for the future now lay.

April had come in with the rains, and by the 10th the redbuds and dogwoods were painting the countryside with their delicate pink and white blossoms.

Daylight was joyously celebrating when Grandfather John Ross awoke. He had slept the night with the window open and a morning breeze was rustling the curtains. It was the kind of day when he felt blessed to be alive. Deep within the chambers of his heart he believed that very day to be the start of a new beginning, and a peace came over him that he had not felt since he was a lad.

The beautiful dawn seemed especially comforting and familiar that day, with clouds resting peacefully along the mountain peaks, like heavenly cathedrals, waiting for God to begin His sermon. Then suddenly near the center of the cumulus glowed a brilliant reflection of light. It was a scene, and a feeling, in this new land of America that Grandfather would never forget. Perhaps, he thought, it was like this when Christ had entered the temple — the mountains celebrated with drums of thunder and the winds strummed the strings of trees and grass like violins, as it came down from the canyons.

Since the past November, John had seen Marie but three times, and she had seemed to be less strident, not as insistent. Perhaps, he thought, he had been wrong about her, though months earlier, in March, he remembered, she had again brought up the topic of marriage.

But John could put her out of his mind, for on the 20th of April, he had received a letter from his army friend, Captain John Dooley, in Savannah. Dooley wrote that in January, Jerome Stanton had died; Agnes was now a widow. But she had not been seen since the funeral.

Grandfather did not need much time to reflect on the situation. The next morning he was on his way. If Agnes needed help, he would be there for her.

Ten days later, he rode Prince into Savannah. The Dooley house was in the old part of town, a large, white, two-story structure. Dooley and his wife greeted John like family. He was shown to the guest bedroom where he settled in, then Dooley and John spent the afternoon talking about old times.

John anxiously asked what Dooley could tell him about Agnes. "Have ye learned anythin' new?"

Dooley had not, other than what his letter had contained. "But I did learn that she lives at Stanton's plantation, Tanglewood. It was where they moved after they were married. And there's another rumor bruited around town that she's being closely watched once again, but by whom, I do not know."

Dooley continued, "It's now the local knowledge that Henry Stanton, the son, inherited all of Jerome's properties — a bit of a shock, for many thought Agnes would probably inherit Tanglewood, the finest of Jerome's plantations."

Early the next morning John rode out of Savannah and took the road northwest to Tanglewood, ten miles from town. Near eight o'clock, he rode down the traveled way to the house, beneath an archway of giant oaks. It was not long before he was met and stopped by a guard, his weapon at his side.

"I've come to see Mrs. Stanton," John announced. We were acquaintances in Scotland. You may just say John Ross is here to see her."

"We don't allow strangers to call on Mrs. Stanton," was the gruff reply.

"But I've known Agnes for many years . . . ," John responded.

"No one is allowed to see Mrs. Stanton," the guard angrily retorted, pulling his pistol and pointing it in John's direction. "Now be off with ya, and don't return unless you're tired of this world."

John was certain he had seen a curtain move at an upstairs window as he reined Prince around and retreated down the long path. A mile farther from the plantation, he stopped at a stream to rest in the shade and wrestle with his problem.

He would have to get into the house some way. He had noticed a small hillock at its northwest, covered with brush. He knew he could get there unseen from where he now rested.

John picketed Prince in a meadow where he could get to water, and found his way to the hillock. He had a good view of the plantation house and guard. It was six that evening when the guard finally left the front entrance area. Ten minutes later, from behind the house came his replacement. Grandfather concluded he would have ten minutes to get inside between the changing of the guard, or he could slip by at night.

Grandfather was unarmed, except for the dirk at his back. But it was all the weapon he would need. He would wait until dark.

At midnight, he slipped from the knoll into the shadows along the house. He was below the upstairs window where he had seen the curtain move. He could see the guard near the roadway, his head bent over and dozing. Grandfather hoped he would not be caught, for he did not want to shed blood and kill the guard.

The windows were fixed — unmovable. In the deep shadows, he took out his dirk and worked on the casing. In a few moments he had the frame removed, then crawled inside the house. While replacing the window, and before he had turned around, he felt the muzzle of a gun at his back.

"Speak now, and softly," came the voice from behind him. ". . . And you best have the correct answer."

"I am John Ross, a friend of Agnes. I have heard she is in trouble, and I have come to help." "John Ross! . . . thank God you're here. I have heard the mistress speak of you many times. Come. Her room is upstairs, first door on the left. Tread quietly, for the house is watched."

When John turned around, the man with the soft, deep voice had disappeared into the darkness of another room. John found the large stairway and began the climb.

Agnes was asleep when he slipped into her room. He stood next to the bed, looking down at her through the dimness of a moonlit night. He had forgotten just how beautiful and innocent she was as he gazed at her golden hair gracing her face on the soft white pillow.

He did not want to frighten her and slowly whispered . . . *"Agnes!"* Her eyes opened wide when he called her name, startled at first. Then she recognized him. "Is that ye, John?" she asked, almost as if she had been expecting him.

"Aye, 'tis. It has been a long time, Agnes, and maybe I should not have come, but I felt it was somethin' I had to do."

Tears filled her eyes. "I'm so glad ye came back, John. I saw ye from the window . . ."

They held each other in the dark until her tears abated. She quickly told John that she had tried to escape from her uncle several times, but had been caught and returned. And then she was forced into the marriage she had not wanted, though Mr. Stanton had been a good man.

He had been a kind man, and she could have run away once they were settled, but she felt duty-bound to stay. And she did not think John would want her after she had married, though she had also thought of an annulment.

Jerome had promised her that Tanglewood would be hers when he died — she would always have a place of her own. But when the will was read, all had been left to Henry, his eldest son. Even the other sons and daughters had received nothing.

Everyone had surmised that the will was not genuine, but it had been signed by Jerome — at least it appeared to be his signature. At any rate, the courts accepted the testament.

But Henry, the suspect son, had told her she could stay at Tanglewood, and he would provide her with living expenses — a situation that had soon turned unpleasant and fearful.

After many minutes of talking, John learned that Henry would return to Tanglewood in two days.

"You must get dressed, Agnes; we're leavin'." John smiled. "And don't ye worry; I'll make an honest woman of ye. After we return to Virginia, we will get married. . . . I have never stopped lovin' ye."

Tears flowed again. ". . . Nor I ye, John."

Agnes hurriedly dressed in her riding clothes and placed a few items in a bag.

"What else shall I take?" she asked.

"Nothin'. . . nothin' at all. We'll get whatever ye need."

The guard was still nodding when they slipped across the yard. It was four in the morning when they rode into Savannah. Ten days later they were in Virginia.

Agnes stayed with Felix and John's mother until she and John were married in the Ebenezer Church on July 7th, 1785. Eight children would be born to their union — Ann, John Jr., Catharine, Jane, Robert, William, James, and Sarah.

Marie wasted no time in finding a wealthy plantation owner to marry. The last Grandfather had heard, she was, indeed, living in Europe. He hoped she had found what she wanted in life.

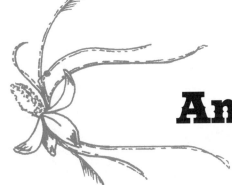

America

Civil War

I HAD FALLEN off to sleep by my campfire remembering all Grandfather John Ross had told me about his life in Scotland, and his early years in America. It seemed our ancestors had been in wars since time began, but I had learned one thing about the Ross history: the men never shirked their duty. When the call came, they were accounted for; they would pull up their loin cloth and wade into whatever was needin' done.

John Ross, Jr. — my father — the oldest son of Agnes and Grandfather John, would carry on the family legacy, fighting for this nation's peace. Pa was twenty-four when he volunteered to fight in the War of 1812 at the Battle of New Orleans, with Andrew Jackson.

A year after he returned home, he married Ma, Susannah Thomas, on April 16th, 1815. Nine children were born to their union, Harriet Jane, William, Thompson, myself — James Franklin, John, Howard, Albert, and the twins, Joseph and Martha.

Ma died on September 22nd, 1831, when I was but nine years old, from complications of the twins' birth. Little Joseph followed soon after, and died on January 14th, 1832. Grandfather John Ross died on July 24th, 1838; and Grandmother Agnes died on December 12th, 1843. I was sixteen when Grandfather passed away, and twenty-one when Grandmother died.

When Grandfather's four daughters married, he gave them each a diamond, the last of his gems. When his sons married, he gave them land.

It now was my turn to stand up for my country and, like those before me, I would do my best.

On Saturday, July 20th, 1861, the assault we had expected never came about as the Union Army continued massing its forces on the other side of Bull Run. Cannon fire and volleys of scattered musket fire boomed and rattled throughout the day, but no major action took place — mostly small skirmishes all along the outposts. It turned out to be another day of anxious waiting, and to keep the men busy I had them helping repair harnesses for the teamsters.

Around noon, Virginia General Joseph E. Johnston's army moved in to join Brigadier General Beauregard's army. Pierre G. T. Beauregard, called by some "the little Napoleon," hailed from Louisiana. There had been concern around camp that he would not arrive in time for the major battle to come. The wounded from the outposts moved through our camp to the rear most of the day.

I didn't know it at the time, but politicians, members of Washington society, and even women with picnic lunches had been clogging up the turnpike between Washington and the Union front with buggies and gigs. They lined along the hillsides to watch the ensuing battle. They had thought it would be a lark to watch the certain Confederate defeat. After all, the Union had an army of some sixty thousand compared to the Confederate's forty thousand.

The confusion of the traffic interfered with the columns of Federal troops moving to the front. Many of the men broke ranks, discarded their spare equipment, including their cartridge boxes, and joined into the holiday air of the day, as if it were a weekend outing.

I had twenty young men under my command, all restless with anticipation. I spent most of the day among the men, calming them as best I could.

Tad Olsteen was a youngster of sixteen, and late last night I had heard him sobbing. It did not help the spirits of the other men, and I did not want anyone bolting under fire, as that could start a contagion.

That evening I went to Tad's pallet to talk to the boy, to ask how he was maintaining.

"I'm okay, Sarge . . . no . . . I guess I ain't okay," he blurted out. "I'm homesick . . . and scared. I don't think I can take much more."

I sat down and explained to him that we all were scared. "But sometimes you just have to face down fear. There's not a man in this army that's not scared."

I asked him, "Tad, would you die to protect your family?"

The enthusiastic youngster responded, "Sure, Sarge, that's somethin' I wouldn't hesitate in doin'."

"Well, then think of our army as the only barrier between the enemy and the safety of your family. We're not the aggressor in this war. They're coming onto our soil to fight.

"My place is twenty miles from here, Tad, and I don't want them over-running my home — or yours.

"When they attack, their objective will be to kill us. To prevent it, we must also be prepared to kill. If we stop them, hopefully it will end the war, and then we can all go home.

"But remember . . . you're here to protect and defend your loved ones."

I returned to my pallet and heard no weeping that night.

I was awakened on Sunday, July 21st, to the bursting of shells. The air was still heavy with night's darkness, but our camp was already at the business of stirring to life. At three o'clock, volleys of heavy cannon fire all along the front had split the night. This would be the beginning of the battle to come. For some reason I had felt a calmness. I was frightened, but the uncertain waiting of the last two days had set my nerves on edge more than the fear of battle.

The men in my command found their own morning meal, then readied their muskets. I made certain plenty of ammunition had been issued to each man.

At seven o'clock our regiment was rushed forward and into line. I was carrying my Remington Army .44-caliber revolver and my .44 Henry when we took a reverse slope position below the rim of the hill, next to our General Barnard Bee's regiment. The enemy had appeared in strength two miles below the stone bridge, and we had rushed up to reinforce the left along that front. The reverse slope of the hill was a good protected position from the blast of cannon fire all along our front.

By half past nine, the outposts of our troops were in retreat across the valley floor, and musket fire could be heard all along our front, but there was still no sign of when the main advance would come.

Then, almost suddenly, an onslaught of thirteen thousand Union troops moved across Sudley Springs and hit our left flank. Colonel Evan's brigade rushed in to meet the Federals head on. Completely outnumbered, our boys then had to retreat across the valley — a heart-rending sight, with men dropping everywhere. Once vibrant men that I knew now lay dead among the brave still standing, firing their muskets as fast as they could reload, their musket muzzles continually winking golden flames. And amidst it all, spirals of gunpowder smoke were settling across the front, engulfing the scene in a ghostly shroud.

By eleven that morning all fury had broken loose. Our entire front was beginning to bend and crumble; it looked like certain defeat. The veterans and old-timers were doing what they could to hold the youngsters in place. And my earlier concern for young Tad had been unnecessary. He was standing up fine.

General Tom Jackson rode his horse, Little Sorrel, up and down our line of defense shouting, encouraging the men to hold. Our battery of six cannons was tearing holes in the Federal line, and we were maintaining steady against the enemy fire.

Than a Captain on horseback rushed up to our position and shouted at General Jackson above the din.

"The day has gone against us!"

Tom Jackson looked at him with a scowl. "Keep it to yourself! We're not beaten yet!"

I heard later, at about this time in the battle, that our General Bee saw Jackson standing on the hill before his troops and in an effort to rally his own men, who were faltering, Bee noted to those around him, "There is Jackson standing like a stone wall!" The name stayed with the General, and he became known as Stonewall Jackson — his determined brigade the Stonewall Brigade.

It was just moments later that General Bee fell, in the heat of battle, mortally wounded.

Captain Robert Ogden Tyler's Federal troops had sallied across the valley with cannon shells falling all around them. Battle flags were flying forward as they worked up the hill and ever closer to us.

Jackson shouted along the lines, *"Don't fire until they're right upon us!"*

My men waited, not budging from their aiming positions. As the Federals came closer, one, then two, of my men fell to the ground.

"Fire!" I shouted, as the roar of detonations began all along our lines.

Our three separate volleys of synchronized fire disintegrated a large part of the charging enemy. The Union soldiers left standing retreated and regrouped with another charge in process. A Captain, on a beautiful black horse, raced back and forth in front of his men encouraging a large regrouped command forward as they fired into our line of defense. I could see him clearly along my front and knew he needed to go down. I had lost six men in the first charge that had almost broken our lines. Without their bold leader I figured the Union boys would lose their confidence. It would be a tough shot, for I knew the officer was never still, riding boldly, racing to and fro along his lines.

But I had picked off many a rabbit moving as fast, and a target a whole lot smaller.

The Union line was getting closer. I lifted my Henry and took a bead on their Captain. For an instant I felt remorse for what I was about to do, yet I knew it was necessary. I shouted to my men, *"Fire!"*

The Captain fell from his horse, and the volleys all across our lines left but half of the enemy standing. They stood in shock, peering at the dead around them, and then in panic they retreated, many dropping their muskets as they ran for safety.

Throughout the valley their officers were screaming at them to form up again, but to no avail, as the troops rushed past them fighting for distance and safety.

At the same time, on our General Beauregard's right, General Jubal Early's brigade was attacking the charging line of Federals with a heavy flanking fire, bringing that part of the Union assault to a finish. General Early was an easily angered Virginian and West Point graduate who had voted against secession, and the Blue Ridge Boys would later be part of his division. Meanwhile, however, confusion reined and the Federals' attempted orderly retreat deteriorated.

Along the crest of the hill, Confederates were cheering. General Jackson began shouting instructions to his troops: "When you charge, *yell with fury!*"

It was half past three when our line surged forward with a ferocious shout. As if by signal, the long gray line moved all across the front, with following units picking up the yell.

The enemy lines completely broke before the onslaught of howling thunder heading their way. It was the first time the Union Army heard the Confederate yell — a sound that struck fear in the heart of many a Union soldier.

Yankee troops fled past their officers on horseback who were screaming at them to stop and re-form, but they ran and kept running, throwing down their rifles and equipment to travel lighter and faster. The retreat turned to panic and then to a rout.

The Northern politicians and civilians who had come to see an easy victory were also in a panic. The turnpike to Washington was full of Union soldiers and civilians in mass confusion fleeing for their lives.

They did not know it at the time, but they were safe, for the Confederates did not follow far past the field of battle.

Our Confederates were overjoyed. Shouts could be heard all along the lines. "We've won the war! We've won the war!"

But General Jackson was not so sure about that, and he told his superiors, "Give me five thousand fresh troops, and I'll march into Washington and drive the Federals clean out of the country!"

The high command refused. "No, General, we've won the war. They'll not attempt another invasion of our lands."

Tom Jackson just seemed to growl to himself, then walked away.

As it turned out, old Tom Jackson was right. He could easily have taken Washington then, and it would have surely put Maryland, an original Confederate sympathizer, and Pennsylvania into Confederate hands, which would have moved the war out of Virginia.

That night I was so tired I went to sleep almost before I had lain down.

About this time, Lieutenant Garrett promoted Corporal Johnston to Sergeant and, at my suggestion, Tad Olsteen to Corporal for his bravery in battle. Johnston would make a fine Sergeant and proved his leadership skills gallantly. I knew my infantry days would soon be over.

Three days later, Major Harmon gave me a pass to go home for a week. The early morning of my departure was cool at daylight, the sunrise painting gold into the purple shadows along the creek bed of hardwood trees.

I had finished my morning meal at seven, and readied my pack for a pleasant ride, though I could tell by the temperature, the day would be hot. As I stepped into the saddle and rode off west on my black gelding, I wondered what my father and grandfather would have thought of my actions had they been at Manassas. My thinking was they would have been pleased. I knew I had fought hard and true, as had other Ross men before me.

By noon I could see the home place in the distance, where Pa now lived alone, and I could see my own land that Grandfather John Ross had given to me — the eight hundred acres I lived on, with our special secret place of pine-covered mountain slope.

When I awoke the following day it took me a minute or two to figure out where I was. I could hear the rattle of dishes from the kitchen, and smell the cooking of bacon and eggs. I closed my eyes; it felt like heaven after my days at Manassas Junction.

I would always refer to the battle as Manassas. The Union Army named their battles after creeks or rivers, the Confederates after the nearest town or crossroad.

In minutes I was out of bed and enjoyed a wonderful morning meal with my family.

I did not have to report back to camp until I heard from Major Harmon. He would send me orders if and when he needed me again. Hopefully, the war was over, but the Major had said he doubted it.

President Jefferson Davis of the Confederacy went from anxiety to elation after the battle at Manassas, and President Lincoln's well-being moved quickly in the opposite direction.

General Irvin McDowell had been relieved as commander of the Union Army as a result of the defeat, and Lincoln appointed General George B. McClellan in his place. McClellan immediately went to work, training and restoring morale. Except for small skirmishes, things had pretty well settled down, though it became apparent that the Federals were not going to go away easily. They were preparing for another battle more earnestly than ever.

I wished that President Davis had given Stonewall Jackson the five thousand troops he had asked for to take Washington and send the enemy north. I had a bad feeling that all the South was doing was letting the Federals rebuild their forces, and then they would attack us Virginians again.

On October 21st of 1861 there had been a battle at Balls Bluff. Union troops had crossed the Potomac River with four regiments of New York and Pennsylvania troops. The first unit had penetrated almost to Leesburg when they ran into heavy fire. They had come into wooded country, familiar to the Confederates. The rebels knew the enemy was on the way and let them advance deep into their trap before opening fire.

The Yankees were overwhelmed by the onslaught, and retreated into their three advancing regiments; they then became disorganized and confused. The Confederates, made up of Mississippians and Virginians, were well used to hunting in that type of woods, and started picking off Yankees like they were hunting squirrel.

In that moment of mass confusion as the Yanks fell back, the Confederates attacked, with the rebel yell reverberating above the snapping of brush and saplings being crunched underfoot as they charged. What happened next was bedlam, as the Union troops retreated.

Balls Bluff was a hundred-foot-high cliff, littered with sharp rock, above the Potomac.

The Union troops were like a herd of stampeding cattle, and when they reached the cliffs they went over, falling, rolling, and sliding to the bottom. Screams penetrated the air as the Yankees fell onto sharp-edged rocks at the bottom. Many of the badly wounded were swept away in the river and drowned.

The Union lost nine hundred, killed or captured; Confederate losses were minimal. Union General McClellan's first battle had been a disaster.

Meanwhile, our Tom Jackson had been promoted to Major General under the command of Lieutenant General Johnston, And Major Harmon sent orders for me to report to the Captain in charge of the teamsters at Manassas Junction by the 25th of October.

It was a morning of unforgettable color the day I left home for the garrisoned Stonewall Brigade. I had stepped up into the saddle of my black mount just an hour after daylight, a day serene and peaceful here at home.

Reds and golds painted the broken hillsides. The sumac had been brushed with a brilliant red, the dogwood splashed in hues of rust, and the shapes of cottonwood necklacing along the creek in the distance were plumed in shades of gold. But the mellow scene turned out to be the last beauty before a dreary and forlorn winter.

It was afternoon when I rode into our rebel camp and reported. I spent the next few days with the teams of horses and mules, working on harnesses and readying the wagons for the campaign ahead.

One month later, orders were received from General Jackson to move the Stonewall Brigade to Winchester, at the head of the Shenandoah Valley, known as the "Breadbasket of the South." Once again the brigade was under the General's close hand, and this time I would be on the other side of the Blue Ridge Mountains, twenty-five miles from home — so close . . . but it might as well have been a hundred miles away.

General Jackson was a stoic, taciturn man, deeply religious as were most Presbyterians, and as I was raised. Before the conflict, he had been a professor of artillery tactics at the Virginia Military Institute, at Lexington, and had been granted a leave of absence for the duration of the war.

One of Jackson's idiosyncrasies was his secrecy. Only he, inside his head, knew what his plans were. He did not even want his brigade commanders to know what was to happen next, except for what lay immediately before them — for fear word would somehow be picked up by enemy ears.

Our brigade, made up almost entirely of young farm boys and men of the Shenandoah Valley, camped four miles outside Winchester. Like me, the men of the valley were direct descendants of those who had fought some one hundred years before in the Revolutionary War. Once again, an enemy was entering their homeland, trying to impose its will upon them. The Southerners had not started the conflict; all they wanted was to be left alone.

The much talked-about problem of slavery had little to do with most of these men of the South and their willingness to fight. A good many did not support the idea of slavery, and felt the states should have worked it out some way. These men were farmers who in the main could not afford a slave had they wanted one; most of the valley farmers could barely provide enough food and money for themselves.

To invade their land by force was wrong, and they would fight to the end to protect it. When the Union Army stepped onto their soil, the South soon developed a deep hatred for the Yankees.

The young men of the Confederacy were proud of the reputation they had gained at Manassas, and they were anxious to celebrate that reputation at a local tavern, to raise a glass or two, and perhaps to find companionship with the ladies. But General Jackson was not about to let them travel the few miles into Winchester — he wanted them ready for action at a moment's notice.

Jackson's young troops were resentful that they could not get leave to town, especially because they knew that the Virginia militia was allowed to garrison there. And Jackson was aware of the grumbling, but he prescribed discipline — reveille, drill, picketing, and taps. He had plans, and he wanted his men tough and as ready as he could get them before spring.

Jackson, furthermore, gave orders against imbibing, orders which, of course, were broken by the men whenever they could lay their hands on the tempting liquid. Many a wasteful and wanton night passed when the men had sneaked ale into the camp and spent long hours drinking. General Jackson knew of it, but he ignored it.

In November of 1861, the weather turned to rain and wind. The landscape was captive to mud. The winds from the north brought bitter cold and the damp sliced to the bone.

Along with the hostile weather, the men became morose, melancholy, and miserable. General Jackson realized he needed to keep them busy, and thus on December 16th, at four o'clock, he trumpeted the troops from their beds for an early morning repast. In short order the infantry was on the march, our wagons close to the rear guard. We were heading for the Chesapeake and Ohio Canal. Jackson was going to wreak havoc and disrupt the use of the canal.

After we arrived, we spent our time in camp in the biting cold of the lonely woods without the comfort of fires, so as not to alert the enemy of our presence. When finally the enemy outposts spotted our brigade, they shelled our position with cannon fire.

On December 27th, the 33rd Virginia Infantry rushed its volunteers into the cold water, and after several hours with pickaxes the dam was leaking.

Having accomplished what he wanted, General Jackson had his infantry on the move, marching back to Winchester. He had started off our wagons earlier in the day to keep our supplies a safer distance from the enemy. In the twelve days we had been away from camp, we had seen just a dusting of snow. Roadways were cleared, and the wagons rumbled on the frozen ground. We buried our heads down into our high-collared coats as we moved into a bitter west wind.

The next day, nearing darkness, I could see the lights of Winchester. The lights in Heaven would not look any more inviting as the welcoming glow I saw in the distance.

On New Year's Day, 1862, General Jackson sent orders to his brigade commanders to fall out. As Sergeant in command, I ordered my men to ready the teams and load up their wagons with ammunition, food, and other supplies. All personnel were to draw five days of rations, and to keep at the ready one day's cooked ration and a full canteen.

Atop his favorite horse, Little Sorrel, Jackson moved his troops out onto the Pughtown Road. Our wagons followed, along with a company of cavalry. Recent rumors had been circulated of an enemy buildup at Romney, forty miles to the west, the direction we were headed.

We had received a hero's sendoff from the townfolk of nearby Winchester, especially the pretty girls, as we passed through the town. I was riding my black gelding alongside the ten wagons I was responsible for, only a portion of the hundred that strung out behind the marching troops.

The day was warm and balmy for January, and many of the infantry boys ahead were peeling their great coats and placing them alongside the road, no doubt hoping to pick them up on the way back. Luckily, I had my men take their coats back up. The morning turned out to be a deception, for snow clouds had suddenly appeared on the horizon. A haze quickly moved across the sky and brought with it a fierce cold wind, then behind the wind came sleet and snow, turning our portion of the world into a blizzard.

Horses and wagons began to slip on the slick roadway, and wagons began to spread out and fall farther behind the troops.

No one knew where we were going, except Jackson of course. Only after darkness did the army stop at Pughtown. It was midnight before we reached camp with the wagons. We had made only eight miles that day.

In the cold morning light we pushed on west. Snow was falling, and the temperature well below freezing. Our supply wagons were slowed by the treacherous going, and we were strung out for at least two miles. When once more we finally pulled our wagons up to the army, the troops were camped, all huddled around fires and sharing blankets in an attempt to get warm.

The next day, again, the infantry pushed on. Where was Jackson going? We had first thought we were headed for Romney, but now we were moving north. At dusk, the troops stopped at Unger's Store, an old trapper's station. Reinforcements caught up with General Jackson there, and it was said his forces now totaled eighty-five hundred men.

Our third day out was even colder. On the morning of the 6th of

January, the infantry attacked Bath. The Federals stationed there put up a token fight, then fled. General Jackson followed with heavy artillery fire until he had pushed them across the Potomac. We lost four men, and twenty-eight were wounded.

With our army's right flank cleared out, Jackson had us backtrack south, taking us into even more brutal weather. The march was a nightmare, and the temperature dropped below zero. Our horses and mules were slipping mercilessly, without winter-spiked shoes. The countryside around had turned into a solid sheet of ice, and then overnight a six-inch snow completely obscured the road, so that we could not tell if we were on the traveled way or not.

The following morning was even worse, for the temperature had dropped to twenty below zero and through the night we had five more inches of snow. The mountain road Jackson had chosen was treacherous beyond the most active imagination. On that Siberian morning, the General was everywhere, helping the fallen and pushing out wagons half buried in snow. Horses slipped down and were thrashing about to get up. There was not a four-horse team that did not have at least one horse down most of the time. As the morning moved along, it turned warmer, and eventually we got underway.

By the 13th of January, the weather had warmed the day, but now brought rain and sleet. General Jackson was a seasoned soldier, and he showed no pity. He would march, and the weather be damned. It was later that I realized this was his way of preparing his men for the hardship of the battles ahead. He wanted them tougher, better, and faster than anyone they faced. Yet we had some thirteen hundred men that had to be taken back to Winchester due to illness.

The town of Romney was then abandoned by Union troops. They had received word of the fall of Bath and, for them, Romney was now untenable. On the 15th of January, our troops marched in and occupied the town.

At this time, our brigade returned to Winchester, leaving others to hold Romney and protect Winchester's flank from attack.

Night had descended on our wagons when we pulled into Winchester, and I had decided to sleep in a hotel bed, for the Major had told me I could have a few days' leave. I was heading for home in the morning.

I walked up the steps into the Sheldon Hotel and opened the large door. Inside, I checked in for the night with the spectacled, balding desk clerk behind the counter. It was only six o'clock, though outside all was darkness and Orion dominated a flat sky of stars. The hotel's dining room was on the left, and through the large double doors I could see tables and a few patrons. I walked into the spacious room and sat down at a far table.

After the hardships of that winter, it felt good to sit back in comfort, and soon satisfied by a warm, well-prepared meal, I climbed the stairs to my bed.

I had received orders to report back to Major Harmon by February 10th, at Winchester. As Quartermaster in charge of the teamsters, the Major was responsible for the moving of supplies and ammunition. It was a hard job, but he was a tough, profane man, and he could move wagons faster than just about anyone in the army — and in General Jackson's army, efficiency and speed were requirements.

In February also, Union General Nathaniel Banks had been ordered by Lincoln into Virginia to clear General Jackson's army from the Shenandoah Valley. General McClellan's forces would soon be away from Washington, and Lincoln was fearful of the capital's vulnerability to attack from that part of Virginia. In but a month, McClellan's army of just over one hundred thousand Union volunteers would be on the peninsula in a massive effort to take Richmond. This overwhelming force of manpower would soon be unleashed on the Confederate armies.

On February 26th, General Banks crossed the Potomac at Harpers Ferry with his forty thousand troops. General Jackson's Confederates were outnumbered ten to one. It appeared to be a lost cause, but Jackson waited and watched, through the eyes of his cavalry and Turner Ashby, the Virginia planter and politician who had become General Jackson's cavalry commander.

On March 6th, Banks' army bivouacked twelve miles north of Winchester. Confederate General Joe Johnston's army was sixty miles east and moving south. The only Confederate army left to defend the valley was our meager group of soldiers under General Jackson, which by this time had dwindled to thirty-six hundred infantry.

General Banks, we had heard, was a high-handed, defiant individual, a politician, and not a military man. With Banks was General James Shields, a complete opposite of the pompous Banks — a former lawyer and politician, and an experienced military man. Their two commands made up the army of forty thousand — Banks with twenty-eight thousand and Shields with twelve thousand.

And back at Richmond, our admired General Robert E. Lee, himself the son of a General and part of one of Virginia's most respected families, was now in charge of all Confederate military operations.

So went the progress of the war.

On the 11th of March, we were up at daylight, preparing for movement. On that afternoon, Major Harmon told me the Union Army was moving toward Winchester. Horses and buggies raced through the streets as the townsfolk left their boarded-up homes, heading south for safety.

General Jackson had ordered his men north, and our supply wagons followed. A west wind had shifted to the north and the temperature dropped. We were to stop our wagons well behind the lines, or when we could hear the close rattle of musket fire.

From where my men stopped, I had a good field of view. The action was directly ahead, with our infantry protected along the reverse side of a slope called Alabama Hill.

I ordered my men to hold up until further orders. The marching Union forces, with bayonets gleaming in the low sunlight and battle flags streaming, were a magnificent sight to behold. The skirmishers and cavalry moving abreast of the endless columns of men went as far as the eye could see.

But it did not seem to worry Stonewall Jackson, for he ordered his troops to attack. The Confederate cavalry seemed to come out of nowhere, attacking the Union cavalry and skirmishers. Behind them came the infantry that had been hidden from the Union's view. In the setting sun, our infantry attacked like amber ghosts wielding gleaming bayonets. The Union front fell back onto its approaching columns. Then, as darkness fell, the Union troops opened up with cannon fire, and the night musket fire looked like millions of fireflies striking golden lamps in the purple twilight.

Overwhelmed by the sheer number of Union troops, our wagons were ordered south as the army retreated. I determined we would no doubt stop at Winchester, but General Richard Garnett, another Virginian, ordered us to a position five miles south. At midnight, we stopped for the night.

At this same time, Jackson was meeting with his Generals in Winchester. Major Harmon told me later that Jackson had ordered them to attack the Union forces north of Winchester at daylight. When Jackson learned that his Generals had moved their regiments five miles south, he was shocked and demanded they be marched back for a daylight attack. The Generals argued that the men would get no sleep, and they were already worn from the day's battle. A livid Jackson realized the opportunity for any further action to save Winchester was gone, and had his Generals report to their units.

General Jackson had his army continue on south. Union General Banks did not pursue, and the Federals set up headquarters at Winchester among the remaining fear-stricken locals.

On the 21st of March, some of Banks' army were pressing south of Winchester to harass the Confederates. General Jackson then received a dispatch from Turner Ashby that most of the thirty thousand Federals were pulling out, heading north and vulnerable. Jackson concluded that McClellan was taking most of Banks' army out of the valley, to add them to his pincer movement on Richmond.

General Johnston's parting orders to Jackson were to hold Banks in the valley, and thus Jackson ordered the men to break camp and march at first light with three days of cooked rations. Two days later, our brigade attacked the Federals at Kernstown, four miles south of Winchester.

The fighting was ferocious, but superior numbers were forcing our soldiers to retreat. General Jackson was horrified that his beloved Stonewall Brigade was in retreat — and why, he wondered, for he knew he had given no such order. General Garnett later explained that he had issued the order, to protect the retreat of Colonel Fulkerson's brigade. Our Confederates had suffered seven hundred eighteen casualties, compared to the Union's five hundred ninety.

At Mount Jackson, the town named to honor an earlier Jackson — Andrew — Stonewall took command of his old brigade, and Garnett was placed under arrest for retreating when no order had been given him to do so. Garnett was to be court-martialed, we heard, and Jackson's Generals were shocked. But one thing they understood from that time forward was that no one retreated without Stonewall Jackson's orders.

The Battle at Kernstown was a Confederate loss, but it turned out to be an accomplishment. Because of the ferocity of our attack on the Federals, Lincoln decided to leave General Banks in the valley, and not move him to the peninsula to help McClellan.

The Valley Campaign had opened at Kernstown — a campaign that would last until late June — and it would be studied by military men across the world as the way to fight a war with inferior numbers.

Retreating south at this time, General Jackson bivouacked and scoured the countryside for men. Hearing the call for help came Jedediah Hotchkiss, the former New Yorker who had founded a boys' school in Churchville, Virginia, in the late '40s. Hotchkiss offered his services as a map maker to the Confederate Army, and in March General Jackson soon learned that the man was a blessing from God. Hotchkiss was well familiar with the Shenandoah Valley from his own earlier geological observations of the area. And while he hated the institution of slavery, as did many others from the South, he loved the valley, and the Yankee invasion drew him into the Confederate cause.

Current charting of the valley and surrounding areas had been inadequate. Hotchkiss joined Jackson as a Captain and Chief Topographical engineer for the Shenandoah Valley District, and Lee and Jackson relied on his precise and detailed battle maps.

When Jackson had first met Hotchkiss, he had peered at the man for a moment, then told him he wanted a map of the valley from Harpers Ferry to Lexington, showing all areas suitable for both offense and defense. General Jackson soon had the knowledge of every stream and trail in the Shenandoah Valley, along with the gaps through the mountains east and west.

In late March of 1862, I was promoted to Lieutenant and put in charge of thirty wagons. We were bivouacked not over twenty miles away from my home, and with the enemy lurking everywhere, I had decided to try for a one-day pass to take care of personal business, see my family, and check on the livestock.

After Major Harmon granted the leave, I was in the saddle by six o'clock, and in three hours I was riding through Snicker's Gap. I feared that the Federals would confiscate my horses, for I had some of the best in that part of the country, and thus I decided to move all but two of them to the hidden meadow that Grandfather John Ross and I had enjoyed so long ago.

By noon the task was done. The sunlit day felt warm and pleasant for March, especially in the protected sanctuary. I spent several hours there feeding my soul, in a different world, where all was peaceful. How I wished that day that the war might be over, and things taken back to the way they were before the conflict. Yet I was old enough to know that nothing ever returns to the way it had been before.

I had been standing along the riffle of the stream, listening to the music of the rushing water strumming over rocks, when I decided to walk out into the meadow of long grass to catch the bright sunlight. I had gone almost to where the horses were pulling at the hay when a dark shadow moved across my shoulders. Startled, I ducked my head to avoid the expected blow. My fear turned to relief when I saw the eagle's shadow racing across the long-grass meadow. Then the shadow vaulted across the tops of the pine trees and disappeared as the eagle screamed, taunting us below with his scorn.

After returning to the house, I had Mary hide the silverware and valuables, and most of the food, in the storm cellar we had secured in the foothills. After I had left again for the war, I found out that ten days later a company of Federal cavalry had stopped at the place, confiscating the two quarter horses I had kept there for the family. They also took my two best draft horses, including the hay, corn, and oats that were in the barn. They searched, but found no larder, and then they rode off. Mary said that the Captain had not allowed his men to bother the family, for which I was thankful.

By April 4th, General McClellan had started his Union army forward toward Richmond. In the west, Kentucky, Missouri, and most of Tennessee, along with parts of Arkansas and Mississippi, had fallen to the Federal armies.

Retreating before McClellan's one hundred seventy-five thousand troops, with forty thousand of them left in the valley, were General Joe Johnston's thirty-seven thousand regulars. It appeared all was lost as our rebel armies withdrew throughout the south.

But we heard that General Lee needed General Jackson to hold fast the Union armies of Banks, Shields, and Fremont in the valley, and he made arrangements to leave General Richard S. Ewell's army in the north to help Jackson, despite General Johnston's protest. We waited word, for as Johnston retreated toward Richmond, McClellan's army of the Potomac followed on his heels.

Following Kernstown, Jackson had bivouacked at Rude's Hill for a few weeks and spent his time studying the maps provided by Hotchkiss. As the enemy approached, Jackson ordered his troops to fall back to New Market. The Federals thought they had Jackson cornered as they hotly pursued us, but they soon found out our boys were hard to catch.

It was a cold and heavy rain that fell the day we were ordered to move down the Harrisburg Road. As usual, only the closed-mouthed Jackson knew where we were going. He had dispatched an order to General Ewell on the other side of the Blue Ridge Mountains to join us at Swift Run Gap. Ewell had eight thousand men when he reported, but he rode into an empty campsite, wondering where Jackson was. Ewell was confused; he had been unsure if he was to take orders from General Lee or Johnston, and now Jackson was also a superior officer.

Later, on May 3rd, Jackson rode his army into Brown's Gap of the Blue Ridge Mountains and out of the Shenandoah Valley he had been ordered to protect. Some said that this was Ewell's duty, but if it was, he was not aware of it.

When our infantry reached Mechum River Junction, the engine of a long line of railcars was belching forth steam, ready to roll. General Jackson had his troops board the cars, and by rail they returned to the valley, arriving at Staunton around noon.

During all that maneuvering our supply wagons moved south, protected by a company of now-Colonel Ashby's cavalry, all heading for the same place — Staunton. The townsfolk there had been nervous and upset, fearing they had been abandoned to the Yankees. By nightfall, General Jackson had sealed off the town; unknown to anyone, he was about to attack Union General John C. Fremont's army — the famed former explorer of the American West.

Jackson marched his army west toward the Alleghenies and took the high ground at Sitlington Hill, joining forces with General Edward Johnson — called "Allegheny" Johnson, after his victories in the mountains the previous winter.

Below the two Generals lay the camp of General Robert Huston Milroy, of Fremont's command, at a mountain crossroad called McDowell. Jackson let Johnson's army take the lead and begin the fight because they were familiar with the terrain, but we could hear it soon become a desperate fire fight. By nightfall, the line of the opposing armies had become entangled in desperate hand-to-hand battle.

The next day, General Charles Sydney Winder, the very exacting new commander of the Stonewall Brigade, entered the fray. As the light faded into night and musket fire stopped, the silence was deafening. The beaten army of Union General Milroy retreated into the darkness. The following morning a rising golden sun shone on an abandoned Federal camp.

General Tom Jackson had his second victory; with his head uncovered and bowed, his men said he stood in a downpour and thanked a merciful God.

Jackson continued to work to turn his infantry into a fast-moving, disciplined force. Shoes wore out, but the troops marched, many without shoes, until their bleeding feet toughened. Jackson's marches were at route step, with a ten-minute break every hour. Dawdlers, or those who strayed from the march, were severely disciplined.

Yet, to the enemy and to our own army, the General appeared to be a madman in his often puzzling ways. His movements often seemed unreasonable and lacking forethought. But the naysayers were wrong. Jackson knew exactly what he was doing by spreading the opposing armies into vast stretches of unfamiliar territory, as he maneuvered inside the circle.

While General Jackson was involved in his marches and maneuvering, General Ewell — Old Baldy they called him — was anxious and uncertain, not happy to just sit back waiting for Jackson to re-appear. On May 17th General Ewell saddled his horse and spent a sleepless night riding dark and hazardous mountain trails to Jackson's camp at Mount Solon, south of Harrisonburg.

Jackson greeted Ewell in his predictably stoic way, the men said, and then led him to where they could talk in private. The two campaigners spoke of the string of defeats suffered by the South and the imminent peril of Richmond. The Army of the Potomac was now closing in on the capital.

General Jackson spread out his maps and pinpointed where he knew the Yankees to be, marking each location. Then he peered up at Ewell, who earlier had been doubting our great General's actions.

Jackson's unpredictable orders and marches were beginning to make sense. The Federals had, indeed, spread themselves thin, Ewell realized, due to Jackson popping up here and there, as Jackson had all the while massed his armies of some eighteen thousand men closer together.

Union General Banks was camped at Strasburg and could be dealt a heavy blow. The only problem was that Ewell had been ordered by General Johnston to confront General Fields and his men. Nevertheless, orders or not, Jackson would not let an opportunity to attack the isolated Banks slip away. He knew it had to be done at once.

General Ewell returned to his troops, and General Jackson issued orders. By three that next morning, our wagons were on the road.

At New Market, our troops added a brigade from General Ewell. General Taylor's Louisiana Brigade of three thousand men had marched into town after a twenty-six-mile walk.

When the rest of Ewell's troops joined us at New Market, General Jackson had sixteen thousand effectives. To cover himself from any repercussion from General Johnston's orders to Ewell, Jackson telegraphed Robert E. Lee, whom he respected as a superior officer:

> *I am of the opinion that an attempt should be made to defeat Banks, but under instruction from General Johnston I do not feel at liberty to make an attack.*

Lee never answered, and predictably Jackson went ahead with his plans. Jackson had us up before dawn with orders to march north. When the men approached Cross Street in New Market, the General in the lead, he pointed east. We all wondered what he was up to now.

Our army moved toward Massanuttan Gap. The day was hot and dust stirred as we passed, settling on horses, wagons, and clothing. We all were covered from head to foot. The men began their strenuous, breathtaking climb up the gap, still only resting ten minutes to the hour.

Late on May 21st, we set up camp near Luray. General Taylor was somewhat confused, for his troops were within twenty miles of where they had started before joining Jackson at New Market. Word quietly spread that Taylor thought that perhaps Jackson was indeed mad.

Though we marched to an ugly war, the springtime Shenandoah Valley was a picture of beauty with its newly planted fields and greening meadows sprinkled with colorful wildflowers. And then Ashby, now a Brigadier General, and General Johnson's Allegheny army joined up with us, making seventeen thousand effectives and fifty large guns.

On the 22nd, we bivouacked south of Front Royal. Strasburg and the Yankees were only twenty miles away.

General Banks had received intelligence information that Jackson's Confederates were eight miles west of Harrisonburg, and that General Ewell was camped at Swift Run Gap. It was far enough for Banks to relax and ride into the countryside.

That same day, Union General McClellan started his push up the peninsula to take Richmond. He was preparing to commence his pincer movement down from Fredericksburg, and things looked bleak for the Confederacy.

But Jackson struck hard and fast, with the dashing audacity of Ashby's cavalry. Ashby, fearless in his determination, cut communications between Front Royal and Strasburg. Then he hit the outpost at Bucklin Station between the two towns, killing or capturing all that were stationed there.

May 23rd broke clear and blistering hot, but weather, time of day, or difficulty of terrain made no difference to General Jackson. A deeply religious man, he believed that faith and prayer would bring us victory against the enemy, blessed by a loving God.

Jackson led us north, the infantry mostly double time, in the stifling heat. Four miles from Front Royal, he suddenly veered right taking a steep trail that rose up before them five hundred feet. The troops were worn by the time they hit the top, breathless, but now they were in the refreshing shade of pine trees with a bubbling brook of cold water nearby.

The men hit Gooney Manor Road running and turned left. It would take them the back way into town. Around a bend, through pine trees approaching the side of the road, was Front Royal.

Federal skirmishers, surprised to see the rebels, especially at that location, opened fire.

Then, at two in the morning, Jackson ordered our attack against Front Royal with heavy force. In no time, the overrun Federals were fleeing north with our infantry nipping at their heels. Our wagons were far enough behind, and we had escaped the steep road into town.

At Cedarville, the Union troops rushed to realign in an attempt to stop the oncoming rebels, but our infantry with their disconcerting rebel yell charged into the Union center. I thought how it must be like the din that Grandfather John Ross, and his father as well, had experienced back in Scotland with the cry of the clansman in the heat of battle.

With the piercing yell, the Federal line broke. They panicked, running to take cover in a nearby orchard, but were soon rounded up.

To keep from being cut off from his supply base, Banks was forced to retreat toward Winchester.

A cool breeze brushed across my face and lifted my eyelids from sleep. Earlier, in the deep of night, discomfort had prowled hot and sultry.

For a moment I had thought I was back at home, until I heard cannon booming in the distance, lighting up the dark sky. But it was not cannon fire; it was thunder. Again lightning flashed, revealing angry clouds boiling overhead. We knew we were in for a downpour, but no angry rainstorm would slow down General Jackson. I had been with him too long to think that mere rain would stop him, not when freezing weather, blizzards, and snowstorms had not.

The night before I had made my pallet where we stopped, and from my bed I could hear the horses and mules occasionally snorting and shuffling nearby. Then I heard men in desultory talk moving about like shadows, carrying bundles of harness. Squeaking leather was thrown over the horses, with a sharp jangle of metal rings and chains in the quiet of the night. Startled, I jumped up to find the pleasant coolness of the morning. It was half past three, and we were to be in line by four. Thanks to my Sergeant, my teamsters had not overslept.

Our wagons were in place with time to spare, but some others were not, and Jackson rode up and down our line of wagons berating Major Harmon about their lateness. We pulled out within half an hour, and apparently satisfied at last, General Jackson left. By five o'clock the sky should have started to lighten up a bit, but it did not, and thunder and lightning followed us down the road.

To the cadence of the marching thunder, we moved quickly north beneath a churning turmoil in the air and dark confusion, it was as if we were hasting down into the valley of death. I wondered if there would ever come a time again when I could stroll peacefully anywhere. Death day in and day out was hard on a man's soul, and I was convinced it left a scar on all decent men.

I rode my black gelding alongside the wagons down through what looked like a coliseum formed by nature, and wondered if the Roman gladiators had felt heartsick, too, as I felt now, when they had entered the arena of death.

The restless sky showered on us later that afternoon, and Jackson pushed everyone hard, not wanting the enemy to get away. Sometime during that night came a heavy rainstorm, and the regiments were bogged down in choking mud.

Jackson received word of Banks' retreat, and hoping to catch him on the march, sent part of the artillery on ahead, to be supported by Major Chatham R. Wheat, of the 1st Louisiana Special Battalion, who would lose his life at Gaines Mill, Virginia, in June. But meanwhile, our weary and plodding infantry continued working its way north, with hopes of catching and cutting off General Banks before he reached Winchester.

Twice the Union Army was cut by the Confederate cavalry, causing confusion and the capturing of supply wagons. But Banks' army was able to move fast down the hard-packed gravel pike, while our troops and wagons were struggling through the mud of a rain-soaked land. The rear-guard action between Banks' retreating army and our rebel infantry had turned into furious fire fights, and we were kept busy capturing hundreds of wagons, their boxes bulging with supplies.

The rainfall slowed down our wagons, strung out for some three miles. My thirty were close to the center, and with constant urging, we were able to keep them tightly together. But Lieutenant Jeffries, behind my group, was having problems and kept lagging farther behind. With the enemy in retreat, being captured was unlikely, but we never knew for certain, with the Federal cavalry roaming the countryside. One thing was sure — if Jackson got wind that his wagons were in jeopardy because of someone's lagging, his voice would be heard.

The Federals' main force was winning the race for Winchester, and once there they could set up a strong defense. But Jackson was still pushing his troops unmercifully hard into the purple of twilight, and when the army stopped, Winchester was but four short miles away. The weary men lay down where they stopped and were asleep immediately from their long day of fighting and marching.

At four o'clock, Jackson roused our sleepy troops, and before daylight we were approaching the high ground south of Winchester. Jackson gave orders to attack, not wanting to give General Banks additional time to set up his defenses. The valley veterans tore into the Federal lines. Banks' troops wavered, and then broke from the onslaught of firepower. Our Confederate lines were fast charging into the breach, and in a mad rush the Federals scattered for their lives.

Daylight came with rays of golden sunlight through a window of purple clouds. Off in the west hung a dark curtain drifting, where the sunlight illuminated sheets of rainfall, hazing a world both bright and dark. Ahead, in the low sky, the heavy clouds could be heard complaining with a scolding thunder and streaks of lightning.

The morning clouds retreated, along with the enemy, before a splaying of light from a friendly sun's far and familiar throne. Amidst it all, the earth was clean and fresh, the day beautiful, the sunlight penetrating into the foothills as the artillery roared and the enemy fled. The Potomac lay thirty-six miles north, and what remained of General Banks' Union army never stopped until they reached the other side of the river.

On Sunday, May 26th, the battle was over. The Federals had five hundred wounded or dead and had lost an untold amount of Quartermaster stores, including nine thousand three hundred small arms, and two rifled cannon. Three thousand Yankees were now prisoners. Of Jackson's army — our men — sixty-eight had been killed and three hundred twenty-nine wounded.

General Tom Jackson turned out to be too great a threat to Washington, and President Lincoln ordered General McDowell to the Shanandoah Valley, overriding McClellan's protests, but relieving some of our concern for Richmond. Lincoln had done exactly what Lee had thought he would do by pulling McDowell north to protect the Union capital from General Jackson's forces.

But the city of Richmond still lay in peril, for McClellan was but a few miles away, and our General Johnston was still retreating. An anxious Jefferson Davis finally received word from Johnston that he would attack the Federals in three days, on the 29th. Only the news from Lee of Jackson's victory in the valley would give some promise to a worried Jefferson Davis.

We bivouacked at Charles Town, the infantry demonstrating against Harpers Ferry only seven miles away.

Lincoln had developed a plan for Union Generals Fremont and Shields to close from the south, and for McDowell and a resupplied Banks from the north. The four armies would cut off General Jackson from escape, sixty thousand troops against our valley army of sixteen thousand.

From Ashby, General Jackson knew of the four movements almost as soon as the Federals began their march, but he did not flinch. He was playing a dangerous game, however, for the enemy knew exactly where he was. But that was his intent. He seemed completely unconcerned about the disaster that steadily loomed ever closer. It seemed, the men thought, that Jackson was the only General in his outnumbered army who was relaxed despite of the impending catastrophe.

Union General Shields' army was near Front Royal. Banks' army had been reinforced at Williamsport and was preparing to march. With McDowell to the south and Fremont to the west, we sat with General Jackson in the middle of four Union armies south of Harpers Ferry.

On the morning of May 30th, Jackson cordially received a delegation of Charles Town ladies. He later rode toward Harpers Ferry, where he could hear the light skirmishing of musket fire. After a bit he stretched out under a tree and went to sleep. His Generals were beside themselves with concern while he seemed in no hurry to escape the four converging armies.

That same day, Jackson sent our prisoners and supply wagons south, with the army following behind. Fremont's army was now a day's march from Strasburg, and McDowell's a day's march from Front Royal. Banks was at Williamsport. It became a race, and we moved south in the middle of the four Union armies closing in for the kill.

But to our troops, Jackson had become the hero of the Confederacy. He was winning battles, while the rest of the South was losing. He was giving the South hope. The men who had cursed and reviled him at every turn now cheered and waved their hats whenever he appeared. The infantry had come to realize that it was Jackson who had turned them into the fighting force they had become, and they were proud to be a part of his army. Our troops were admired by all wherever we went, with townsfolk cheering and throwing flowers as we passed through village after village.

Meanwhile, the Union's pincer movement was only hours away from snapping shut on us. That day we lost a wagon, and two of my men were captured by the enemy. The wagon had broken an axle, and I had stayed behind for a time to help. I could see the men would soon have it fixed, and so I instructed them to follow as fast as they could, and I returned ahead to my other wagons. But they never showed up.

That night as we reached Winchester, rain began to fall. Jackson awoke at three the next morning to a gloomy day and sent orders for General Winder to evacuate Charles Town.

In a turbulent rainfall we moved our wagons south with our flanks protected by cavalry. The wagons were bursting full of the goods we had captured at Winchester. The army had never eaten so well, and the troops finally had shoes to wear, though doubtless they would not last long with the miles soon to be traveled.

I rode along our wagons encouraging horse and man to keep moving, until that night when we stopped in our muddy tracks to rest six miles south of Winchester. Then into the rain we continued south, leaving a disappointed Winchester that had been liberated for only six days, for they had welcomed the security of their own Confederates in their streets.

We knew that to snap the Union trap, General Fremont needed to advance; but he delayed, overestimating our strength, we concluded. Having been once deeply stung by Jackson, Banks was slow to move, until the 10th of June. And Shields, as well, rested after taking Front Royal.

Thus, when our Confederate Army had neared Strasburg, General Jackson decided to swing west, hit Fremont, and open up the pincer. General Ewell attacked Fremont hard, and the Federals retreated from the onslaught with the Confederates on their heels.

Our wagons were out ahead of General Winder and the Stonewall

Brigade. Though weary and bone tired, we were making forced marches of thirty miles a day and would soon catch up with the rest of the army.

On June 1st, General Winder and the Stonewall Brigade was spotted and harassed by Federal cavalry south of Winchester, but the cavalry was no match for the hardened veterans. Winder was now beyond the Union's trap, and Jackson stopped again, the men said, to praise a merciful God.

South of Strasburg we had lost ten wagons when Lieutenant Jeffries had let his teamsters lag too far behind and they were nipped off by the Federal cavalry. Major Harmon was furious, and I felt sorry for Jeffries, but he had been too lax with his men. It was a hard lesson learned, and he never let his wagons fall behind again.

Jackson had us moving south, and along the way he was burning bridges. No army could stop our worn and tattered troops. We could march thirty miles a day, then without rest fiercely tie into an opposing force. And all the while, the rains continued, and the swollen rivers and creeks were running bank full.

Around noon that day there seemed to be a pileup of the wagons at a low water crossing. With our wagons stalled, I rode my black to the front of the caravan to see what was holding things up.

Normally a dry wash, the channel was running three to four feet of fast water. The ramp to the crossing dropped six feet, and stopped at the water's edge were four mules refusing to enter the running stream. The teamsters were whipping the mules unmercifully, but they would not budge. They were determined not to cross the wash.

I had never owned mules myself, but Pa had a pair I had used at different times and he had told me of a trick you could use, though I had never tried it.

I rode my horse down the bank and up to the left front mule, which seemed to be the stubborn ringleader. I crowded up next to him, then leaned over, bit its ear, and shouted. That mule left the ground on all four legs, honking a series of brays as the team of four hit the water, splashed across the stream, and charged up the far bank. After that the rest of the teams crossed the gully without any problem.

By June 6th we had moved to Port Republic, and the army now occupied the heights between the North River and the Massanuttens. Richmond at this time was having its own problems. McClellan's army of one hundred fifty thousand were only a few miles from the city, while we had only fifty-four thousand troops to oppose them — nearly three-to-one odds. And since May 29th, both armies had attacked and counterattacked with hardly any ground changing hands.

Fremont's cavalry continued to attack the rear guard of our Confederates as we moved into Port Republic. General Ashby's cavalry attacked and captured sixty-four Federals, but before the day was over, Ashby lay dead.

However, with no time to grieve over his General's death, Jackson immediately began preparing a battle plan to engage Shields and Fremont at the same time. By daybreak of June 7th, General Ewell was confronting Fremont at Cross Keys. Jackson had the bridge burned at Conrad's Store, and put troops to guard the one remaining bridge at Port Republic.

On Sunday, June 8th, the battle continued. Shields entered the fray, coming to Fremont's call for help, to attack Jackson from the rear. Instead, Shields' army hit Ewell's front head on and became engaged in a ferocious fire fight with our Confederates.

Early in the day we almost lost all of our wagon train on the main street of Port Republic. As Jackson watched from the heights, he saw that Captain Samuel Moore and twelve men were all that stood between the Federal cavalry and his wagon train. But with eyes only upon the prize, the Yankee horsemen never noticed the Captain and his men. Besides not seeing Moore, I do not think the cavalry gave the teamsters a thought as to putting up any resistance. But they were in for a surprise. Several of my teamsters and I sighted down rifle barrels from behind our wagons and fired into the fast-riding Federals as Captain Moore opened fire. The Union cavalry fell back, along with twenty empty saddles, to regroup. We knew there were too many Federals and that they would get us eventually, but before they could charge again, Jackson had a six-gun battery of cannon into position and opened fire, driving the cavalry from the town.

Then Cross Keys became another Confederate victory. Fremont's infantry of ten thousand fell back in disorder before Ewell's five thousand effectives. The North lost six hundred eighty men; half were dead. Ewell lost forty-eight killed and two hundred forty-seven wounded.

That night Jackson ordered Ewell to leave a brigade at his front and bring the rest of his army to Port Republic to join him in attacking McDowell's forces across the swollen river. Federal forces were isolated on the other side of the stream with no way to cross or get near the one bridge that was controlled by Jackson's artillery from the heights that overlooked the town. On that same Sunday, General Joe Johnston was wounded and carried from the battle in the lines before Richmond. General Robert E. Lee was now placed in command of the Army of Northern Virginia.

Monday's battle began at dawn, led by General Winder and his Stonewall Brigade. They crossed the North River bridge, forded the South River, and quickly hit McDowell's front. The battle was nip and tuck until Ewell's brigade came up. Taylor's men moved to the right, making room for Ewell. By the time Ewell's third brigade had marched into line, the Federal army collapsed and melted away. It was just eleven that morning, and we had defeated another Federal army. The Yankee casualties for the day were one thousand eighteen men, five hundred fifty-eight of them held as prisoners. General Jackson's casualties were eight hundred, the most we had suffered in battle.

The Shenandoah Valley campaign was over, and before the sun set that Monday, our troops were on the march for Brown's Gap. Jackson, with sixteen thousand troops, had defeated an invading force of sixty thousand men.

General Lee, in his diplomatic way, told Jackson he should come to Richmond, but that his movement should be kept secret — no one was to know of his intentions. Lee was a man after the General's own heart, and whatever Lee suggested was taken as an order.

On June 17th, at midnight, General Jackson issued marching orders, and before daylight we were moving our wagons down the road toward Richmond.

On June 23rd, Jackson mounted Little Sorrel and rode to meet with General Lee at High Meadows fifty miles away. Fourteen hours later, in the late afternoon of the next day, he arrived at Lee's headquarters. It was a war meeting of Generals — Lee, Jackson, James Longstreet, Ambrose P. Hill, and Harvey D. Hill, Jackson's brother-in-law — called to plan Union General McClellan's removal from the peninsula.

Jackson and General J. E. B. — "Jeb" as they called him — Stuart's cavalry were to dislodge McClellan from the left as the rest of Lee's army cut them down. Jackson was to have his men in line by June 26th.

Jackson rushed back to his troops, and the next day he received precise battle orders from Lee for timing and troop placement. Jackson was to be in position Wednesday night on the Hanover Courthouse Road.

On Thursday, the battle began — they called it the Seven Days' Battle hereabouts — that drove McClellan from the peninsula. The Confederates now had a General in Robert E. Lee who would take the fight to the enemy.

By July of 1862, General John Pope had taken command of the Union armies in Virginia, a pompous man, thoroughly detested by all of us in the South.

On the 19th, we were headquartered with General Jackson at Gordonsville, and General A. P. Hill's division was sent to serve under Jackson. Our cavalry was keeping tabs on the enemy, and when Jackson received word that Union General Pope had occupied Culpeper, we could see he was pleased.

But Pope had made a fatal error. He had split his massive army, and General Jackson issued marching orders. General Ewell in the lead was soon meeting resistance; it was Banks' Yankee division, and that day we had run into an army of bluecoats willing to fight.

Cedar Mountain — more hill than mountain — was nearby and Jackson seized the high ground, placing Ewell's batteries on the heights and his infantry at the base.

A ferocious battle ensued, with both sides winning and losing throughout the day. When it appeared that the Federals were about to get an upper hand, General Jackson mounted Little Sorrel and rode to the front. With the rebel yell, he charged the enemy. His troops rallied around him, following into a fierce barrage of bullets. Like madmen they, too, yelled — at the top of their lungs — and the surge of our Confederate gray broke the Union lines.

"*Press 'em!*" Jackson shouted, as the Yankees raced in fear to get away from the persistent hail of bullets that followed them north.

Tom Jackson had defeated Banks again; but it was a hard-fought win. After gathering up the spoils, we retreated to Gordonsville, before Banks could find reinforcements. While garrisoned there, I had taken twenty wagons to our warehouses along the Virginia Central Railroad to pick up supplies. We thought we would be safe from the enemy, but one of my teamsters was picked off by a sniper from the nearby woods.

The following weeks saw mostly skirmishes and minor engagements between the major battles. On August 27th, the infantry marched into Manassas Junction along the Alexandria and Orange Railroad and captured warehouses of food and supplies, an abundance of foodstuffs and badly needed shoes and clothes. Our men simply helped themselves to what they needed, and there was still enough to fill a hundred wagons.

It felt strange to me, returning to the site of the first battle of the war so close to home, but there were many times I had been closer, without the chance to see my wife and children.

We learned that General Pope was on his way to crush Jackson's little army. But what he did not know was that he was being pulled farther and farther into a trap. General Lee had General Longstreet's division moving up from the south, to catch Pope in the middle.

An official from the War Department in Washington was on his way to Pope when some of General Jackson's troops wrecked the train. The man was captured and taken to a physician to tend his broken leg. As he lay on his pallet, he could see the lonely dark figure of a soldier sitting at a nearby campfire, motionless, and bowed in prayer. When the official questioned the doctor as to who the lone figure was, he was told it was our General, Tom "Stonewall" Jackson.

Surprised, the courier asked to be lifted up to where he could look upon the famous warrior. He saw the disheveled figure of a man in an unkempt uniform. General Jackson, unsmiling, peered over at the injured man for a moment, then turned away. After a closer look, the man could not believe he had just witnessed the famous Stonewall Jackson.

"Oh my God! Lay me down again!" he moaned. His words spread, and our troops adopted the cry. "*Oh my God! Lay me down again!*"

On the 28th of August, near the stone bridge, General Pope's infantry approached, and as the sun went down, our troops attacked. When the fight ended for the night around nine o'clock, once more the men fell asleep where they had stopped.

Pope now believed he had Jackson in a corner. He was certain his sixty thousand troops, thirty thousand from the southwest and thirty thousand from the east, would smother and annihilate Jackson's twenty-three thousand. There were times we worried about it as well.

General Richard Ewell, meanwhile, was wounded and had lost a leg, and General William B. Taliaferro took three wounds and was carried from the field. He was the third General of the Stonewall Brigade in three weeks to go down, and General William E. Starke now took command of our famous brigade.

On the morning of August 29th, the main body of Pope's army came down the Warrenton Pike and its batteries opened fire on our right. But General Jackson had to hold Pope there until Lee brought up General Longstreet. Everyone wondered where General Longstreet was, for he was to have taken position on the right. If Pope charged now, it would be disastrous.

Then the call went down the line, *"Longstreet's come!"*

The Federals went for our left. All day long our boys repulsed attack after attack. If the Yankees had cut through the Confederate lines and captured our supply wagons, the battle would have been lost. Yet, through it all, General Longstreet still had not entered the fray.

The combined Union armies of Generals George McClellan, Ambrose E. Burnside, and John Pope, some one hundred fifty thousand regulars, were bearing down on General Lee's army of seventy-two thousand. We learned that throughout the day, Lee and Longstreet could hear General Jackson's guns, which had reached a crescendo of firepower by evening. And we later heard that Lee had suggested that Longstreet attack and relieve Jackson's beleaguered army; but Longstreet thought they had better wait for his cavalry reports on what was at his front.

Jackson wondered what had happened to Longstreet, for we were hard pressed. As the sun fell behind the hills, the fighting finally stopped.

Dawn of the next day, August 30th, brought forth a bronze sun to a countryside of retreating shadows that were already hot. General Pope did not attack, and the morning slowly wore on.

Around noon, word had it that Jeb Stuart reported to Lee that the Federals were massing three lines along our front. Lee alerted Jackson by courier. At three o'clock, without a warning of cannon bombardment, the Union infantry came down on our left flank.

Shocked into action, our boys came racing out of the woods to man the lines. This was by far a heavier force than the day before, when our men could barely hang on. We were outnumbered three to one by the attackers, and our lines were starting to collapse. Jackson again appealed to Lee for help from Longstreet. It was a sure sign, we thought, of Longstreet's foot-dragging to go on the offensive.

Longstreet stood on the ridge where his and Jackson's lines hinged together. He watched the Union army charging across the valley beneath the sights of his battery of eighteen guns. For an hour his cannoneers watched, anxious to get at the mass of Federals streaming across the open field. Still Longstreet waited. He would wait until the final Union reserves had been committed.

Jackson meanwhile again sent a plea for help. Finally, Longstreet gave the order for his batteries of cannon to open fire. Cannonballs ripped across our front and into the charging Union left flank, and the effect was immediate. The assault stopped, and among the carnage of fallen men, the blue-clad Yankee troops slowly began to retreat. Cannon fire was tearing them to pieces, and the retreat became a rout.

History had repeated itself. The Federal army was soundly defeated again at the Second Manassas. And we were on the move, chasing Yanks.

At Chantilly, the Federals stopped to put up a resistance, but their hastily built fortifications could not hold the Confederates and General Lee's forces soundly beat them again.

With Virginia finally cleared of Yankees, General Lee decided to move into Maryland. On September 4th, we crossed the Potomac River. The infantry cheered. They would no longer have to fight on their own soil. They intended to show the Yanks how it felt to have their homes invaded, but they were treated so well by the folks in Maryland that they acted in kind.

Most Marylanders' sympathies lay with our side, but because of its location it had been forced early into the Union.

On September 15th, our army defeated the Federals at Harpers Ferry and occupied the town. Jackson captured eleven thousand troops, seventy pieces of artillery, and warehouse after warehouse of supplies, along with badly needed shoes and clothes. That same day, General Lee sent orders to Jackson to bring his army to Sharpsburg.

At the Battle of Sharpsburg, by the end of the second day we held the field. The next day, the armies faced each other without a fight. General McClellan, even with superior numbers, had turned timid. Sharpsburg had been a ferocious battle that turned out to be a draw on the field, but Lee, concerned of the Federals receiving reinforcements, retreated his army back across the Potomac. Because we had abandoned the field, it was considered a Union victory, their first in the north.

With winter coming on, General Jackson moved us to Winchester. We heard that Lincoln was disappointed with McClellan and replaced him with General Burnside. Under pressure from Lincoln, Burnside began massing troops along the Rappahannock River across from Fredericksburg.

General Lee wired Jackson to proceed. General Longstreet's First Divison and Jackson's Second Division moved in and occupied the heights above Fredericksburg.

On December 12th, a cold and foggy morning, in the quiet of a lifting mist, Union General Burnside crossed the river and attacked our entrenched lines, only to be repulsed.

The next day the landscape was covered with an even heavier fog. At ten o'clock the sun began to penetrate through, and as the wispy curtain rose on the scene below, it revealed a massive force.

Union cannons began to roar like drums, and at half past ten General Lee put his artillery into action. Soon three divisions of Federal troops began to advance, with their brigade colors gleaming in the sunlight. It was an awesome sight. Charge after charge of Union men advanced, only to be thrown back by our Confederates. By the time sunlight began to fade, the ground lay covered with blue-clad soldiers. Those still left standing were in full retreat.

Throughout the battle, my men were kept busy hauling ammunition from the railcars sided along the Richmond, Fredericksburg, and Potomac Railroad, five miles south of our lines.

The Battle of Fredericksburg was another Confederate victory, and then with both armies in a holding pattern, we went into winter quarters.

A spirit of revival swept through the Confederate armies that winter, and none more so than General Jackson's army. We had morning prayers and evening services at least twice a week. Sundays were a day of rest, with mail service banned; we spent the entire day in worship and study of the Holy Word.

On April 5th, 1863, I was home on leave. Major Harmon had been reluctant to let me go, but once again I needed to help out with the spring planting. I had finished with the row crops two days earlier, and planned to leave the following day for the front. My orders were to report back to my command by April 25th to General Elisha F. Paxton's brigade near Hamilton's Crossing at Fredericksburg.

I had just finished my morning meal, and it was a beautiful Virginia day, when the war seemed like a fitful dream that lay far away and in the past.

I stepped outside the house and walked to the barn, treading in the morning darkness upon familiar earth, carrying an old lantern shining a ray of golden light along my slow-moving feet, wading in the morning's purple shadows.

I opened the hinged door and stepped into the barn, inhaling that familiar aroma. Inside I hung the lantern on a post where I entered a stall we used for milking our cows. It gave young B. J., my son of ten years, a reprieve from the chores he had been doing while I had been gone.

After I had finished with the milking, I turned the cows out, and left the barn carrying a full bucket of milk into a gleam of lemon sunlight. I paused there for a moment to watch the glow moving across the lonely and empty land, antique gold upon the dark shadows of the grass and indigenous trees. In the near foothills the golden glow sprang suddenly to life on a meadow of blue wildflowers.

The Union army controlled the area at that time, and I had to lay low. But I knew my hiding places and stayed close to home, especially if a patrol of cavalry were to happen by. Our farm was out of the way of any vital interest to the military, however, and only once while I was home did a patrol pass by, but they never rode up to the house.

After the Battle at Fredericksburg, Abraham Lincoln had decided that

General Burnside was not the man he wanted to command the Army of the Potomac, and our Confederates now faced General Joseph Hooker.

On April 29th General Jackson received news that General Hooker was no longer in his front, but had moved and was preparing to cross the Rappahannock. We received orders to advance at once. It was a typical spring day, with fruit trees in full bloom, clad in pink and white blossoms. In the woods and along the hills wildflowers of all colors abounded along our traveled way, as we passed the lonely farmsteads.

That night we camped at Hamilton's Crossing, and all visitors who had come to see the famed General Jackson were turned away, for he was praying. The next day Jackson went to General Lee's headquarters, and together they came up with a plan to stop Hooker and hopefully crush his Union army in the process. We thought that could be a tall order, however, as the Federals outnumbered our Confederate army by more than two to one. But the Generals reasoned that Hooker would strike through the wilderness, to try to turn us left.

General Lee would keep a smaller army where he now stood, for any frontal attack, and would send Jackson along with General Richard Anderson's division to a position northeast of Chancellorsville.

On May 1st, around midnight, Jackson awoke, and we were on the road by three. At eight Jackson joined with General Anderson, who had already formed his line guarding the Old Turnpike and Plank Road. Jackson ordered General Lafayette McLaws' division ahead to engage the Union troops in the wilderness. General Jeb Stuart's cavalry was now in position to protect Jackson's left flank.

At sundown Jackson met Lee on the Plank Road. They left the road, found a log to sit on, and went over the day's happenings. Then General Stuart came rushing in and joined the other two Generals with some vital information. It seemed Hooker's right flank was in the air and not anchored. Earlier that day General Lee had reasoned it would be disastrous to attack Hooker's front.

When Jackson asked Lee what he should do, Lee simply pointed to Hooker's right flank. "You should go there." That was all the command Tom Jackson needed.

By four o'clock, from a nearby neighbor, Jackson had learned of an old abandoned road around Hooker's flank and to his rear. Lee showed up and asked Jackson how many troops he wanted. He would take twenty-eight thousand and leave Lee with fourteen thousand to hold the front.

General Lee hesitated for only a moment, then gave his approval.

The next morning, clearing the way took time, and the infantry was not able to get on the march until eight o'clock. Due to the downed trees and invading brush, our wagons were inching behind the slow-moving troops. We could have waited until almost mid-morning and easily caught up, but Jackson wanted his supplies at hand. All that day we crawled behind the struggling infantry in the tangle of woods.

The late afternoon was calm, and we later learned that the Federal troops had been relaxed along the right flank.

Shortly after five o'clock, Jackson attacked with General Robert E. Rodes at the forefront. The ferocious rebel yell at first surprised the resting Federals, and then they were terrified as the charging gray line came down upon them. They ran pell-mell away from the charging fury, with their worthless breastworks facing the wrong way.

Darkness did not stop Jackson. He called up General A. P. Hill's division to relieve the worn-out Rodes. *"Press 'em!"* the concise Jackson told Hill. *"Press 'em until they're destroyed!"*

In the darkness, Jackson and his aides rode on ahead to find the enemy, only to realize the Federals had abandoned their lines. Jackson sent back word for General Hill to rush on in the darkness to catch the enemy. But as Jackson and his men rode back into our own lines, some of the men, thinking they were the enemy, opened fire on the group. Both General Jackson and General Hill were seriously wounded.

It was a sad day, with both Generals down, as General Stuart took command. He was known to be a good cavalry officer, but an inexperienced infantryman.

The next day, a Sunday, General Jackson awoke minus an arm the surgeons had removed. He sent a message to General Lee of his injury, and of Stuart's command of the corps. Our Confederates had notched another victory, Jackson's greatest, and even the perfectionist Jackson praised his officers.

We all thought that General Jackson was getting well. He had gone to the Chandler home to recuperate, and on May 3rd and 4th he seemed to be improving. The peaceful country setting, among the Chandler family's Southern hospitality, seemed to agree with him.

On May 6th, the Federals had retreated back across the Rappahannock. Their casualties were seventeen thousand two hundred eighty-seven, ours twelve thousand eight hundred twenty-one — numbers that were almost impossible for us to imagine.

On May 7th, General Jackson was in pain. He was said to have pneumonia.

On Sunday, May 10th, 1863 — a day none of us will forget — General Jackson died. He had always said he wanted to die on a Sunday, and God had granted his wish. But with his death went the South's chances of winning the war.

After the battle at Chancellorsville and Jackson's death, General Lee reorganized the Army of Northern Virginia into three corps, under Longstreet, Ewell, and A. P. Hill, who had recovered from his injury.

To the west, at this time, things were going badly for the South, but in Virginia, General Lee seemed to have the Federals figured out. Lee was an able commander of the offensive, but we all knew he would soon feel the loss of Jackson, for Longstreet, a great General — the best fighter they had, his men said — could be contrary at times with Lee. Ewell at one time had the fire, but unknown to Lee, his offensive fervor had diminished after he had lost his leg at the Second Manassas. And Hill's bravery and audacity were well known, but he was enduring a sickness that often took the edge off his decisions.

General Lee was now at his maximum strength of some seventy-five thousand — sixty thousand infantry, ten thousand cavalry, and five thousand artillery. He would have no more, for there were very few replacements to be found in the South. The rich industrial North, however, seemed to have an endless supply of new flesh, and the Federal force was well over one hundred thousand effectives and growing.

In the Confederate Army's reorganization, our brigade — the old

Stonewall Brigade — was in Early's division of Ewell's Second Corps. In June we were moving down the Shenandoah Valley and clearing out Yankees. On the 13th, we were almost to Winchester.

It felt good to be close to home again, and removing the Yankees from our God-given land. I had to fight myself from becoming too bitter toward our enemy. And it did not seem to bother me as severely, as it had in the past, to daily look upon the bodies of dead Yanks laying in a heap or heading for the burial grounds.

At times I would try to move my mind from the war, and between fire fights I would turn to nature as we traveled north. The land and planted fields were surely a beautiful sight. Intermittently, all seemed peaceful as we traveled the old roads, filled with long past memories.

I was within ten miles of home when we went by Snicker's Gap, and my heart skipped a beat and ached. We never stopped; and the caravan moved on.

General Lee had decided to bring the war to a head, and crossed the Potomac into Pennsylvania. If the South were to win, it was now or never. By June 24th, our division had cleared Hagerstown, and we were in Chambersburg, Pennsylvania. At the same time, Federal troops were pulling stakes at Manassas to head off Lee, hoping to prevent him from reaching Washington.

I was amazed at the groomed lush fields, fat livestock, and surrounding wealth of this area, compared to the war-ravaged countryside in Virginia.

On June 27th, General George Meade relieved General Joe Hooker of Federal command of the Army of the Potomac. Then, on July 1st, the battle of Gettysburg began. Although Lee had issued orders for no major engagement, our armies stumbled onto one another. Looking at the raging battle with his field glasses, he saw General Rodes' brigade assault the Federal line and turn it into a rout. Lee decided to attack.

Observing from Seminary Ridge, Lee watched his army drive the Federals from the field, pushing them through Gettysburg. The Federals retreated onto Cemetery Hill where they were frantically digging in to make another stand

At half past four that afternoon, with a good four hours of daylight left, General Lee sent orders to General Ewell, now occupying Gettysburg, to carry Cemetery Hill — though Lee made the order discretionary — *"if practicable."* By half past five, Ewell still had done nothing, as Lee anxiously watched. Yet during that time Federal reinforcements were arriving to strengthen their position. At seven o'clock Lee rode to Gettysburg to find out why Ewell had not attacked. Ewell gave Lee the excuse — lame we all thought — that because of the lateness in the day, he was not sure of success. One could only surmise how much General Lee missed the dogged energy of General Jackson, who would not have hesitated in taking the position.

While General Ewell dallied, General Winfield Hancock was rushing reinforcing regiments of his Federal troops forward onto Cemetery Hill, Round Top, and Little Round Top.

By morning, the Federals had a formidable defense. General Meade, as well, had reached the position on Cemetery Hill and continued to rush troops into position. The Federals were now entrenched with reinforcements coming in by the minutes.

Early that morning of the 2nd, Lee's orders to General Longstreet had been for him to attack the Round Tops as soon as possible. We all knew, however, that the glum Longstreet did not agree with the move, liked nothing about going on the offensive here, and took no initiative. He delayed his start with excuse after excuse. It was four that afternoon when Longstreet began his bombardment and assault. Yet, even with the late start, General Longstreet came close to taking the Round Tops. Had he proceeded when ordered, they surely would have been easily ours, for while early on that first day of action, we had outnumbered the Federals, but by nightfall things had switched. By then the Federals had eighty thousand effectives compared to Lee's fifty thousand.

Meanwhile, General Ewell, upset by Lee's censure for not taking Cemetery Hill the day before, was determined to take Culps Hill. Our General Harry T. Hays took the hill in some brutal and hard fighting, but the Federals rushed in reinforcements and our rebels were driven off the high ground.

General Ambrose Wright's Georgians also had assaulted on Cemetery Hill, a move that had reached the crest, holding for a time before being driven back. Once again, had help arrived at that moment, we would surely have won the day.

That evening, General Lee was determined to succeed the next day, and ordered Longstreet to attack Cemetery Ridge early that morning. Lee knew that if the South were ever to win the war, it had to be now. He knew we could not endure a sustained battle. We had neither the resources nor the manpower. To move to another line to the south, as General Longstreet had wanted, would cut off the supplies, and leave no way to retreat should such a circumstance be necessary.

It was still dark when I was awakened by cannon fire all along our front. Our line, General Early's division, was just east of Gettysburg. To our right along Seminary Ridge was A. P. Hill's corps. From Seminary Ridge south into the woods, facing Cemetery Ridge and the Round Tops, was General Longstreet's corps.

The bombardment in the early morning darkness of the 3rd of July turned bright and ferocious. Shells were bursting throughout our campsite, and after the devastating carnage would come the agonized moans and screams of the wounded.

My mind flashed back to Grandfather John Ross and his tales of raging battle in Scotland. I wondered, again, would it ever end?

During the assault, my men were working to calm our horses who were raring and straining to a certain stampede. By ten that morning, thanks to our God, the bombardment ceased.

I made a quick assessment of the damage and found I had lost three men, six horses, and four wagons beyond repair. With dispatch, I put the men to work repairing the wagons that could still be usable.

Before I had a chance to eat a long-delayed morning meal, Major Harmon ordered me to take thirty wagons near a mile west of Seminary Ridge for more ammunition. At half past noon, we had made our way to the Hagerstown road, behind the lines of General A. P. Hills' corps.

It was after one o'clock, when we reached the pack train, and my men were about to load ammunition when from along the breadth of Long-street's and Hill's front came the roar of hundreds of cannons that began bombarding the enemy. My heart skipped, for I knew that it must be the opening of a major assault on the Federals.

Around three o'clock, we had reached the crest of Seminary Ridge on our return, when the bombardment stopped. Now amidst the deafening silence, from where our wagons rumbled, we had a panoramic view of the mile-wide open field separating the two armies.

And then, from the forest of green trees below marched our three brigades of General George Pickett's division, and six brigades of General

James Pettigrew's. Pickett had been a classmate at West Point with General Jackson, as well as with Union General McClellan.

Forty-two regiments formed the two formations, a mile long, with perhaps a thousand feet separating the two lines. They moved into the valley with flags flying and lines dressed to perfection, descending with golden bayonets gleaming in the sunlight. Officers moved back and forth in front of the marching lines, some prancing on horseback, others on foot, shouting orders and urging the men forward. As I watched down that vista of summer green, I had never seen in my lifetime a more beautiful sight that soon turned ugly.

As our troops neared the halfway point, the Federals opened fire with batteries of cannon. Our men loyally marched on, helpless, as exploding shot cut gaping holes along the lines. Scattered throughout, they fell to the green and turned the ground red. Lines would redress and continue on across the valley as flags fell, only to be picked up by another brave soul. Our dead and wounded littered the ground as the line determinedly moved on. In short order they were within four hundred feet of the trees on Cemetery Ridge where victory would be ours.

Then they were at a stone wall that gave them their first protection from the onslaught of Federal firepower, and from behind the barrier they fired their rifles. Officers urged them forward again, and they spilled over the wall, where the fighting turned into bitter hand-to-hand combat. We were winning the hard struggle, as the blue coats faded away. But in the melée, General Garnett went down as did our General Lewis Armistead. I remembered how the troops liked to tell the story of General Armistead at West Point, when he was expelled for breaking a plate over the head of his classmate, now General Jubal A. Early.

Snatching away our victory there at Cemetery Ridge, came a reinforcement of Federal troops. We had none. The fray turned to disaster, and those that could made their way back across the valley of death from where they had just come. In bitter retreat, many fell beside their dead comrades.

Of the more than twelve thousand men and nine Generals in the assault, only five thousand men and two Generals would make it back to our lines. Generals Longstreet and A. P. Hill subsequently prepared for a counterattack that never came.

Union General Meade, it was said, was overjoyed to come out of the scrap with a victory, and thus never pursued, though many on the Federal side thought he should have. I was not so sure. The Federals no doubt knew they had faced a master of defensive warfare in our General Longstreet. Even after the charge had failed, he was his old combative self again, barking orders as he waited for the anticipated assault. Had Meade counterattacked, the outcome at Gettysburg might have been different.

When all was done, General Lee took the blame for the defeat. But as I look back on Gettysburg, Lee was gravely let down by his Generals, though not by the men in the lines. They gave all they had and would have succeeded if they would have shared quick and decisive action from their leaders. First, there was Stuart, who had never returned in time to be Lee's eyes, causing him to blindly stumble upon the enemy — though his blunder was not disastrous, for Lee quickly moved to the advantage.

Then, Ewell not taking Cemetery Hill at a time it easily could have been was a serious blunder. And Longstreet's slowness and foot-dragging the second and third days was surely as severe. And, as well, Pickett's part in the final assault remained a mystery, for where was he during the charge?

Lee had relied on his division and brigade commanders to fight the battle, and his plan would have worked well if Stonewall Jackson had still been with us. But we could see that after Gettysburg, General Lee realized he would need to become more involved in any battle.

He would not have to worry about the reticent General Longstreet, however, for the Confederacy would no longer have the manpower to mount an offensive that could end the war. We knew that General Lee could only hope for a Federal mistake.

At Gettysburg, General Stuart's cavalry had suffered its first defeat from the confident and newly promoted Brigadier General George Armstrong Custer's cavalry brigade. The Union cavalry, once a joke, had come of age, and Custer's Michigan boys had much to do with turning it into a potent force, one unfamiliar to us.

In the darkness of that sorrowful night, Major Harmon ordered our wagons back to the Potomac. The next day, July 4th, the two armies again faced each other without firing a shot, this time quietly caring for their dead and wounded. Around noon, rain began to fall in a steady downpour. That night, our army retreated down Pennsylvania's muddy roads.

The next morning General Meade discovered that the Confederates were no longer in his front across the valley. Concerned that Lee was maneuvering to another line, and reluctant to turn loose of his strong position, he stayed in place.

Pressured by Washington to follow General Lee's retreat, Meade finally moved, but he was wary of Lee and was not going to be pulled into a trap. The Federal army nipped at our heels as we plodded toward the Potomac. Then, on the 12th, Meade caught up with us at Falling Waters, where we engaged in a fire fight.

It had not rained for a day or two, but the skies were threatening again. The Potomac River was flooding without a way for Lee to cross. Safe in the comfort of home, the powers in Washington pressured Meade to attack while General Lee was vulnerable, but Meade was not that certain of success. He was facing the man the men called the gray fox. It was said that Meade knew for certain he would not rush in, only to find his army had been destroyed. With Lee hamstrung at the river, he would take his time. Perhaps, it was thought, he could destroy Lee piecemeal.

Lee's savior from disaster was Major Harmon. We had reached the Potomac two days ahead of the army, and the Major, seeing there was no way General Lee could cross the swollen river, started barking orders.

We scoured the countryside for timbers, tearing down abandoned houses, barns, and sheds. We soon had enough to suit Harmon, and he immediately had us building pontoons. Once finished, we floated them down river to Falling Waters where we linked them together and floored them. We laid cut branches over the planks, to deaden the sound of our artillery, wagons, and feet that would cross the floating bridge.

General Lee's army started across in the darkness of July 13th, and finished the next morning. By the time Meade had advanced on the 14th, all that had not crossed were the rear guard entering the pontoon bridge. Lee's army, safe on the other side, had diverted disaster, the bridge was cut loose from the Maryland bank, and we were safely back in Virginia.

In late July of 1863, I went home for a week. The day before I was to report back to my brigade, I traveled to the upper pasture. It was a beautiful day, with the sky an unending depth of blue. I spent some time where Grandfather John Ross had always liked to go, but I also went to a favorite place of my own, off in the southwest part of the sanctuary, where a timber of northern red oak grew. Along the scattered trees, some eighty feet tall, lay a grassy meadow along the slope of an escarpment.

As a boy I had scoured that nearby eroded slope for fossils. Hundreds of ancient shells were still scattered there among the morning glory vines clad with their pink, blue, and white blossoms. I lay for a while in the wildflowers and sunlit grass, feeling the warm sun rays and smelling earthy aromas so familiar to my memory.

Toward the evening of that July day, late in the war, I whistled for my black, mounted up, and headed back to the house.

After Gettysburg, Union General Meade received reinforcements, increasing his army to eighty-five thousand effectives, with another ten thousand en route. We received none.

On October 14th, 1863, Lee and Meade fought a battle near Culpeper; on the 16th, General Lee retreated, and Meade did not pursue.

That next year, on the 17th of January, 1864, my son James Robert was born. I learned the news when Mary's letter finally caught up with me, in March. On February 29th, Ulysses S. Grant was promoted to Lieutenant General, with the command of all Union armies — the same position General Lee held for the South. The hero of the Union's western campaigns was now called upon to take command of the Army of the Potomac. He was Lincoln's man, and a fighter, despite the fact, it was said, that years earlier he had shared no fondness for his experience at the Military Academy at West Point, graduating twenty-first out of thirty-nine in his class.

General Lee hated being committed to the defensive, but he had no choice, for he did not have the resources to launch an offensive. He could only hope for the enemy to err, and then punish him with a counterattack.

In early April, Union troops began massing along the Rapidan in a thirty-mile front from Fredericksburg to Cedar Mountain. General Lee prepared for the assault and ordered all surplus material to the rear.

That winter I had been promoted to Captain and put in command of sixty wagons, two Lieutenants, six Sergeants, and about a hundred teamsters.

On April 23rd I was called to Major Harmon's tent and asked to volunteer for special duty. He then laid out the assignment. I was to proceed to Culpeper, twenty-four miles northwest of our encampment. Of the four warehouses there, two — north of town, along the Orange and Alexandria Railroad — were still full of badly needed supplies. He suggested I might require fifty wagons.

I peered at the Major from beneath the brim of my cap and looked into a taciturn face. Only one who knew him well could detect the light in his eyes.

"I know!" he immediately retorted. "It's a dangerous mission, with the Union cavalry in the area, but the General wants those supplies that were left behind, and there's no one else I can trust to get it done."

I felt duly complimented, of course, as the Major continued to explain that it might be a week before the first Federal brigades moving south would reach Culpeper. General Lee, he noted, had pulled all his forces to set up his main line of defense south of the Rapidan, thus permitting me friendly travel until I would cross the river; then I would have eight miles in hostile territory.

"But before I forget," he said, "you'll have no cavalry."

The Major's final comment was sobering. Nevertheless, I was eager for the task. But I wanted to handpick my men, each of which would be armed with pistols and rifles. "And," I told him, "I'll need a few extra men for a makeshift cavalry of my own."

The Major wished me well as I said I would be ready to move out in the morning.

"Good luck to you," he added, and dismissed me from the tent.

I spent the rest of the day choosing the men I wanted, mostly farm boys who could ride and shoot.

It was daylight when we pulled out of camp the next morning. I had with me Lieutenant Brad Jones, five Sergeants, and eighty men, traveling that lazy spring day just south of the Rappahannock River.

The cottonwoods and oaks had been busy sprouting leaves, cloaking their dark branches with a misting of green. Along the countryside, thickets were blossoming in pink and white blooms, calling out for someone to gaze upon their beauty. The greening slopes were longing to be loved. Riding by, I returned that intimacy. The love of nature and the land was something I had learned from Grandfather John Ross, and I have never forgotten how his eyes would take on a look of internal peace whenever we were alone with nature's bounty.

"Love the land, James," he had told me, "and it will love you. It's a law . . . a spiritual law."

Except for the occasional boom of cannons far in the distance, it was difficult to believe we were at war. I rode my black gelding along the lumbering wagons. By noon we had reached the fork of the Rapidan River. We stayed south of the Rapidan and followed a trail west. Fifty wagons take up much space, and I estimated our caravan stretched out for nearly a mile.

The afternoon was owned by a golden sun, and I had guessed the temperature to be hovering at a gentle seventy degrees. I could not have asked for more perfect conditions, except that we needed a rain, for we were raising too much dust off the roadway. I was concerned that after we had crossed the river, the moving cloud might be seen by the enemy.

Very few locals appeared on the road, but we did meet an Alabama regiment of Confederate soldiers marching to the east. Around four o'clock we passed a farmstead where a man was plowing up an eighty with a pair of black mules and a flock of crows following. I dismounted, walked into the field, picked up a handful of dirt, and let it slide through my fingers. I loved the smell of newly turned earth, for it reminded me of home. As the farmer tooled a turn near the road, he stopped.

We spoke a bit about the weather, but neither of us would mention the war that soon might easily destroy his hard work. I asked if he knew of a back trail, a way we could get to Culpeper without using the main road, and with a stick in his hand, he cleared the ground and drew three lines in the dirt.

"That's the Rapidan," he told me, "that's the Orange and Alexandria Railroad, and that's the main road into Culpeper."

Then he drew a crooked line meandering off the road and entering the town from the northeast.

"That's the back way," he said, "through a thick wilderness of trees — and narrow at times — but nobody's used the trail for years. I doubt there's many alive that even know about it."

We were twelve miles from Culpeper on the unseen course, ten by the main road. I copied the map to a crumpled piece of paper, and quizzed the farmer about each bend and turn. Then I mounted my gelding and raised my hand in appreciation. "Much obliged, sir; you've been a help."

I had been mulling over in my mind all day as to how I could keep a mile of strung-out wagons from being seen by the enemy; perhaps the trail was the answer.

Before dark, we crossed the Rapidan and camped to the north. I had not wanted to camp in enemy territory, but I was not about to be trapped on the south side of the river in the event of rain during the night.

The trail was supposed to leave the main road close to where we had crossed the river, and I found the path, almost overgrown with forage. As the wagons moved along, I sent Sergeant Dooley back to brush out our tracks at the entrance.

We had made about sixteen miles that first day, traveling from daylight to dark. We camped in a clearing of heavy timber, a stream of branch water running through the meadow, with enough grass to accommodate our caravan of hungry horses. If the farmer was right as to the additional two miles the trail added, we had another ten to go to reach the warehouses.

The dawn was overcast, and when we moved out, the sky looked like rain. Three hours later of slow going, we had traveled about three miles. Nature had almost closed off the trail, and I sent a crew of men on ahead to cut the choking brush and move the downed trees. We hoped that we might use the hidden path on our return as well, knowing we would have to keep the enemy unaware of its location, even if we had to lead them off in the wrong direction, away from the wagon train — though that might be easier said than done.

We were making our way along the north bank of a stream, where intermittent white riffles were eagerly rushing over rocks and gravel, singing to the dark, silent pools. The wind was now from the north, pushing low swirling clouds across the sky, and with a sweep of God's hand, the light of day had turned to darkness. Protected as we were in the woods, sharp gusts of wind nevertheless penetrated the surrounding cover. Roaring by above our heads, the winds angrily tossed limbs about. Then from the truculent clouds, thunder rumbled and lightning flashed, splitting apart the sky, and it was all the men could do to calm the animals.

A heavy rush of rain hit us hard, dimpling the creek water and tattooing the ground. It raised a heavy, musty smell as the thirsty dust soaked up moisture. Across the creek, behind a curtain of rainfall, stood a hazy forest of dim and ghostly trees. The countryside had first turned melancholy in the steady downpour, and then, from along the horizon, a golden light shone through small windows of the clouds. The sun splayed through the breaks and began to paint the country in long, wispy strokes of lemon light. Brightly it penetrated a world of darkness. In an hour the storm had passed, leaving us with a clearing sky, an arching rainbow, and a sweet aroma of cleansed air.

But then we had another concern, with the mud. Fortunately for us, the wagons were empty; had they been full, I don't know if we would have made it through the water-soaked trail.

By nightfall, as the sun sank behind the far blue hills, we could see the Orange and Alexandria Railroad tracks. We made our camp out of sight, and I ordered no fires. After eating a cold supper, I had a meeting with my officers to make sure they knew their duties. If we were discovered by Union cavalry, Lieutenant Jones was to move the wagons back across the Rapidan as fast as he could. I and Sergeant Dooley, with his twenty mounted men, would stay behind to lead the enemy away from the wagons.

After our meeting, I had taken Dooley aside and asked him if he might be acquainted with a Captain John Dooley from Savannah, who had been a close friend of my grandfather's and who had fought in the Revolutionary War.

"He was my great-uncle," the Sergeant replied. "How strange that they knew each other — and in war, as well."

Around ten o'clock that night, I slipped into Culpeper. On the far side of the tracks I could see the warehouses along the siding. The north buildings contained our supplies. At the railway depot was a lonely square of golden light shining out of the open door onto the platform. The sound of a teletype broke the silence, except for the footfalls of my gelding. The streets were empty, but I could hear voices riding on the breeze, coming from the hotel.

The hostler was still at his tasks when I rode up to the town stables. Claude Berry was his name, and the man I wanted to see. I had become acquainted with the old man years past, and whenever I was in Culpeper I would stop by to visit. He saw me ride up, and greeted me, wondering what I was doing in those parts.

"Passing through," I told him. ". . .Thought we might visit a spell, for it's been a few years."

We settled in a back room of the stable, for old Claude had acknowledged that the town had "enemies" — "If ya know what I mean," he added. We continued our conversation.

It was midnight before I returned to camp, but I had learned a wealth of information. The Federals had a cavalry unit that had come in two days earlier from the west, and had bivouacked four miles south of town. They probably determined any rebel assault would come from that direction. The main Union army, Claude had added, was forty miles north and on the move. They could be in Culpeper in two days, and that would mean more cavalry could be nosing around the next day. The cavalry had left guards posted at the warehouses day and night. We would need to move early in the morning, I decided.

When I had ridden by the warehouse, I wondered where the Union soldiers were — perhaps they were asleep, though I had been at least a thousand yards away in the dark and could have missed them.

I had our men up at two the next morning. By half past three, Sergeant Dooley's men had killed four and captured twelve of the warehouse guards. Even though we had the advantage of darkness and surprise, we lost two men. At four o'clock the wagons were being loaded at the warehouses.

There had been eight guards at the south warehouse, an unusual number I thought. They had put up the toughest fight. While the wagons were being loaded from the north building, Jones, Dooley, and I broke into the well-guarded south warehouse. It looked empty. Two rooms were quartered at the south end of the building, one of them locked. By lantern light, we forced the lock and opened the door. The room was mostly bare, except for ten large wooden boxes, covered with canvas, in the shadowy southeast corner.

As we pried open a box, gold bars gleamed in the soft lamplight. I could barely lift an end of a box — there was surely five thousand pounds of gold in those ten boxes, well over a million Federal dollars.

We decided our find was the spoils of war, and thus now belonged to the Confederacy. We placed one box in each of ten wagons, covered with our other supplies.

With two men loading each wagon, we had the warehouse empty and wagons moving by six that morning, and by seven o'clock the wagons were on the hidden trail. Dooley and I had brushed out the tracks leading away from the warehouses, and every fifteen minutes we would check on the prisoners. At half past seven, to our dismay, we found one was missing. We knew this meant that the Union cavalry south of town would be heading for the warehouses within the hour to check on their bounty.

And thus I took Dooley and his eighteen horsemen and moved south to hold the horse soldiers away from an all-out search for our wagons. We were not but a mile south of Culpeper when we dismounted, taking refuge behind bushes and trees on a piece of high ground each side of the roadway. In moments we could see the Federal horsemen bearing down on us at full speed. They were within a hundred yards when we opened fire. All pandemonium erupted, with men and horses falling. But we broke the charge, and the remaining horsemen raced for cover. There must have been ten dead Yankees lying on the ground.

We had surprised them this first time, but the tough fighting was to come. The Union Captain had over a hundred horsemen to our front, compared to my nineteen. When they would discover so few of us were holding them, they would run us over like a charging bull. I had calculated to hold them another hour, and by then our wagons would be moving fast and safely away.

The Yankee cavalrymen were being particularly cautious, for I could see their scouts working in the brush around both our flanks. As stealthily as we could, we began retreating under cover to keep from revealing our numbers.

I believed that the Union Captain assumed we were a much larger force, trying to break our supply wagons through to the south. But, in sum, we had stalled them an easy two hours before they determined to make their charge.

We lost two men fleeing from the Federals, and just west of Culpeper on the highest ground we dug in and made our final stand. By that time we were completely surrounded. There would be no escape. We held them there until noon, before we ran out of firepower and they overran our position. I had taken two wounds, one in the shoulder and one in the thigh. I was nearly unconscious when we were captured, and remember little. But we had given our wagons plenty of time to escape. I found out later that ten of my men were dead, leaving only seven, with just one escaping injury. I do not know how many Federals we killed.

It was months later before I learned of the wagons' successful return to our lines.

I spent a week in a makeshift Union army hospital, along with Sergeant Dooley, who had been hit twice, once in the stomach. That first day the doctor told me my wounds were not serious, but Sergeant Dooley's were. If Dooley made it through the night, he had a chance — and he did.

The Yankees sent us to a prison in Michigan, and two months later we were back with our unit, part of a prisoner exchange.

On May 1st, 1864, Union General Grant had set up headquarters at Culpeper, and on May 4th he launched his army into the Battle of the Wilderness. The fighting was bitter, with fierce attacks and counterattacks. By Saturday, the 7th, Grant was getting whipped unmercifully. General Lee's plan of defense was working, and General Longstreet's brigades were performing with precision. In the close-quarter fighting, Longstreet had been wounded, but his efficient commanders carried the day.

In the Wilderness fight, the two sides together lost twenty-five thousand men. Grant tried to get his troops to Spotsylvania before Lee, but Lee was already there. In the ensuing battle, Grant lost seven thousand men to Lee's two thousand three hundred.

Union General Philip Sheridan's cavalry, made up of three divisions, and Jeb Stuart's Confederate cavalry, heavily outnumbered, had a running battle from the 9th to the 11th of May. Then on the 11th, Jeb Stuart was killed at Yellow Tavern.

On May 12th, at the Battle of the Mule Shoe, Lee once again prevailed. For every move Grant made, Lee had an answer. Again Grant moved to Lee's right, only to be confronted where he stopped. On May 21st, at the Battle of Cold Harbor, Grant suffered a terrible defeat. In two months his casualties totaled fifty-five thousand men, compared to Lee's twenty-seven thousand.

On June 17th, Grant had moved his left wing south of Petersburg with eighty thousand troops. He faced fifteen thousand of Lee's shrinking forces.

On June 24th, General Early's division of sixteen thousand men was in the Shenandoah Valley, sent there by General Lee to protect it and the Virginia Central Railroad — and to threaten Washington.

On July 2nd, Sergeant Dooley and I reported to General Early's division at Winchester. On July 6th we were at Harpers Ferry, and on July 9th at Frederick, Pennsylvania.

On August 4th, to combat the threat of Early attacking Washington, General Grant sent Sheridan to drive Early from the valley. Sheridan was also to destroy all crops and anything else of use to the Confederates with his thirty-eight thousand effectives — infantry and cavalry.

Meanwhile, General Grant now had Richmond and Petersburg under siege, in much the same manner that he had taken Vicksburg.

In September, General Sheridan caught up with our division at Winchester. Three days later we were routed at Cedar Creek and retreated south. Our losses were grave, totaling five thousand three hundred casualties; but likewise, Sheridan's totaled five thousand five hundred thirty. However, we had lost one-third of our forces, compared to less than a fifth of Sheridan's. Our crippled army's losses were disastrous, and our brigade was never the same after our defeat. We knew that the Shenandoah Valley was now lost to us for good.

The Federals began their program of destroying all crops and burning anything useful, and I later learned that a company of Sheridan's cavalry had ridden into my place along the Blue Ridge and had harassed my family. Mary told me that many of the men had entered the house and had searched for valuables, tearing apart household items and furniture, taking things outside and destroying them, including our clothes, which they ripped and threw to the wind. Some put on Mary's dresses and danced around the yard like village idiots, all of which went on as they hooped and hollered as if they were at a drunken revelry.

My eldest son, B. J., nearly twelve, was dragged outside and beaten. The Sergeant accused him of being a Confederate soldier home on leave. B. J. was a large boy for his age, and he had been the man of the house for the last three and a half years. Mary began pleading to the Captain, who had stood by watching. She finally convinced the officer of B. J.'s innocence, and he had the thrashing stopped.

While all of this transpired, other Yankee troopers under the Captain's orders were riding the homestead, recklessly burning our crops and out-buildings. When they finally mounted up and rode away, the barn and crops were burning. They had shot the livestock in the corral and barn, and all that was left was a house in shambles. By God's mercy, Mary's hidden supply of foodstuffs were sufficient for the season ahead, and they had not found the rifle B. J. used for hunting, so that he still could provide most of the table meat that winter.

After our merciless defeat at Cedar Creek, General Early established headquarters at Staunton where we spent the winter. The siege and defense of Petersburg lasted through the winter of 1864-1865, with nothing gained on either side.

By the last of February 1865, Hancock's division was closing in on us. They were marching thirty miles a day and were only seven miles from our campsite when we began retreating to Charlottesville.

Ten miles east of Staunton, General Custer's division hit us as we neared the town of Waynesboro. Custer, only recently promoted to Major General, had just turned twenty-five, but he was renowned as a ferocious fighter, and our depleted army was no match for his well-armed cavalry. Our undermanned army collapsed, and the battle was over.

General Early and a few staff members managed to escape over the mountains, and perhaps another hundred or so escaped the roundup of prisoners. I was one of them, along with Lieutenant Jones, Sergeant Dooley, and ten of my men. We took off by horseback, and the Yankees soon dropped the pursuit. There was nothing left of our Stonewall Brigade, the once powerful unit that had been the pride of the Confederate Army.

By mid-March of 1865, General Early had returned to Richmond. He had left town with a division of men and now he returned with none, for no division was available and Lee had sent him home to await orders. None ever came.

My twelve men and I reported to Major Jenkins, the Quartermaster in General Ewell's division. On the 20th of March an orderly, along with the Major, caught me with my men working on our well-worn wagons and repairing harness.

"That's Captain Ross," the Major said, pointing in my direction. The orderly saluted and handed me a message. I was to report to General Lee immediately.

An hour later, I was at Lee's headquarters in Petersburg. I saluted a Colonel sitting at a desk just inside the door. He looked at the message and took me into a fair-sized room where General Lee was perusing a number of maps scattered across his desk. The Colonel spoke to the General, "Sir, this is Captain Ross."

Lee looked up from his maps. He smiled as I saluted. We shook hands and then he motioned me to a chair near the window. He moved another close to mine and sat down across from me.

General Lee was a handsome man, with a gentleness to his visage despite the fact that he looked every inch the military figure. I had seen him from afar astride his famed horse, Traveller, but this was the first time I had been close. His hair had turned pure white, though at the Seven Days' Battle, early in the war, I remembered his hair as dark.

Lee thanked me for what he called the successful warehouse mission at Culpeper. "It was a masterful job," he said, "particularly the seizing of the Federal gold."

The gold had already been put to good use for needed supplies from overseas that our army otherwise could not have purchased. The General went on, to my humble amazement, to apologize for the "sacrifice" he called it, that had caused my capture.

"But we worked hard for your exchange," he added. "And President Davis has asked me as well to give you his thanks."

You must only imagine how these words affected a seemingly insignificant farmer such as myself. I thought of Grandfather John Ross, how proud he would be. I recalled his own favored meeting with his Chief, a hundred years before. My heart nearly burst with gratitude and joy. This was certain to have been how Grandfather must have felt that day.

"I appreciate your kind words, Sir," I responded to the General, as evenly as I could, fearing a quiver in my voice.

As I spoke, however, the General's look turned melancholy, as he deeply sighed. "It is a nasty war, James Franklin, and I see nothing of good from it. The best of our country has been shattered . . . but we will just have to carry on and do the best we can."

"Sir," I somewhat shyly expressed, "I have felt all along that in a free society states should be able to secede if that's what the people want."

Lee cleared his throat and solemnly added, "Yes. But even so I agonized long over resigning my commission in what once had been our nation's army, the Union army. Yet I was left with no choice. Circumstance led me to go with my state and my people." He paused and smiled again.

"But enough of that kind of talk, Captain Ross. We have a job to do, and there's more awaiting before we rest. I thank you again for a task well done."

He excused me from the room, and as I walked out the door, I recalled that in our conversation General Lee had called me by my given name. I felt proud to be fighting for such a great man. At that moment in time I would have done anything he had asked, for while General Lee was ferocious in battle, he remained a kind and thoughtful man. Was it any wonder he was cheered everywhere by his men?

In late March of 1865, General Grant's Army of the Potomac began its offensive south of Petersburg. General Sheridan was to attack our General Pickett at Five Forks, but bad weather delayed the assault for three days because of the rain and muddy conditions.

On the last day of March, Pickett's Confederate division, with twelve thousand infantry and cavalry, repulsed Sheridan in some hard fighting. Yet the feisty Sheridan was not satisfied, and called for an infantry division to assault the rebels early the next day.

Union General G. K. Warren's infantry did not arrive until mid-afternoon, and Sheridan was furious. Unbeknownst to Sheridan, however, the late start would work in his favor. Pickett, thinking the Federals had put off their attack until morning, went far to the rear of his lines to General Thomas Rosser's shad bake — fish Rosser's troops had caught in the Nottoway River. Pickett had told no one where he was going.

At four o'clock, when the attack came from out of the pine trees along Hatcher Run, no one knew where General Pickett might be found or what to do. His Confederates were in total confusion, asking "Where is Pickett?" I believe that same question was asked at Gettysburg.

General Sheridan hit hard and fast, and Confederate resistance was piecemeal at best without someone in command. Pickett heard the battle in progress and rushed to the front, but by the time he arrived, half of his division had either been killed or captured. Pickett had failed his men, and Lee's right flank was gone.

With Five Forks in the hands of the enemy, General Lee had two choices — retreat or surrender. He issued orders for the army to abandon Petersburg and Richmond.

The next day, on Sunday, April 2nd, General A. P. Hill was killed by a Union soldier. That same day, our President, Jeff Davis, left Richmond by train.

On April 3rd, the Confederate retreating vanguard column included General Longstreet, along with Generals John Brown Gordon, William Mahone, and William Nelson Pendleton. Most of these twenty-two thousand effectives made the withdrawal from the front in good order. The four divisions of General Richard H. Anderson, combined with the remaining troops of Generals Bushrock Johnson, Henry Heth, Cadmus Wilcox, and Pickett, badly whipped the day before, marched northwest disheartened and weary along the banks of the Appomattox. When they met up with General Longstreet's confident veterans the next day, their spirits were lifted.

The struggling Confederates marched for Amelia Courthouse along the Richmond and Danville rail line, to get necessary supplies. Military supplies were there, but no food. General Lee had thirty-three thousand soldiers and no rations. The next warehouse with supplies was at Danville. Lee sent orders to have the food supply sent to Burkesville Crossing, but now it was a race against both the Yankee General Grant and hunger.

On April 5th, General Longstreet took the lead. Behind came Generals Anderson and Ewell, with Gordon bringing up the rear. The disheartening news came back from Lee's forward scouts that the enemy had won the race for Burkesville. Lee studied the enemy's position with his glasses and determined they were too well fortified to attack. He then decided to veer west to the vicinity of Farmville, on the Appomattox River, where rations could be sent by way of the Southside Line.

A day earlier, General Ewell had sent us into the countryside to scour the communities for food, but there was little could we find, not nearly enough for a marching army.

Ewell and Anderson's divisions fell far behind General Longstreet's corps, and at Sayler's Creek we were torn to pieces by the Union army. General Ewell surrendered, and the terrible, bitter war was over for my men — those that were left.

On April 9th, 1865, four days later, as General Lee approached Appomattox Courthouse, General Custer raced on ahead and captured the rations meant for Lee's army. General Lee was now completely surrounded, and without food. He painfully decided that the loss of life would be too great to try to fight his way through the enemy. His weary troops had marched the last forty miles in three days with nothing to eat.

When he surrendered the Army of Northern Virginia at Appomattox, General Robert E. Lee had thirty-three thousand men with him. The first thing he asked from General Grant was that his troops be fed; the request was granted.

The conditions of the surrender were for all prisoners to lay down their arms. After the ceremony of turning in our weapons was completed, we would be allowed to return to our homes.

On April 10th, 1865, with tears in his eyes, General Lee issued his last orders to his troops.

General Orders	*Headquarters Army of N. Va.*
No. 9	*April 10, 1865*

After four years of arduous service marked by unsurpassed courage and fortitude, the Army of Northern Virginia has been compelled to yield to overwhelming numbers and resources.

I need not tell the brave survivors of so many hard fought battles, who have remained steadfast to the last, that I have consented to this result from no distrust of them. But feeling that valor and devotion could accomplish nothing that could compensate for the loss that must have attended the continuance of the contest, I determined to avoid the useless sacrifice of those whose past services have endeared them to their countrymen.

By the terms of the agreement, officers and men can return to their homes and remain until exchanged. You will take with you the satisfaction that proceeds from the consciousness of duty faithfully performed, and I earnestly pray that a merciful God will extend to you His blessing and protection.

With an unceasing admiration of your constancy and devotion to your Country, and a grateful remembrance of your kind and generous consideration for myself, I bid you all an affectionate farewell.

General R. E. Lee

On April 11th, after a hearty morning meal, I mounted my black. I was allowed to keep the gelding, as I was a farmer. It was an amazing sight — men I had known and stood beside in the fiercest of battle, taking off in many directions. I rode with another Confederate, whom I knew only slightly, heading for Leesburg.

We talked little, for there was not much to talk about when you were grieved. All of our good men had been killed — for nothing. Many called our dead the best men of the South. I allowed that was proper and true, for I knew many of them, and there could be none better.

My mind went back to some of the worst of the times. My Lieutenant Jones would never return to his home. He had been killed at Sayler's Creek. The Union batteries had opened up on us from the high ground into the bottoms, where we trailed our wagons. They had cut down our troops — many without guns, shoes, or hats — and the carnage was devastating. My men were scattered about, trying to control their frightened teams, as other animals plunged out of control, dragging their traces across the countryside.

I had parted with Sergeant Dooley at Appomattox, after saying our farewells. He was onward to Atlanta, Georgia, with a fear in his heart of what he might find when he reached home — as it was, I thought, with all men returning to a war-ravaged land. I, too, wondered what I would find this time when I got home, and prayed to Almighty God that all was well.

Stirred from my thoughts as I rode, I became aware of nature around me at peace. The birds were fluttering in and darting out of the springtime brush, singing their sometimes happy, sometimes haunting, familiar songs. Nearby came the humming of a riffle, calling for me to come and watch her playful joy, splashing over smoothed, water-worn rocks, and to then calm down in a deep, serene pool.

My spirits were nourished as I rode the creek bottom of the fair, greening land, the sunlight warming my back. I thought I did not care what the politicians did from that point on, as long as they might leave me alone.

I loved the wilderness, where I could always feel the presence of God. As I continued on toward home, my thoughts went rambling into many directions. Thinking back to my youth, I remembered a poem penned in the back of the family Bible and a moment in time that Grandfather John Ross and I had shared.

There is no place like home
It need not be of gold
A clapboard shack suffice
If love awaits, untold

I returned home to Snicker's Gap the day John Wilkes Booth shot Abraham Lincoln at Ford's Theater. Lincoln died the next day, April 15th, 1865. His assassination was the worst thing that could have happened to us all, for it turned the reconstruction of the South into a living hell. Abe Lincoln had been prepared to forgive and return to normalcy; but those now in power had different ideas.

I had counted twenty-four horses in the upper pasture, including six fillies and four colts, a goodly number for any breeder. When the Confederacy had become desperate for horses I had let them have twenty of my quarter horses. I received nothing for them, as I was paid with Confederate currency, which turned out to be worthless paper.

Still, I was luckier than most. Though I had a shambles of a house, I could rebuild, and I had land and my beautiful horses, saved only because the Union never knew about the hidden pasture. Mary had kept the taxes paid up those five long years, or I would have lost it all.

Pa and his place came through the war in good shape as well. The Yankees had mostly left him alone, except for taking his horses and crops. But my three brothers did not fair as well. Bill's and John's places were completely destroyed, and they would have to start again from the ground up. And my younger brother, Howard, had died from wounds he suffered at Gettysburg. Pa had thought Howard was improving, but he died two months later, on the 14th of September in '63.

The morning of April 20th, 1865, was like a world lighted by the dawning sun, and washed clean from the rain the night before. And it was then that I felt the lingering melancholy begin to leave me, which had been with me the past week. I would come through this ordeal after all, for the worst had not been done to me — I was still alive.

And while I did not take to the haughty dictates of the victor, I knew there were worse things than defeat. I still had my home. I had my family. And I had my God.

Grandfather John Ross had often told me he had lived in three different worlds in his lifetime, one of them warring, and the last the best. Well, maybe it falls upon all men to live in three different worlds. I had lived in two — before and during the war, and now my third was just beginning. I would endeavor to make it become full with God's promise.

I had decided that government — even the Union — was a necessity to quell the winds of anarchy. But at the same time, I knew that too much government could take away our freedom, and incentive to succeed.

As days and weeks passed by through that postwar year, I could feel myself growing stronger. Whatever circumstance came along, I could meet the challenge. I found renewed incentive and responsibility for my family's well being and to perpetuate my wonderful Grandfather John Ross's endowment to me. I determined to continue to be a doer and not a wisher, as Grandfather often admonished, for I have found that those who only wish will still do so on their deathbed.

Grandfather had taught me that we have a responsibility to leave this earth improved from what we first found. And we must teach our children right from wrong, particularly from the Holy Word.

This reconstructed new nation will only be as great and as successful as its individual people, both North and South.

My thoughts were passing through my mind like a whirlwind. And it was then that I determined to begin to pen the going and coming forth of the John Ross clan, for all those of us to follow.

This is part of my responsibility here on this earth, to tell what went on before and what should come, what plans I should lay out for my remaining years here in God's land.

As I penned these tales, and alternately pondered our future, I determined that perhaps we would go West, to start life anew in my third world, out where it was said to take true character to survive, out in a world free of barrier, where accomplishment was what you made it — a land of new horizons.

But the first thing I would do was rebuild the farm — to better than before, for I never once thought of selling the place in its present condition. I would have bigger barns and a sixteen-foot-square birthing stall. It would be a family endeavor.

I determined to begin anew in Virginia for the moment, starting that day. I knew that with God, things always came together for the best.

Less than a week later, I heard that General George Custer was in Washington, D.C., and I wrote to him.

Dear General Custer,   *April 20, 1865*

We met many times during the war, though on opposite sides. Your tenacity in battle was a sight to behold, and although my enemy during the war, I admired your abilities from afar.

It is my understanding that you had numerous mounts shot out from under you during the conflict, but at Sayler's Creek, the last week of the war, I would have sworn you were riding one of my own bred quarter horses that I had sold to the Confederacy, a beautiful black I had called Dandy. His ancestor was a gray-white stallion named Prince, originally owned by Count Richard Sheffield of England during the War of the Revolution. Wherever he is, call him Dandy, and he will come trotting.

I have heard you to be a fair man and my reason for writing is this: I have five excellent quarter horses from the same lineage I would like to sell. My farm was destroyed during the war, and I need to rebuild. If you or anyone you know would be interested, please contact me.

I am located near Snicker's Gap, Virginia. Those around the area can tell you where I live.

Your Obedient Servt.
James Franklin Ross

It was the 10th of May before I heard from General Custer. He was interested in acquiring several of my stock, if they were as good as Dandy. And he wrote that Dandy was the best horse he had ever owned — then the General struck out the word "owned" and wrote "acquired."

Custer planned to be at my place around noon on the 15th.

I decided to bring only the five of my quarter horses from the upper pasture for the General to look at. Something inside me was telling me yet to be cautious of a victorious enemy, as he might wonder how I had managed to come by that many horses.

When the General and his aide rode into the yard, I immediately recognized him. The men dismounted and introduced themselves. I had thought the other military man looked familiar — it was no aide after all, but Lieutenant General Sheridan.

Mary had our chicken dinner ready when she came out of the house, and she invited the Generals in to eat. They politely demurred, but strong and persuasive Mary insisted.

Later, again outside, we went to a makeshift shed where the geldings were waiting, and I turned them loose into the corral to parade themselves. General Sheridan whistled. "Where'd you find those horses? I've never seen better horseflesh in all my days!" He wanted the gray.

"Four hundred for him, and three hundred for any of the others," I told him, "and you take your pick."

The price was fair, for there were no horses in these parts better bred, and they knew it. Sheridan looked at Custer for a moment and then sarcastically remarked, "You know, Captain, we could confiscate those horses if we wanted."

I knew they could, though I answered, "But you're decent men, General, and I need to rebuild." I smiled and said nothing more, but I knew as did they, that they had been responsible for my farm's destruction.

"What would you take for all five?" Sheridan asked.

I thought carefully a moment. "Fourteen hundred dollars!"

They walked away and talked it over between themselves, heatedly at first, and then Custer said something that seemed to calm the bravado of General Sheridan. They walked back, and Custer affirmed, "We will take the five."

Sheridan wrote out a bank note, and I had my money to rebuild.

The two officers mounted their geldings and led their newly purchased quarter horses down the road to Washington.

Custer had been riding Dandy, and the gelding had remembered me, for he must have caught my scent. He had walked right over and nuzzled my outstretched hand.

As the Yankees rode from sight I remembered that Sheridan had called me Captain. It was my conclusion that they must have done some checking before they had come by to see me. And I thought I was surely relieved that I had decided to only show them the five horses.

By August of 1865 we had the house in fair shape, at least good enough to where Mary and the girls could finish. B.J. and I had completed framing the barn by that time, and were nailing on board siding.

America

New Horizons

*O*N APRIL OF 1866, we had a good birthing of horses. A magnificent gray stallion had sired a colt and two fillies. In May, along with the three existing mares, I had also bred two three-year-old fillies, soon to be four.

In July of that year, Custer purchased two more horses from me, a gelding and a mare for four hundred dollars, the mare for his wife Elizabeth, and the gelding a gift for his brother Tom. He soon would be transferred west, to be stationed at Fort Riley, on the plains of Kansas, arriving in November of 1866, to command the newly established 7th Cavalry with a peacetime rank of Lieutenant Colonel.

I had wished him well, and he rode off leading the two horses. I liked Custer, though there were many who did not, either from professional jealousy or from personal conflict I would assume. The often brash young officer had passed so many older military men in rank that it no doubt had galled the most of them. And after the war was over, some set about to destroy his character and reputation.

Custer was said to be an impetuous fellow, and that his headlong charges into battle in the war were often reckless, but it could not be denied that when he rode into trouble, he would find a way to escape. His "Custer's Luck" had brought home victories and promotions. The way I saw it, Custer had as much to do in bringing about an end to the Civil War as any other Union commander.

But I was glad he had not brought General Sheridan with him again, for there was something about the man that set my teeth on edge — probably, I might deduce, his earlier threat to confiscate my horses.

The summer heat of 1867 was in the air the day that B. J. and I were cultivating the corn at Pa's. Pa was a getting on in age, and he had a lot of acres to work. Each year my brothers and I would help out until all the crops were harvested.

To let the Belgians have a rest, I had tooled to a stop at the end of the field, near the road to the house. I had a jug of water wrapped in burlap under a nearby tree, and I walked over to hoist a drink. In the distance, a man walking the county road turned and stumbled along down our way, his tired feet dragging and raising scuffs of dust from the well-beaten earth. I waited, standing under the oak, until he walked up to me and introduced himself.

"Isaiah Washington," was all he was able to say, and then he staggered forward and fell into my arms. I steadied him for a moment and lifted the jug for him to drink. After a refreshing swallow or two, we rested under the tree. Isaiah was a dark-skinned mulatto looking for work.

Until the war ended, he had been a slave, and had never been beyond his owner's plantation, or the state of Louisiana. His master had been a good man who had seen to it that Isaiah and his children had been educated. And although they worked hard for the master, Isaiah and his family enjoyed as decent a life for slaves as could have been, and they respected the man for this. Isaiah had seen firsthand how other slaves had been treated by brutal owners, and he continually thanked a kind and merciful God for his blessings.

But his owner had been killed in the war, and Isaiah had stayed on at the plantation where he had grown up, for although he was free, he had no place to go. When the man's grieving widow sold the plantation in 1866, Isaiah finally had to leave.

It was before daylight on a cold February morning when Isaiah and his family walked away from the place and never looked back. They had trudged along the back roads as they moved east, then north, never straying far from the creeks and rivers.

By day Isaiah would stop at the farmsteads, asking for work; but he was finding only minor jobs, for almost everyone was destitute after the war. For the odd jobs he did find, he would take his wages in food, for cash was scarce. At night the family would camp in the deep woods along the streams, far from homes and civilization. Isaiah was adept at making fish traps, and his family lived mainly on a diet of Isaiah's catches, as they continued their way to the north.

It had been four months since Isaiah had left the plantation, and in the main he had been treated fairly by the farmers where he had stopped. But they were having troubles of their own, without taking on more mouths to feed. He had almost given up finding a refuge for his family when he walked down the roadway to Pa's.

I did not know what Pa would say, but Isaiah was famished, so I took him to the house. We caught up with Pa inside the barn, and after I had related Isaiah's plight, Pa seemed to be mulling the situation over in his mind.

It was dinnertime, and Aunt Jane stepped outside to let us know it was time to eat. Pa had invited Isaiah in for dinner, but Isaiah declined to go inside the house. After several invitations and refusals, he finally agreed to come into the kitchen to eat. And that was fine with Pa, for he always ate in the kitchen. Aunt Jane laid out a meal fit for a King — well, a country King anyway — and we partook of her fried chicken, green beans, potatoes, and white gravy.

After Aunt Jane had said grace, we all set to and ate heartily, including Isaiah. Then suddenly he stopped and would not eat any more. Pa finally got it from him that he had felt guilty, eating so lavishly while his family hungrily waited along the banks of the Potomac River.

I had never felt prouder of Pa in all my life than that day when he said to Isaiah, "You finish eatin', and I'll have Jane fix up a meal for you to take back. You get your family and bring 'em here. I've lots of land, but not much money. I'll build you a house where you can stay, and I'll expect you to work — but you'll not lack for food, and I'll see to it your children will get schoolin'. You'll have enough to buy what staples you'll need and, if it's a good year, a small stipend. If what I've said meets your approval, you and your family are welcome." Months of anxiousness on Isaiah's face were replaced with a smile. It seemed the hardship for his wife and five children, camping along the rivers was finally over. He had found a place for his family.

Isaiah excitedly accepted Pa's offer, and Pa sent B. J. to saddle up the roan for Isaiah to go and get his family.

Some thirty minutes later, Isaiah was riding off down our road.

The Washingtons stayed in Pa's barn for almost a month until we had built a place for them to live in, a small house northwest of the barn, on a slight knoll next to the apple orchard. Everyone helped with the construction, including Isaiah and his oldest son, Joshua, who was about B. J.'s age.

The Washingtons were good people, and it was not long before B. J. and

Joshua had become acquainted and were riding horses together across the countryside.

Three years quickly passed and on July 20th, 1870, when I was forty-nine years of age, I knew that the day was at hand for our move to the West. Mary was thirty-eight, my eldest, B. J., was seventeen, my youngest, James, was six. The three girls Susan, Harriet, and Virginia were fifteen, thirteen, and ten.

There were those who thought we were mad to pick up and frontier into the untamed lands of the West, especially at my age, but we were determined, and the war had left a lingering disappointment. Reconstruction had been a bitter dose to swallow.

Pa had never said much about it one way or another, until I went to see him for the last time. He told me he envied my going, and were he younger he would do the same. His words made me feel better, and when we shook hands that day, he hugged me for the first time.

After I had mounted my gelding, Pa placed a coin in my hand. "It was one of your great-grandmother's, and I think she'd want you to have it. . . . Be careful," he almost whispered.

I could feel emotions about to break down, so I quickly reined the gray around and to a fast walk went down the lane. At a rise in the road, I looked back and Pa was still standing by the corral fence watching. I don't know why, but I knew I would never see him again. I paused what seemed like a long time, then raised my hand into a sweeping wave. I knew if he had called me back and asked that I stay, I would not leave.

I looked at the gold coin Pa had given me, and ancient piece that I had seen but once before when I was a boy.

I reined the gelding into a trot, as if he was eating up the roadway. As I approached the house, I realized I could not have had a better father. Though harsh and stern at times, he was a devoted believer in God's Word, and now was I. He had taught me well.

I had sold the farmhouse and four hundred acres of pasture and crop-land, along with most of the livestock, to a man and his wife from

Pennsylvania. Then I held an auction and sold the rest of our stock, equipment, and goods. The four hundred acres of high pasture and foothills I deeded back to Pa. I could not bear to see it out of Ross family hands.

I had received forty-two hundred dollars from the sale of the farm, along with a note for an additional thirty-eight hundred due in ten years. The auction took in seven hundred.

On the coming Monday morning, we would finish loading up the spring wagon and head for Harpers Ferry. We would meet up with the Baltimore and Ohio railway train on Tuesday, and if everything went well, we would reach our destination, Junction City, Kansas, sometime Friday. I had rented a stock car all the way through to Junction City for the horses. B. J. was taking his black stallion; I was taking my gray-white, three of my best mares that would foal the coming April, a gray gelding, two colts, and five fillies, one to three years of age. All the quarter horses were from the line of Count Sheffield's stallion, Prince. My brother Bill took my remaining horses, and would pay me later.

I would try to sell our wagon at Harpers Ferry, but the two Belgian draft horses I would also take along.

We were to homestead one hundred sixty acres in Geary County, Kansas, eighteen miles southeast of the town of Junction City, which was just outside the Fort Riley garrison. It was not far from the river town of Manhattan, which now was also the site of the land-grant Kansas State Agricultural College. I was thinking to the future for our children, while hoping to establish a new home for us all.

The area we hoped to obtain was upland, the only available there. The rich river bottom at Manhattan and Junction City had long been taken. At Leesburg we had garnered some of the information regarding the homestead opportunity, but we would need to do the necessary paperwork with the land office in Junction City. We would have to make certain improvements within a year to maintain possession, but we knew we could do that easily enough.

As we had fixed pallets on the floor the night before we were to leave, I lay awake with many thoughts. I stood before the threshold of new beginnings, and I hoped I had made the right decision to go West.

The children had been anxious to be on the way, but I knew that later, when we were in the middle of nowhere on the open Kansas prairie, they might be dispirited and long for the Virginia they had left behind.

I spent most of the day before in the upper pasture, where Grandfather

John Ross had taken me when I was a boy. It brought back many tender memories as I listened to the waterfall splashing into the pool below, and surveyed the rhododendron slope above me.

As I was about to leave the meadow I stopped, turned, and peered back one last time.

"Good-bye, Grandfather . . . ," I whispered, and sadly wondered if he had felt as melancholy when he had left his home in Scotland.

The Monday morning sky was overcast when we pulled out of the yard. We left with hope in our hearts but warm tears of remembrance in our eyes.

About five miles out, a drizzle began to fall, but by the time we had traveled another two miles it had stopped. When we reached the heights and looked down on the Potomac, the sun was breaking through the clouds. It was around four that afternoon when we rumbled across the bridge into Harpers Ferry and found a hostler close to the depot to stable our animals.

Down the street I had spotted a sign advertising wagons for sale, and sold the owner ours for fifteen dollars. Then we checked into the hotel two blocks away, and that evening ate in the dining room. The youngsters were excited, for they had never eaten in a hotel before, and it became a wonderful first experience for them. Susan's blue eyes sparkled when her Ma told her she could order whatever she wanted from the day's menu.

We ate an early morning meal and went to the stables, but it was nine before B. J. and I had the horses loaded in the railcar. The train was to depart at ten, and we had hardly finished loading when I heard a train whistle east of us and coming closer. We were at the depot when the engine pulled in and stopped, hot steam hissing and trailing upward from beneath the cars. Inside the depot building I could hear the telegraph ticking away a message into the unknown. In half an hour the engines had been switched and hooked onto several stock-filled railcars.

The family stepped up into the parlor car, and with suitcases in hand I followed behind them. From habit, I reached down to hitch up my gun belt, but I had forgotten I had no gun. I did, however, have Grandfather's dirk sheathed at my back beneath my clothes.

The men of the South had not been allowed to own guns — the price of defeat in war. I had been forced to lay my Remington revolver and Sharps rifle in the stockpile of Confederate weapons at Appomattox. I had not told them about the dirk.

I would be free of those suffocating bureaucrats once we were west of the Mississippi. Beyond the river, I would leave behind the stains of war and bondage of defeat.

Early the next day at Marietta, Ohio, we switched from the Baltimore and Ohio to the Marietta and Cincinnati railcar. Late that night we again switched trains in Cincinnati, to the Pacific Railroad.

The parlor car we boarded in Cincinnati was more plush than the other two lines. Ornate brass lamp fixtures hung between the windows on red velvet. We sat on cushioned seats of fine cloth. In the far corner of the car stood a polished black cast iron stove. Eleven others filled the car, two men, a lone woman, and four other couples.

Around noon on Thursday we crossed the Mississippi River into St. Louis, where we had a two-hour wait.

I told Mary and the children to stay where they were, and I would be back within the hour. It did not take me long to find a general store. The clerk, a tall, boney lad that needed to sit down at the dinner table more often, asked if he could be of help.

"I'd like to see your pistols and rifles," I quickly told him.

After looking them over for a short time, I told the young man that I wanted two Remington army .44 revolvers, two Winchester .44 carbine rifles, two cartridge holster belts, and two hundred rounds of ammunition.

The clerk whistled. "Gosh, mister, you must be gettin' ready to fight a war!"

"No," I smiled at him, "not a war; but where I'm going I don't know what kind of skunk might be lurking in the woods."

I paid the clerk, loaded one of the revolvers, put it in the holster, and threw it around my hips. A gun once again alongside my right leg felt reassuring. I loaded the rifle and told the clerk to wrap the other rifle and handgun.

I stepped into the rail car with time to spare. Mary peered at my guns, but smiled and said nothing. I handed B. J. the package.

"These are yours; you've handled guns all your life. They're for hunting and protection. Never use them against another unless forced upon you. . . . But if you have to, put your bullets where they'll stop someone from returning fire."

Early the next morning, July 25th, 1870, we stopped in Kansas City, and by mid-morning we had rolled into Topeka, Kansas. The sun had passed its highest arch in the sky when we crossed the Blue River into Manhattan. An hour later, the Fort Riley stables flashed by north of the train, beneath a rimrock bluff. To the south meandered the Kansas River.

Peering out of the window to the southwest, I could see the confluence of the Smoky Hill and Republican Rivers. Minutes later the racing wheels sang across the Republican into Junction City, where we rolled to a jerking stop.

Kansas had been a state for but nine years. Abilene, twenty miles west, had recently become the first cattle town, and received much renown for the cattle drives from Texas that ended at the railhead there. It was widely known — even in the East — that Abilene had become a wild and lawless community. The town government had named a reluctant grocer to be Marshal, but he held no sway, and the cowboys did as they pleased.

But on the day we pulled into Junction City, the Abilene Marshal was Thomas James Smith — Bear River Tom, they called him — hired in May. He had been a New York police officer, and a Marshal in Wyoming. He handled the cowboys in Abilene masterfully — mainly with his fists — and he soon had things under control — that is, until November, when two disgruntled farmers caught him by surprise one night and chopped off his head with an axe.

The next year, in April of 1871, the Abilene town council would hire the renowned Wild Bill Hickock, quick on the trigger, and a bad man to get crosswise with.

We had come to Kansas at the beginning of the state's reputation for gunfighting, and it would last until the 1900s. The Jesse James gang, now in operation, would terrorize the state's banks until April of '82, when Jesse was killed by Bob Ford, one of his own men who no doubt like the others had dreamed of fame. And the infamous gunfights in Abilene, Dodge City, Ellsworth, Wichita, Caldwell, Newton, and Medicine Lodge lay in the days ahead.

When I had stepped off the train in Kansas, I looked at a never-ending azure sky, and a land with a diverse panorama of horizons. No place I had ever been or seen was anything like what met me that first day. And though I have come to be familiar with the endless gentle roll of the valleys and hills, I am still enthralled by the simple beauty when I stand along the rim-rock and peer across long vistas of virgin land.

By the time we had gotten the stock and walked up the slope to the dust-blown main street of Junction City, the hour was approaching four. A young hostler sat on a chair in front of the stables, and after bedding down the horses, we talked. He was abrupt and disgruntled for one so early of years, but after a while he mellowed. His name was Spencer Jones, and he had rolled into Junction City two years earlier, he said, and had opened up the stable. Later, when we became more familiar to each other, he told me he had ridden with Jesse James, but when he had turned twenty-one, he determined he had to get away from robbing banks or he would end up at the end of a rope in some Godforsaken place. As the years passed, I found Spencer to be a kind and generous man.

Later that afternoon of our arrival, we checked in at the hotel. The next morning when we walked downstairs to breakfast I noticed that B. J. had strapped on his gunbelt, and he looked every bit the man he had become.

I deposited forty-five hundred dollars at the Wells Fargo office. Then B. J. and I went to the land office, where the clerk showed me the map of what was available. After studying it, I said I would take the southeast quarter of the available section, which was down the road from the schoolhouse a half mile — a school that doubled as a church on Sundays.

The clerk looked up at me. "Ya can't have a quarter; I can only let ya have an eighty."

I explained that I had been told me in Leesburg that the homesteads were to be a hundred sixty acres.

"Well . . . that was a year ago," the man replied, and looked over at B. J. "What about him? Let him take an eighty, and you'll end up with your one-sixty. He's eighteen ain't he?"

"Well, he will be soon."

"Close enough," he shrugged.

We took the necessary papers, with B. J. signing for the east eighty; I signed for the west.

We passed the rest of the day rounding up a spring wagon, implements, and the staples we would need for a month or two while we settled onto our new piece of land.

On July 27th, 1870, at the break of dawn, we were crossing the Smoky Hill River. B. J. was handling the reins of the Belgians, pulling the spring wagon full of goods. Susan, our eldest daughter, was riding along with him. I had the reins of a new buckboard, with the rest of the family in the buggy. Our quarter horses trailed behind the wagon.

A flour mill sat on the high east bank of the river, pounding away. We stopped and bought a hundred-pound sack and moved on. After a couple hours, we crossed Clark's Creek at a low-water crossing. It was not long thereafter and we were angling up Humboldt Creek.

Every so often we would see a farmhouse off in the distance. It was for certain a vast and lonely country we traveled through.

At late afternoon, we breasted the rimrock and stopped to look at the view back down the valley. If I was a reading my map correctly, I thought we should not be much more than a mile to our homestead. The young-sters in the spring wagon had fallen behind, and were slowly making their way south toward us, perhaps a mile back down the valley.

It felt as if we had entered another world, looking down a hundred feet over the valley below. I peered at Mary. She never said a word, but I could tell she was disheartened after surveying the ground. There was hardly any soil cover, with broken slabs of ledge rock four to twelve inches thick scattered everywhere. I would not have to travel far for foundation and fence rock. I felt a cause for discouragement, too, but those rolling flint hills were breathtaking, and the thick bluestem grass seemed to flourish everywhere. It would make exceptional pasture for the horses.

We waited at the high point along the rim for B. J. to catch up. By the time we had reached the west line of our homestead, the soil looked better; the surrounding country had a nice depth of earth cover.

A quarter-mile from our west line on high ground grew a dense grove of oak trees. We reined our horses, with the quarter horses following, into the shady patch, and stopped where we would build our home.

That night we slept with the stars, taking refuge under the wagon when the rain fell; but it was a gentle summer shower that nicely cooled the sun-parched countryside.

After a hearty morning meal that Mary and the girls quickly put together in their rugged new surroundings, B. J. and I began hauling rock and laying up the foundation for our house. Two days later the lumber dealer from Junction City hauled in the material I had ordered on our arrival. By the first of September, we could move into our home, and though it was not yet finished, it was weather-tight.

For three months, while the house was being built, we had hauled water from Humboldt Creek three miles away. Then, with that main task completed, we dug a well just southeast of the house, a two-week venture through the rocky earth. We had gone down some twelve feet when we hit ledge rock. The rock was damp, but no water lay on the ledge. Lucky for us, the ledge was in layers, two to eight inches thick. After a couple more days, using sledge and pick, by nightfall we managed to cut down another five feet into the rock. Yet all we had managed from our hard work were several small areas seeping water from between the ledges.

On the third day we went out early to dig deeper, but to our surprise, the hole had four feet of water in the bottom. I thought about going even deeper until B. J. reminded me that God had surely blessed us with our needs, so maybe we should leave well enough alone. And we did. I never knew for sure if he was just trying to get out of some messy wet work or if he truly believed we had received the goodness of our Lord, but years later I knew it to be the latter. The well turned out to be a good one and never once went dry.

The next April, in 1871, B. J. found a spring near the northeast corner of the lower end of our land. We cleaned it out to allow enough water for the horses and other livestock; it saved us from having to haul. Later, as time went on, I piped the water into a tank to make it easier for the animals to drink.

The Kansas days were long, from light until dark. The nights were short, and sleep came easy. Each day, except Sunday, our day of rest, I was worn, but it was a good feeling with accomplishment.

I often asked myself — as I traveled that train here to Kansas, and as I had gone about my new homesteading tasks — what made a man risk all to go into a hostile land, a land nearly empty of civilization, his nearest neighbor miles away, the nearest lawman or doctor days away? It might have been much easier to have stayed put in a long-familiar environment.

And then I recalled the pain of rebuilding the land of the South, wasted by the war. I knew that as my Grandfather John Ross had done, I had left my homeland in the hopes of a better life for my family, and in the need to be removed from the painful memories of brother fighting brother.

On the 12th of April, 1871, the Kansas land was wide awake after a long winter of hibernation. A township road ran along our west line, and on the far side a farmer had parked his buggy along the trail, looking at the distant acreage. After we had introduced ourselves I learned that he and his brother owned the half section that ran to the Humboldt road.

He was disgusted with the property. "We homesteaded a year ago," he said, "thinking we were getting farmland. Instead we got three hundred twenty acres of nothin'. I don't think there's a place on the whole piece where you could put in a plow and grow anything." The two men were considering pulling their stakes and heading for Oregon.

I recognized how fortunate we had been to get our land, for on our one hundred sixty acres, I had planned to break up the east eighty for raising feed — probably oats, barley, and corn; and if I were to raise my horses as I had planned, that would leave a small eighty acres for pasture. I knew that would not be enough grass for a herd, and I had hoped I had not seemed too anxious when I asked the man if he would consider selling his piece.

I offered three hundred twenty dollars, and he grumbled, but ended up agreeing, for he had been trying to be rid of the pastureland for some time, but had no takers.

The next day we met at the land office, then settled up at the abstract office.

That Sunday I walked the new acreage. I surely did not think God would mind my looking at his handiwork on the Sabbath.

I knew that land was a treasure to me, as I passed through the thick bluestem bending in the wind. I had gone a mile, to the edge of Humboldt Road, and for a time stood beneath the rimrock, beside a large half-buried stone clad in gray patina. The rock and I, knee deep in grass, were locked together in God's bounty through the passing of time.

Back on the rim, I peered down vistas of canyons and beyond to a sweeping distance colored in mauve, and I wondered who else, before me, might have stood there on the cliff of time and admired the view of another sunset.

It was coming onto dark when I went back to the house through an unbroken ground of tall bluestem grass and intermittent rock, a peaceful, empty land in the silent hills. I had been told this West was a lonely land, and maybe it was for the unbeliever. But I knew, as my footsteps passed through my grass of horizons west, I was not alone.

The following morning I had gone outside in the early darkness to tend my chores, and thought of Grandfather John Ross and our week together at his favorite place in the Blue Ridge Mountains. And then the pages of my memory turned to Pa back home in Virginia. At that moment my heart ached for all my family, those passed on to their Heavenly Reward and those we had left behind — especially Pa.

The scars of the war were deep upon my soul, but I had mostly recovered from the loss of freedom I had felt. The country and the people in Kansas spoke nothing of the war, nor did I; it was better to leave it in the past.

As the morning turned gray, I stood by the barn and watched the horses, their heads down, chewing on the prairie hay I had scythed and pitched over the corral fence. I watched the sunlight slowly paint a golden hue upon their flanks. I glanced around the countryside, resting my eyes for but a moment on a thicket of newly blossoming redbud.

The soft, cool wind stirred the strands of my thinning hair and arrested my rambling thoughts for a moment. We had a lot to do in this new land, and I knew there would be many more hardships to endure, but I also knew we would succeed.

I stayed near the barn as the sun rose above the vacant hills, gradually bursting forth and showering warm light across the rolling bluestem. As I peered at the horizon I felt the guiding hand of God resting on my shoulders. Nearby, out of a soft breeze that drifted down through the branches of an oak, covered with the familiar chartreuse misting of budding leaves,

I heard the voices of my Confederates, as we sat around the campfire, pouring forth our souls into the hymns of long ago,

> *From every swelling tide of woes, there is a calm, a sure retreat. . . . There is a scene where spirits blend, . . . There, there on eagles wings we soar. . . .*

Epilogue

*J*AMES FRANKLIN ROSS died on January 10th, 1894, on a cold, blustery day when the winds sang lonely songs in the Kansas prairie grass and cedar. He had spent twenty-four years in the Flint Hills he had grown to love, but even so he had always remembered Virginia, where his spirit remained in the foothills and hidden meadows of the Blue Ridge Mountains. It was right for a man to love at least two lands in a lifetime without being capricious; and so it was for James.

By the time of his death, his children had already scattered into the Kansas winds, making roots of their own. He had become a successful farmer and rancher, as he had long dreamed, never straying too far from raising the best quarter horses in the country. The Count of Sheffield's proud stallion, Prince, now had offspring spread across the Kansas prairies.

A potbelly stove in the corner glowed red and the church was warm the day of the funeral, but outside the frosty windows hung a low southern sun that had no effect on the zero temperature or the blanket of snow covering as far as the horizons. It would take most of a day to dig James Franklin's grave through the three feet of frozen ground in the Upper Humboldt Cemetery. He would lay alongside his daughter Susan, who had died eleven years before.

After the minister had read the Twenty-Third Psalm, James's daughter, Harriet, sang his favorite song, "Dixie." You could almost hear him whistling it on the rocky Kansas hillside as he moved along slowly astride one of his stallions.

> *I wish I was in the land of cotton*
> *Old times there are not forgotten,*
> *Look away! Look away! Look away! Dixie Land.*
> *I wish I was in Dixie Hooray! Hooray,*
> *In Dixie land, I'll take my stand*

To live and die in Dixie,
Away, away, away down South in Dixie. . . .

One hundred eight years have passed since James Franklin died. My brother and I would visit the isolated and lonely Upper Humboldt Cemetery each May on Memorial Day, to flower the three graves of James Franklin, Mary, and their daughter Susan Pepper, just to let them know they had not been forgotten. Now that my brother has passed on, my daughter Marcia or special friend Kathy Oller go with me.

Many of the stone markers at the old bluestem cemetery are gone; others have fallen over. But those that remain are still faintly legible. As near as I can tell, no one had been buried there for close to a hundred years.

Then, in 1999, I was amazed to see a new stone grace the prairie hay slope. The names of a man and wife, showing only their dates of birth, were carved into the granite.

But sometime in future days, two more kindly souls will be there, adding family to those long ago pioneers, and leaving their own mark on the wheel of time.

— *Harold G. Ross, 2002*

Cover artist . . . Tom Bookwalter, a nationally known illustrator and graphic artist, is currently a graphic design instructor at Kansas State University, Manhattan. Bookwalter's work appears in national magazines, annual reports, calendars, posters, and brochures. He has been honored by the National Geographic Society, the East and West Coast Society of Illustrators, the International Society of Business Communicators, and the Greater Jackson (Mississippi) Advertising Club. His clients include Rockwell International, 3M Company, Hewlett Packard, Ford Motor Company, VISA, IBM, United Technologies, Honeywell, Levi Strauss, AT&T, the National Football League, *The Washington Post*, and Miller Brewing, as well as the Department of the Navy, the Federal Reserve Bank of Kansas City, and the United States Information Agency.

Bookwalter attended Peru State University in Nebraska and earned his B.A. from Emporia State University, Emporia, Kansas. He attended the prestigious Art Center College of Design in Pasadena, California.

Bookwalter is represented nationally by the Neis Group, of Grand Rapids, Michigan; Munro Goodman Artists Representatives, in Chicago and New York; and the Image Mill, Des Moines, Iowa.

Line graphics artist . . . Rodney Hoover is a freelance specialist in landscape and rural art in Manhattan, Kansas.

Also by
Harold G. Ross

Throughout My Passing Day

Where Eagles Fly

Along Golden Hills

Homage to the Gods

Brannick and the Untamed West